IT ENDS WITH HER

IT ENDS WITH HER

BRIANNA LABUSKES

This is a work of fiction. Names, characters, organizations, places, events, and incidents are either products of the author's imagination or are used fictitiously. Any resemblance to actual persons, living or dead, or actual events is purely coincidental.

Published by Thomas & Mercer, Seattle

www.apub.com

ISBN-13: 9781503953130 (hardcover)
ISBN-10: 1503953130 (hardcover)
ISBN-13: 9781503954090 (paperback)
ISBN-10: 1503954099 (paperback)

Cover design by Damon Freeman

Printed in the United States of America

First edition

To Katie Smith and Abby McIntyre
For Wednesday nights at Olivia's

The world breaks everyone and afterward many are strong at the broken places. But those that will not break it kills. It kills the very good and the very gentle and the very brave impartially.

—*Ernest Hemingway*

CHAPTER ONE

Clarke

March 4, 2018

Special Agent Clarke Sinclair barely flinched as the icy drops of rain slipped into the space between the collar of her leather jacket and her neck. It didn't matter. The cold. The wet. The thick Missouri mud coating her boots. Nothing mattered.

Except that wasn't true. The girl had mattered.

Charlotte.

Charlotte, who was now being lowered into the ground, while the quiet little cemetery held its breath and the sky turned gray in mourning. The girl's parents stood at the edge of the grave, beneath an overlarge black umbrella, and the space between their bodies spoke volumes even at a distance. Would they ever recover? Probably not.

When she felt the press of a shoulder against her own, she didn't need to look over to know it was Sam. Her partner had been scouting the edges, on the outskirts of the tombstones, looking for the bastard, while she'd taken up a post on the far periphery of the group, hesitant to move any closer lest she disturb the already-fragile tableau. They were both dressed casually, not necessarily wanting to broadcast that the FBI was patrolling the scene.

"I really need you to not talk to me at the moment," she said, her voice so quiet it was possible it got drowned out by the rain. But he stiffened next to her, so she knew he'd heard.

There were three heartbeats' worth of silence before Sam broke it. Always had to poke. Always had to prod.

"He's not here," he said.

She rounded on him. "Are you kidding me? What did I just say?"

Sam stared back at her, the water catching on his eyelashes and running into the canyons that shaped the landscape of his face. His hair, a touch too long, like always, was slicked back, the abundance of silver in it almost masked by the dampness of the strands. He'd turned toward her when she'd shifted, his feet slightly staggered, his stocky body held at the ready like a boxer waiting for the first bell.

"You still have a job to do, kid, or did you forget that part?" The gentleness in his tone made the scolding sting worse than it would have if he'd raised his voice. He'd always been like that, ever since he'd secured her a place at Quantico. Always the disappointed father figure to her unruly, rebellious teenager. There were days when it seemed like he actually saw her as a capable adult, responsible enough to take care of herself. And then there were times when she didn't know if he would ever see past the damaged girl he was always trying to save.

Resentment licked hot at the edges of her frayed emotions, so intense it felt almost like hatred.

"No, you don't get to pull that shit," she said. "Not you. Not now."

His thin lips pressed together so tightly that the pink of them disappeared into a straight line. "Do you think I don't care?" It was just a slight head tilt toward the grave, but she caught it.

"I think this guy has gotten the best of you three times now, and your massive ego can't stand it," she said, not because she believed it but because she wanted to see him blink. "Do you know how many dead girls I found when I was in Florida? Before you dragged me into this cesspit of a situation? Zero, Sam. Zero."

He wanted to say something. It was there on his face. Maybe about how she'd been wasting her life chasing after pricks committing white-collar crimes that didn't hurt anyone but their millionaire investors. Maybe about how he'd seen that life she'd been living, with her broom-closet office and stained takeout containers, and was not impressed. Maybe about how she'd once been an FBI prodigy who wouldn't have blinked twice at stumbling upon a dead body but had now gone soft after trading it all for the safety of a desk job in a field office.

Maybe it wasn't important what he was going to say. Whatever it was would have been painful. The movement in the corner of her eye caught her attention anyway. The burial was over.

Sam sighed, and she felt it. The weariness of it sank into her bones as easily as the rain was soaking her jeans. He reached for her then, but his stubby fingers hovered uselessly just behind her elbow before he let his hand drop. "I'm going to do another pass."

She just nodded. Because what else was there to say as the mourners trudged over the saturated earth to the soundtrack of quiet sobs?

Sam took off, blending into the shadows of the trees ringing the cemetery. Clarke watched him go with little hope. She knew if Simon Cross was here and he didn't want to be found, he wouldn't be found.

It had been more than a year since the bastard had first started contacting them with his mocking Polaroids and pretty postcards of unfamiliar places they grew to know too well, and they still hadn't gotten the drop on him. In her experience, that type of communication with authorities meant mistakes. It meant that he thought he couldn't be caught, which was a dangerous mind-set for criminals. They began to take shortcuts. Hubris turned meticulousness into sloppiness in the blink of an eye.

But not Cross. He was fastidious, bordering on perfect, and far too brilliant to do something as amateur as show up at his victim's funeral. He'd led them on a countrywide scavenger hunt and hadn't left a single fingerprint or fleck of DNA behind, and they thought he'd make the most basic mistake in the book?

No. He wouldn't be there.

She didn't want to be impressed. She wouldn't be impressed. Three girls were dead, brutally murdered because they happened to have red hair and bad luck. Lila Teasdale. Eve McDaniel. Charlotte Collins.

Even the elaborate clues he set up in his sick little game weren't about the girls. They were about manipulation and control and power. That's what it came down to. The postcards that promised false hope if only the FBI could solve the clues in time. The relentless countdown that ticked away the seconds until the next deadline. The dead girl as the final prize in a twisted scavenger hunt Clarke had never wanted to play in the first place.

All of it. The whole mess was about Cross's fingers curled around puppet strings, him watching with glee as they all danced so prettily.

Clarke shifted as the mourners swept by her. It was a bigger crowd than it had seemed when they'd gathered around the grave site. Their collective grief had made them smaller, had weighed on their shoulders until they curved into themselves, had erased boundaries so that one body seeking comfort was swallowed up by another desperately wanting to offer it.

The gravitational force of it all pulled her along, dragged her in. Suddenly there were people around her, on all sides. She lost track of herself, of who was behind her, who was beside her, which she never let happen. It was because she'd been off balance, unfocused.

Sam had been right. Again. She still had a job to do.

Clarke slowed a bit, not enough to disturb the wave of bodies trudging toward cars but enough to maneuver out of her vulnerable position.

A flash of movement caught her attention, and she turned to steady the woman to her left whose heel had sunk in the softened earth. As Clarke's fingers pressed into the thick wool of the woman's coat, she heard her name, whispered like a vow into the wind. She whirled to find nothing but air beside her and the retreating backs of mourners who all looked the same.

The rain. The rain was too heavy to really see.

She crushed the palms of her hands to her eyes to clear away the excess water, then took off running, no longer caring about making a scene. She latched onto one arm after the next, studying the face of each shocked and angry person she dared to disrupt. There was hardly any air left in her lungs to utter a "Sorry" to them as her fingers grasped for the next suit-encased shoulder.

Not him. Not him. Not him.

Desperation and the rain had turned her vision into something she couldn't rely on, but as the adrenaline crashed back to normal levels, everything righted itself a bit.

Had she even seen him at all? Or was her mind playing tricks on her, as it so liked to do? It had taken years to banish the voices in her head that whispered insidious lies, the ones that were crafted to undermine her grasp on reality. The fragile stability she'd established in the quiet spaces between the doubts shook at the mere thought of becoming untethered once more. Those days were supposed to be a memory.

But still she felt the breath on the soft spot just behind her jaw.

Scrubbing there, as if that would rid her of the sick shivers it sent along her skin, she crested the little hill at the edge of the cemetery, ignoring the glares from the men she'd just assaulted. Sam didn't ignore them, though. He was watching. He was wondering about their anger.

"What did you do?" he asked, his gaze lingering over her shoulder.

"Oh, that's nice. Thanks for the trust." Years of practice had made her an expert at deflection. But years of knowing Clarke had made her easy for Sam to read. His eyes flicked over her face, and she immediately regretted drawing his attention. He always saw too much.

"What happened?" The lazy edge was gone from his voice this time. It was sharper now. Pointed.

Every instinct honed from years of training, from years in the field—God, even from years at her boring desk job—was throbbing at her to tell him. To say the bastard was here, to call in the cavalry, circle the wagons, scour every inch of this place. If she didn't, it would be more than just grounds for termination; it would mean their blood would be on her hands. Any girls that came next. If nothing else was certain, there was that. There would always be more girls.

But the words didn't come out. Instead, she shrugged. "It was nothing. I thought I saw . . ."

Sam's entire body went rigid. "You thought you saw?"

"It wasn't him," she said.

"That's not like you."

It wasn't. Not at her job. She didn't make mistakes. She didn't panic. She was a professional.

"First time for everything." She didn't meet his eye as she pushed past him to slide into the passenger seat of their rental.

They were quiet as they drove past a dilapidated McDonald's and strip malls advertising fake tans and cheap wigs. But when they pulled into their little motel, Sam reached over, his thumb resting on the sharp jut of bone at the edge of her wrist.

"You know I can always tell when you're lying to me, right? You have a tell."

She knew. "I have to change. We're leaving for the airport in a half hour."

"You twist your hair around your finger," he said, ignoring her attempts to pull away.

"Sam . . ." What was she supposed to say? She got spooked by a shadow? That she wasn't even sure if she could trust her instincts anymore? That it was Sam's fault anyway, because she'd been doing just fine until he'd thrown a grenade into her life, one he knew she wouldn't be able to handle?

Sam. If it weren't for him, she wouldn't even be here, chasing after the bastard.

It wasn't like she'd been happy in Florida. It wasn't like she'd been happy anywhere. But there, well, she'd come as close as she'd thought would ever be possible. Her position may have shifted away from the excitement brought on by chasing down big bad wolves in the night. But the nightmares had stopped. Waking up drenched in sweat with the claw marks from her own nails leaving drops of blood on the sheets was no longer a thing. She'd even walked by an AA meeting. Yes, she'd kept on walking right back to one of the bottles of wine she'd kept in the fridge, but she'd paused to read the flyer at least. It had felt like growth.

When she'd been the hot, young recruit in DC, the idea of voluntarily moving to Florida to ride a desk was as foreign as somehow living a normal life. She'd just graduated from Georgetown with a master's in criminal justice and the belief that submerging herself into a life of monsters would be enough to keep her own at bay. Special Agent Sam Gallagher had the right connections to open any doors her degree and her field testing couldn't.

The help hadn't always served her well. Even though Sam was openly gay, there'd been rumors that she didn't earn her spot through merit, a cringeworthy suggestion she hadn't had to live with for very long. At the young age of twenty-five, she'd helped catch the infamous TST Killer, and it had promptly shut up the gossipmongers. Or at least made them whisper behind her back instead of deliberately loud enough for her to hear.

The rush from catching the bad guys didn't last forever. It was like a drug: with each progressive hit the high would be shorter, until she was all but shaking in withdrawal in the months between cases. It got to the point that it was either leave it behind or burn in the flames.

Her coworkers had been smug when she'd put in for a transfer after only three years of being with the bureau. But celebrating when the mighty fell was so purely human she couldn't even blame them for it.

Plus, those two years in Florida had been the closest she'd ever come to normal.

The highs hadn't been as intense, but the lows hadn't crushed her, either. Maybe happiness wasn't something everyone could get. But emotional stability was certainly underrated.

Then Sam had come along. Because he always came along.

At first he'd just wanted her on his team. Didn't she miss fieldwork? Didn't she realize she was wasting her potential? He'd call or visit to try to persuade her, and it had become a joke between them. Until it wasn't anymore.

Sam had hopped on a plane straight from the autopsy of Cross's first victim, turning up at her door at one in the morning with a plastic evidence bag and regret stamped into the deep furrows of his brows. She'd almost collapsed to the floor right then because she'd known whatever he was about to tell her would be devastating. He wouldn't have looked like that otherwise.

When he'd handed her the bag, she'd wished she'd allowed herself those few seconds of unconsciousness. She'd taken it with shaking hands.

Catch me if you can, Clarke. Don't worry, I won't be gone for long.

The message was scrawled on a piece of thick, plain ivory paper.

She'd met Sam's eyes. It wasn't the first time some psycho had tried contacting her directly, especially following the arrest of the TST Killer. It was the first time Sam had come down in person, though.

There was a selfish part of her that resisted. She wouldn't even deny it. The deep cracks that spiderwebbed her psyche were too fragile to handle hunting another serial killer. It had taken five days of Sam camped on her ragged, little beige couch for her to give in. Of course she had, in the end.

He'd promised it would be only for as long as it took them to catch the bastard. Then she could return to Florida and put it behind her, go back to her life of almost contentment. Now, after months of hunting him, she realized the end that Sam had promised her was not going to come anytime soon.

The note they'd found pinned to Charlotte's body guaranteed that.

You couldn't solve my puzzle in time? I guess you'll have to try again, pet.

"Maybe I shouldn't have . . ." He dropped his head, looking tired. So tired. "Maybe I shouldn't have dragged you into this—what did you call it? A cesspit. Maybe if I cared about you a little less, or a little more, I wouldn't have. I don't know."

And wasn't that everything that was wrong with them?

"I get it," she said. In his position, she would have done the same. That didn't make her like it. That didn't make her not resent him. But she understood it. "You had to."

"I didn't," he said, still not looking at her. "I really didn't."

The rain kept up its steady patter against the windshield, and it was as if each drop washed away some of the anger she'd been holding on to. The anger she'd been holding on to so as not to feel anything else. The rest, well, that was much harder to deal with, to understand. Anger she knew.

The problem was that a small part of her had thought they'd be able to save Charlotte.

"I have to go change."

He nodded in acknowledgment. "I'm sorry, kid," he whispered as she was closing the door. The apology lashed against her like the quick slap of leather against skin.

She took the stairs two at a time, fumbling for her key card. Once she was safely in her room, she leaned back against the cheap wood of the door.

Had it been him at the cemetery?

She didn't like it, this not trusting herself. Because reality was a fleeting thing, and she knew that too well. The idea of losing her shaky grasp on it terrified her.

Her eyes caught her reflection in the mirror above the dressers that ran along one of the walls of the motel room. There was a flush running up the long length of her neck, but her cheeks were pale, and her pupils were dilated, eating up most of the green of her irises. Her shoulder-length brown hair was dripping onto her soaking-wet shirt. It clung to her body, highlighting the thinness of her frame, all the hints of curves long faded from endless weeks of forgetting to eat.

She glanced away, not wanting to see how fragile her control was, and that's when she spotted the flip phone sitting on the counter below the mirror. It was small and silver and years out-of-date from the sleek iPhones everyone carried these days.

And it wasn't hers.

Before she knew it, she was sliding on a fresh pair of gloves and crouching so she could get a better look. It didn't seem to be rigged to anything. Bombs weren't really his style.

She shouldn't pick it up. Even if it wasn't going to explode. But she did anyway.

Carefully, she grasped it between two fingers and thumbed it open.

The background was just the default factory setting. She navigated to the contacts, then the phone log, and finally the texts. Everything was blank. She dropped it back on top of the dresser before shrugging out of her soaking-wet clothes. By the time she'd wrapped herself in a too-small hotel towel, the phone had gone to sleep again. A few buttons brought it back to life, but there was nothing waiting for her to find.

She plucked her own phone out of her purse and fired off a quick message to Della LaCroix, the tech genius on Sam's team.

Need a favor. Can you look at something for me? Don't tell Sam?

The second text was to Sam. She hesitated over the wording, his whispered "I'm sorry" lingering in the little space where someone less cynical than herself might call her heart.

He's been in my room—can just tell.

She pressed her lips together until she felt the sharpness of her teeth against the flesh, but she decided to leave the message at that, with no mention of the phone.

This was wrong. Hiding it. There were procedures. Rules to follow. Probably for good reason, definitely for good reason. They could make plans, trace the phone, lull him into a trap. All good options.

Except she was herself. The person who always had one hand hovering over the self-destruct button. Because something dark and dangerous whispered to her that they had gotten nowhere from following the rules. The phone would be clean, and he was too smart to fall for any of their traps.

But maybe. Maybe if Clarke didn't turn it in like a good little FBI agent, if she hid the phone away like a guilty secret, he would think she was getting sloppy. And then he would get sloppy, too.

So she didn't do all the things she was supposed to do, all the things she'd been trained to do; she just stood in the middle of the shitty hotel room, with its ugly walls and its cheap carpets, and mentally traced the thin white scars that ran along her inner thighs. They made her miss the weight of a razor blade in her hands.

The vibration from her own phone pulled her back. She glanced down; it was just Della.

For you, anything.

Maybe in a different life there would have been a twinge of guilt for dragging Della into her lies. At this point, it was all just background noise.

Maybe in a different life that twinge would have been enough to get her to call Sam, confess everything. But this life was what she had, and so she studied the flip phone instead. There was nothing to find, but it kept her mind from looping in on itself as it was so prone to do.

And then it rang.

Everything in her stilled. Her heart, her lungs, her thoughts.

She flicked the phone open to answer it but didn't say anything as she held it to her ear. There was silence there, but she refused to break it.

The voice finally slithered through the open line. "Hello, Clarke."

CHAPTER TWO

Bess

July 7, 2018

Bess Stanhope hated the smell of beer. She also hated when her boyfriend would get that look in his eyes after he'd tossed back a few. One time he'd thrown the contents of the half-drunk red Solo cup in her face, and her hair had smelled of hops for days. She'd scrubbed her scalp raw when trying to wash it out, but nothing erased the memory of the expression on his face when he'd done it.

He was drinking now, and she wished she'd stayed home. But he'd begged her to come with him to the lake house to celebrate the Fourth. Three days later and the party still hadn't stopped, and she was so tired. The frazzled edges of her nerves were raw and pulsing after the constant barrage of misogyny and alcohol that was the mainstay of this getaway weekend.

It was only 10:00 a.m., but a group of the revelers was lying out on the docks, basking in the harsh rays of the summer sun, with a cooler full of Coors Lights. The bros were all decked out in Ray-Bans and red swim trunks as if it were an agreed-upon uniform, down to a cookie-cutter girlfriend draped off one arm.

Every so often one of the ladies would get tossed into the frigid water, sinking under the mirrored surface with an angry-cat shriek, after putting up a faux fight that involved ineffectual swats at sweaty chests. The boys would high-five one another, then adjust their backward-facing baseball caps for no apparent purpose, while the victim sputtered to the surface. Few women looked good with wet hair, but these ones came close.

Bess wanted to plunge a screwdriver into her own eyes.

She stretched out her legs, which looked stubby in comparison to the gazelles on the docks. Her neon-pink running shorts rode up high into the creases of her thighs, and the blades of grass were sharp against her pasty skin. She tipped her face up to the sun, drinking in the closest thing to silence she'd had since arriving at the lake house.

The name itself was a misnomer. She'd been picturing a little cabin by the water, but they'd pulled up to a three-story mansion, BMWs and Mercedes lined up like haphazard soldiers in the driveway.

It was a far cry from their tiny place in Brooklyn. And an even farther cry from what she was used to before that. Growing up, she would have thought this place a castle out of the fairy tales her mother liked to tell her while they'd huddled under thin blankets in their studio apartment. The cold that had turned Bess's fingers numb was always just woven into the story as part of their adventure. They were exploring the North Pole, not freezing because they couldn't afford the expense of turning up the thermostat.

Jeremy, on the other hand, was in his element. Though the excess was beyond their means now, he'd slipped back into it like a well-tailored jacket. While she found a familiar comfort in the nights they had to eat ninety-nine-cent tacos from the vendor at the end of their street, it chafed him. He missed filet mignon and Dom.

Austin, their host, had greeted Jeremy with a "Yo-o-o-o" and a handshake-hug bro bump that let them assert their heterosexual masculinity and establish affection at the same time. Austin had turned to her next, and she blinked against his shimmering goldenness—his tawny hair that draped over hazel eyes, his bronzed skin on display thanks to low-riding blue gym shorts—before he'd gathered her in his arms in an embrace that lasted three seconds too long.

Jeremy was pale in comparison, with close-cropped brown hair and deep-chocolate eyes. He would refuse to put on sunscreen this weekend, and then he'd burn and swear he didn't, even when she could leave ghost handprints on his back.

She suspected Jeremy had always been envious of Austin, whom he'd been friends with since their high school football days. Neither had been a true star, so they hadn't been able to ride the glory into college. Jeremy had struggled his way through a business degree, with a GPA that had reached only the low threes, with her help. Austin had pursued debauchery, paid for by his trust fund, but had come out of it with "Harvard Business School" on his résumé.

Bess wondered if Austin kept Jeremy around as a funhouse-mirror version of what he could have become. A way to make himself look better. She wondered what that made her.

The problem was that Jeremy's temper—never very far from the surface—flared so easily around Austin.

They'd had a few good weeks recently. Before that there had been months of tension and whispers and walking on eggshells. He'd told her all that was over. He'd been working toward his new promotion, and now that it had been announced, things would be good again.

She'd let the bubbly effervescence born from that promise carry her into this holiday weekend even though she'd known with all the outside forces adding pressure it would be a tough one.

They'd only just dropped their suitcases in the corner of their spacious bedroom on the third floor when they started fighting. They had their own bathroom en suite, and Bess had eyed the walk-in shower with a longing she usually reserved for red wine and cookie dough.

He came in behind her, pulling out his dick so he could piss in the toilet. She hopped on the swirled-marble countertop, watching his back, trying to avoid catching her own reflection in the mirror.

"So you think he's hot?" Jeremy asked, finishing off. He walked over to the sink, nudging her out of the way to wash his hands.

"What? Who?" She was genuinely confused by the question.

"Don't be stupid."

"I don't know what you're talking about."

He turned cold eyes on her, and she took a quiet breath. Those eyes were so quick to warm with humor and affection most of the time. But she knew this would be one of those moments when the rage froze them over, and she lost the Jeremy she loved to a monster. She braced herself.

"You're such a lying whore." His voice lashed across her like a whip as he pushed her back up against the mirror. The faucet dug into the small of her back, but she barely even noticed that bit of pain as his forearm came up against her throat. "You know what I'm talking about. Austin. You practically threw yourself at him."

Bess clawed at the thick arm cutting off her air supply and met his stare dead on. She kicked out with her leg, but he blocked the blow. It did make him release her, though, and she slumped back, gasping for air.

"I don't know why you do things like that, that make me hurt you, Bess." His voice turned soft and soothing. He ran his fingers down the side of her cheek. Hers were still protecting her neck.

She shook her head. "I'm sorry. He's nothing compared to you, baby," she murmured, laying a shaking hand on his bicep. The muscle flexed beneath her fingers. "Look at you. How could I want anyone but you?"

He nabbed her fingers to bring her palm up to his lips and laid a gentle kiss there before scooping her off the counter, into his arms. He carried her like a baby into the bedroom and deposited her onto the soft yellow down comforter. He bunched her short sundress up around her waist, pulled her panties down, and pushed into her in one swift move. She didn't dare cry out as he met dryness and resistance. He thrust into her as the other arriving couples chatted just outside their door.

In the very best circumstances, Bess wasn't the type of person who fit easily into a new, large group. She'd long been envious of those who could seamlessly blend into the personality of the crowd, feeding off the energy. But she only ever felt drained by it.

She'd tried to rally and, with the help of red wine, make that first night bearable, but she was still sore from that afternoon, and she was tired of explaining away the blooming purple-and-green marks on her neck.

He doted on her to compensate for her quietness, and the other girls cooed over how sweet they were. The perfect couple. It turned the alcohol sour against her taste buds when he smiled at the compliments and pressed his lips against the cheek he was so careful not to bruise. They'd learned long ago injuries to the face were harder to hide.

Jeremy wouldn't be pleased that she wasn't down at the docks with him. She watched him as one of the leggy blondes plunked herself squarely onto his lap. She watched his hand graze the underside of the blonde's breast as he pulled her close to whisper something in her ear, and she knew he was probably hard as a rock against the leg that did not have a dimple of cellulite on it.

There was nothing in her but relief, though. Relief at not being the center of his attention. Just five minutes of not having his suffocating gaze directed at her every move was glorious.

It was time. She'd gone into the bathroom that first day, after he'd attacked her, and had quietly vomited into the urine he hadn't flushed from earlier, and as she'd lain in the fetal position with the tile blessedly cold against her flushed cheek, she'd known. It was time. Time to finally leave.

She was prepared, to some extent. A while back, she'd signed up for self-defense classes, telling him she'd joined a book club. In reality she'd spent every other Wednesday night in the small but well-lit basement of her local church.

"Make yourself big," the teacher, an aging hippie with long, stringy gray hair, would yell at the self-conscious circle of women. "Don't be afraid to use your voice."

The moves never seemed to work on Jeremy, but it was nice knowing she had them at the ready anyway.

Still, she'd stayed with him. When he was kind and sweet, he was the boy she'd met in freshman English who secretly loved Shakespeare and brought her iced green tea to class. When he wasn't, well. She kept surviving those times, her battered body stitching itself back together, and as the bruises faded, so did the feeling of certainty that she had to leave. Because he would be happy and smiling again. Until he wasn't.

Fingers of tension coiled around the base of her neck, pulling the delicate muscles tight. She shook her shoulders, trying to loosen them, then pushed to her feet.

She tightened the laces of her shoes, smiling down at the happy, bright yellow of them against the lush lawn. It was late in the day to start a run, and the air was already suffocatingly hot, but she needed to feel the pavement beneath her, to eat the miles away and challenge her lungs until they burned and clawed at her throat. She shook out her legs and pushed her unruly dirty-blonde hair back into a ponytail.

It was just this one last weekend. She could do it—she could get through it. Had made it through worse. Plans would need to be made, of course, when she got back to the city. He wouldn't just let her go;

she wasn't naive enough to think that. But there was something in her that hadn't been there before. A certainty. A determination she could cling to when he turned soft eyes in her direction, and the memories of harsh words and harsher blows receded.

Yes, there were plans to be made. There wasn't much she could do at the moment, though.

So she flipped to an old Guns N' Roses song on her iPhone and took off at a light jog, skirting the house and finding her stride on the empty two-lane road that led back to town.

CHAPTER THREE

Clarke

July 13, 2018

Clarke pulled the faded photograph from her bag and held it up. Her eyes flicked between it and the building on the other side of the street. The store's sign had long succumbed to weather or neglect, but it was a match. **Gary's**. She flipped the photo over to read the now-familiar scrawl.

Four days.

The plastic bag protecting the picture was the only thing stopping her from tearing it to shreds.

It had been four months since Charlotte's funeral, and nothing had changed. Only the scenery. And even that was all starting to blur together, one miserable town after the next.

She'd thought maybe Cross was getting careless with the addition of the phone. But it hadn't rung since that first time she'd found it. Instead there had been two months of silence after Charlotte's death. Then the picture had arrived. It was of a pretty redhead with a round face, caught midlaugh and mid–eye roll, like she'd been secretly delighted the photo was being taken. There was an innocence in the captured moment that made the next realization much harder to swallow. Cross had his next victim.

The countdown didn't start with the pictures of the girls, though. No. He liked to let Clarke and Sam figure out exactly whose death they would be responsible for before sending them on the chase.

Della ran the photo through her face-recognition software and came up with Anna Meyers, a pastry chef from San Francisco. She specialized in cupcakes and had been missing since April.

Cross let them sit with the knowledge for two weeks. Two weeks of not being able to do anything, of realizing the bastard had Anna, while being helpless to even know where to start the search.

Then the first clue had arrived. Apart from the pictures of the girls, that first clue was the only thing he ever mailed them directly. The rest would be left at the locations, for them to figure out, for them to find.

Weeks after Anna's sweet face had first landed on their desk, they were nearing the end of the countdown for finding her. Four days. That's how long they'd had to figure out the latest clue was at Gary's. If his pattern held, they'd have three to find the next location. Failing to do so would cost them their final prize. Anna.

After sliding gold aviators down over her eyes, she surveyed the street. It was on the outskirts of Sweetwater, Texas, a town that seemed like a place where housewives forced bleached-blonde daughters into beauty pageants and beefy sons into football helmets as soon as they could walk.

Gary's was a mutt—a mix of a liquor store and a BBQ joint and a dirty video shop rolled into one place. The flyers hanging by frayed edges on the outside walls touted a "Buy one, get one" deal, but she didn't want to know if Gary's mixed and matched services.

The store sat right outside the town's dry-county limits, where it could lure in the husbands who wanted to numb the boredom with a fifth, and the teens who thought they were rebels without a cause.

An old lady in a purple muumuu sat in a beach chair a few houses down, cradling a sawed-off shotgun. A standing fan, with a cord running back into the weathered little house, swiveled in a sad, slow arc beside her. Otherwise the block was empty.

Beads of sweat ran down Clarke's back, collecting above the waistband of her jeans as she crossed over the road to Gary's. She wished she could strip out of the black leather jacket she wore over her holster, but she didn't want to draw even more attention than she already had as a stranger in a place that did not seem particularly welcoming to them.

She checked the sign one more time and tried to ignore the guilt that licked up her spine at going MIA on Sam. When the tip had come in during the early hours of the morning, it had been more sleep-deprived desperation than conscious thought that had her on a plane to Texas. Sam wouldn't see it that way.

Regret had no place here, though. Explanations and reprimands would come later, but for now she had a job to do.

So she slid the picture back into her purse and pushed through the door to Gary's.

The air conditioner was a little window unit with ribbons blowing in its gentle wake, and it let out a cough when she walked in.

Her sunglasses caught in the tangled mess of her sweat-drenched hair as she pushed them up to eye the large man at the cash register.

The man—or Gary, as he would now be known in her head—was neck-deep in a magazine that was surely a part of the store's stock, and didn't even glance up at the small chime that welcomed her in. Her gaze slid to the back row of coolers, where stacks and stacks of pretty brown bottles nestled in cardboard six-packs. Ignoring their siren's call, she grabbed a king-size bag of peanut M&M's instead and rested her hip against the counter.

Gary grunted as she tossed the yellow bag down, letting out an annoyed exhale of breath at being interrupted.

He was wearing a dirty wifebeater that didn't quite cover the beer gut that was making a break for it over the top of his faded jeans. His dark hair was slicked back from a bloated face whose main attractions were dark beady eyes and a bulbous nose. The capillaries in the skin that stretched over his flared nostrils could only have gotten that way from years of alcohol abuse.

"That all?" His voice was a slow drawl as he typed the price into a midnineties cash register, with the lazy movements she'd come to recognize as Southern through and through.

"I have a package to pick up as well," Clarke said.

"We don't do packages." His words crept to a crawl as if he were talking to an idiot. Asshole. "Check the post office. One fifty."

Clarke dug for the wadded bills she knew were floating at the bottom of her jacket pocket. "You have a package for Clarke Sinclair," she said this time, dropping the money into his sweaty palm.

He actually looked up at that. "Christ. You're Clarke Sinclair?" His eyes skimmed over her body, assessing. She wondered what he saw. It wasn't a pretty sight, she was sure. Her dark hair was currently staging a rebellion because of the heat, and her green eyes were red rimmed and bloodshot from lack of sleep. The pit stains under her arms were evident even beneath her jacket. "I've been wondering. Not what I expected, to be honest."

A barbed comment lodged in her throat, but she swallowed it. "You've had the package for a while?"

"A couple weeks." He lifted an exposed hair-matted shoulder as he reached beneath the counter. But then he hesitated. "Got ID?"

"Did they ask you to check?" she asked, but was already thumbing open the black leather case. The gold on the FBI badge caught in the light as she flipped it to reveal her ID card. There was fresh panic in Gary's eyes as he took it in.

"No one said anything about FBI," he muttered, his fingers tightening on the cardboard he still clutched.

"Relax," she said. "Not here for you, Gary."

It didn't seem to ease the tightness in the man's once-soft face.

She nodded to the box, and all of a sudden he was eager to hand it over. They both eyed the little brown package that he set in front of her. The top of it was blank except for her name in thick black marker, scrawled in that same haunting handwriting.

Instead of picking it up, she slapped a printout down onto the laminate. "Was this the man who dropped it off?"

Gary studied the sketch, squinting. But then he shook his head. "Nope. Not the guy."

"Did you know the person who left the box?"

The bastard had a habit of using random messengers, so she wasn't expecting much.

Gary's eyes shifted toward the door, but the rest of his body language was open, if nervous, so she chalked it up to wanting to get her out of there as fast as possible, and not as a marker that he was about to be deceitful.

"Normal guy. Didn't know him, though. Just said I had to make sure it was really you. That's it. Swear."

It fit the bastard's MO, and Gary was clearly so preoccupied with his own criminal activities that it wasn't likely he would lie to her about something else.

It also meant Gary didn't know anything of value, and she could get the hell out of the store. Get the hell out of this goddamn trash fire of a state.

"Okay, thanks," she said, pulling out gloves from the stash she kept in her purse, even though she knew the precaution was useless. They never found any evidence on the clues.

But she was already toeing the line with the big boss. Roger Montoya's endgame was the FBI-director spot, and he didn't take kindly to his agents flouting rules and regulations. Especially her.

Wearing the gloves would also save Clarke a lecture from the crime-scene guys, and she liked staying on their good side. So, despite her annoyance at the waste of time, she worked her fingers into the stubborn blue latex before finally picking up the package.

It was only then, as she was about to leave, that she glanced up to the little white security camera perched in the corner above the door. She stared down the lens, then flipped it off, before she headed back into the oppressive Texas heat.

CHAPTER FOUR

Adelaide

April 1993

Adelaide Young clutched Mr. Koala to her chest, hoping that his worn fur would block the noise of her racing heart. It pounded as if she had run and run and run as fast as she could across the playground. But she was just sitting in the back of Ms. Jacob's big black car.

The sight of it had scared her at first, and Adelaide had not been able to relax until Ms. Jacob had climbed out of the monster and smiled at her.

Ms. Jacob often looked like a rainbow, with flowy, jewel-colored skirts and chains with oh-so-pretty crystals dangling from them. And she always smelled like cookies. Adelaide had taken to crawling onto Ms. Jacob's lap, laying her head on her soft chest, and sucking her thumb in the way that used to make Mommy and Daddy angry, but they weren't there to be angry anymore. Ms. Jacob wouldn't get angry. She would just stroke Adelaide's hair and hum, and the vibrations would tickle Adelaide's cheek.

Adelaide didn't know why her mommy and daddy weren't there anymore. She just remembered she'd been so excited to build sandcastles at the beach and collect seashells in her new purple bucket and hunt ghost crabs while perched on Daddy's shoulders. She remembered Mommy and Daddy shouting a lot as she kicked against the back of Daddy's car seat.

And then she'd woken up in a strange place with bright lights and people dressed all in white and blue. The smell in the air had burned her nose, and the people there liked to poke at her with needles. She had not liked it. And she had not liked that Daddy no longer came running when she screamed. She'd tried over and over, yelling until her throat felt like she'd swallowed a bumblebee. And even then, he hadn't come.

One of the ladies had brought her Mr. Koala, and that had become the one thing she had from the before time. Before the endless stream of towering grown-ups and their pats and their hugs and their words that she could never quite understand even though she knew what the words meant. Before the scary places that didn't have the painted-butterfly walls of her room, that didn't have her shelves of books or her baskets of stuffed animals. Mr. Koala had not even been her favorite among them.

It was at one of the scary places that she'd met Ms. Jacob. She'd bent down so Adelaide didn't have to hurt her neck to look up at her face. She had soft honey hair, like Daddy's, and when she smiled, she had dents in her chipmunk cheeks.

Those dents were out now as she helped Adelaide climb down from the monster car. Adelaide was sweaty in her jacket that was too heavy, but she didn't want to take it off.

She stared up at the house that was bigger than the one she'd lived in with Mommy and Daddy. That one had been only one level, her bedroom snuggled up against theirs, which snuggled up against the little kitchen and living room. They'd had a big backyard for her to play in, though, and Daddy had even built her a tree house the summer before, when she'd turned six and was big enough to play in one.

Ms. Jacob stood beside her, and Adelaide slipped a hand into hers. The fingers tightened once, and Adelaide felt better for a second, before Ms. Jacob began tugging her toward the happily painted red door.

"You're going to love it here, Addie," Ms. Jacob chattered down at her. Ms. Jacob liked to chatter, like a songbird. Always talking, always talking. Adelaide liked it because it meant she didn't have to talk. "You remember Mr. and Mrs. Cross, don't you? You liked them."

Adelaide did remember them, but did not remember liking them. Mr. Cross was a very tall man with white hair like Grandpa had before he went away. His voice sounded like a whale when he'd talked to her, all loud and slow. He smelled stinky, too. Mrs. Cross was as round as a ball. She had squeezed Adelaide tight against her soft stomach, so that Adelaide thought she might not be able to breathe.

"You're going to be a good girl, aren't you Addie?" Ms. Jacob squatted down beside Adelaide on the porch. No one in the before time had ever called her Addie.

She nodded because she knew that's what Ms. Jacob wanted her to do, and she liked making her happy.

"That's my girl," she said, cupping Adelaide's face. She placed a kiss against Adelaide's forehead, and Adelaide leaned into it, liking the feel of the dry lips against her sweaty skin. It reminded her of Mommy.

Ms. Jacob pulled back and pushed a bright red corkscrew curl behind Adelaide's ear. Then she made a face, sticking out her tongue and crossing her eyes. Adelaide giggled, and Ms. Jacob seized the moment, turning to knock on the door. It opened in an instant as if the Crosses had been standing right behind it, waiting for them. Adelaide scooched closer to Ms. Jacob, wanting to disappear behind her thick tree-trunk legs.

Ms. Jacob wouldn't let her hide, though, and pushed her ahead, saying she needed to run back to the car for Adelaide's bags.

Mr. and Mrs. Cross smiled so big Adelaide wondered if their faces hurt. Hers used to when she smiled that big.

Mrs. Cross pulled her against her stomach again, and some of her shirt went into Adelaide's mouth.

"Addie! Welcome to your new home."

"Who are you?" The boy was leaning against the wall just inside her new bedroom. It was painted bright pink, with soft pink curtains and a pink comforter and pink pillows and a pink poster of a white fluffy cat hanging over her bed.

Her favorite color was purple.

She eyed the boy. He was small, not much taller than herself, with shaggy brown hair and dark brown eyes. His clothes hung on his skinny body, his jeans slipping down narrow hips as they made an effort to sink to the floor. A worn leather belt tightened past the last notch with a crude homemade hole was the last defense against gravity. The arms of his multicolored striped T-shirt ended below his elbows.

"Your new sister, Simon, you know that," Mrs. Cross said, bustling into the pink room with Adelaide's little rolling suitcase. She had been so proud of it when she'd gotten it for her last birthday. It had her name on it in gold sparkles. She'd zipped her toys into it and rolled it back out to her tree house and pretended she was running away to the circus but had never actually wanted to leave.

Mrs. Cross unzipped it now while the boy continued to watch Adelaide. "You know what? Why don't we let you settle in, Addie, before we unpack?" She turned toward Adelaide, cupping her cheek with plump, damp fingers. Adelaide had liked when Ms. Jacob had done it, but she didn't like the feeling of Mrs. Cross touching her.

Simon watched Adelaide flinch away, and his thin lips curled into a smile. Mrs. Cross didn't seem to notice.

She bustled over to Simon, turning him around and marching him out of the room. "Let's leave her alone, Simon. We'll come get you for dinner, my dear. Hot dogs and macaroni! Yum," she called out, closing the door behind her.

Adelaide crawled on the small bed and buried herself under the covers, bringing her legs up to her chest. The hot, thick tears ran down her cheeks, and she pushed Mr. Koala into her mouth so Mrs. Cross wouldn't hear her crying.

It wasn't long before the door opened and then closed again, and Adelaide clenched her eyes shut, so that maybe they would think she was asleep.

After a few minutes of silence, she couldn't resist peeking, lifting one lid so she could see who was standing over her, breathing quietly.

"They're not so bad, you know." It was the boy. He'd been watching her cry. She sat up, scooted back against the wall, and hugged her knees to herself, resting her chin on them. "I'm Simon."

He held out a hand and she shook it, pretending the adult act wasn't strange to her. He smiled into her eyes and she warmed. "You're Addie, right?"

"Adelaide," she said, her voice so soft she didn't even know if he'd heard her.

"Adelaide," he repeated before dropping her hand and walking around the room, assessing it. "I'm eleven. How old are you?"

"Seven."

He nodded wisely. "Seven's a good age. Seven's a good age."

She nodded, too, not knowing what that meant, but he sounded like a grown-up when he'd said it, so it must be true.

He picked up one of the Barbies perched in a little pink-and-white convertible. He studied the face before tossing it to the floor. The pretty blonde hair spread over the carpet after her head bounced off the hood of the toy car.

"I've been here three years. The family before that had six other foster kids," he said, moving on to the next basket. He dug in. "Now that—that sucked."

She giggled nervously at the word Mommy had always told her was a bad one. But Simon said it as if it were nothing.

"They weren't as old as dinosaurs like the Crosses, but at least you don't have to fight for food around here."

"Are there any others here?" Adelaide asked, braving her first full sentence. He turned with a smile, holding a floppy yellow duck half his size.

"Nah," he answered. "There was Matthew, but he isn't here anymore."

"Did he go away?"

Simon threw the duck back into the bin. "Not like your parents."

Adelaide fought the tears in her eyes, not wanting to cry in front of this older boy any more than she already had. He wasn't looking at her, though. He'd found a rubber bouncy ball, which he seemed to deem satisfactory. He turned, in a swift move, and chucked the ball toward the wall next to her head. She ducked, and the ball hit the space where she had been with a *thwunk* before bouncing back to him. He caught it with one hand, laughing a little-boy laugh.

"You are *such* a girl. I wasn't going to hit you." Adelaide didn't know if she should believe him.

She didn't say anything, and Simon lifted a narrow shoulder. "Fine, don't believe me. No one ever does."

There was silence for a minute.

"You wanna play catch?" she asked. His face brightened instantly.

"Well, come on then," he said, tearing out the door and down the stairs. She scrambled off the bed, her little feet struggling to keep up with his longer strides. The screen door slammed, a shot that rang out in the quiet of the house, as she saw him burst through it into the light of the warm spring day.

CHAPTER FIVE

Clarke

July 13, 2018

It never got easier. Even though she knew what was in the box, knew the contents weren't dangerous, it never got any easier.

Emotions gnawed at her gut, warring for dominance. Dread, disgust, excitement, a sick twist of curiosity. It was those last ones that made it hard for her to look in the mirror some days.

The box was so innocuous. Plain and brown and just sitting there where she'd placed it on the bed's comforter. It should look scarier than it did. More intimidating. It was like the bastard himself in that way.

He liked to vary it, the packages he left for Clarke and Sam. Just another way to keep them off balance. Sometimes it was a cardboard box, but sometimes it was a hollowed-out book tucked onto a library shelf; sometimes it was an empty beer case stacked in the dark corner of a bar. The constant was what was inside each. And what it meant.

She'd already kicked off her boots by the door, but all of a sudden her jacket was too restrictive. It needed to come off. Once it had, she palmed the now-exposed gun at the side of her breast, sliding it from the holster. The weapon joined her badge, which she'd slapped down on the bedside table.

Her toes dug into the faded worn-down carpeting as she paced the length of the room, keeping the box in her sight line at all times. Like she would a rabid dog.

The Swiss Army knife was in her hand before she could second-guess herself. She flipped open the deceptively sharp blade before tossing it once in the air, then catching it by its handle.

There was playing fast and loose with procedure, and then there was consigning it to hell. Most of the time she toed the side of the line that kept her in a job. She solved cases, and that was undeniable. If a few rules were broken while she was doing it, well, mostly the higher-ups looked the other way. The ends justifying the means.

Still, there were certain lines that couldn't be crossed, ones that would let a bad guy walk because of her stubborn disregard for rules. Processing evidence on her own should earn her more than a slap on the wrist or one more note in her file to add to the long list of notes in her file.

She'd also run out of fucks to give, though, around the same time they'd found Charlotte. Or maybe before that. Probably before that.

Maybe she had a blind spot when it came to the bastard. Maybe everyone knew it but let her work the case anyway. They were the ones who set her loose on him in the first place; they could be the ones who cleaned up her mess.

So she slipped on a fresh pair of gloves and sliced through the packaging tape so she could pull back the flaps. The photograph came unstuck from the bottom of the box with ease.

It was actually a pretty scene—a cabin, on the edge of a lake, that looked like a lovely little hideaway. There was a dock that jutted out in the water, with a boat moored at the end of it. *No Worries* was painted on the stern in purple letters. She flipped the picture over.

Three days.

"Goddamn it." Clarke threw the knife into the thin wall closest to her. It sank to the hilt of the small blade. Her legs gave out and she dropped onto the carpet, her back leaning against the bed. "Goddamn it," she said again, quietly this time.

Almost unconsciously, her fingers found the dark ink of her tattoo, a constellation captured on skin, just below the crook of her left elbow. It was her little piece of the sky that she could always keep with her, and the emotional permanence of it and the stars had become her anchor. If ever there was a time she needed a reminder that the world was bigger than anything that seemed unbearable to her, she would just let her fingers trace over the geometric pattern. The sheer weightiness of it, of the universe it represented, made her feel light and floaty in the kind of way a razor blade used to.

By the time she held up the photo to the light to see if there were any watermarks lurking beneath what her eyes could see, she realized she was just delaying the inevitable. Putting it off wouldn't make it any easier, though, so she crawled to her bag, the rough carpet leaving raw burns against her kneecaps. She ignored the sting as her fumbling fingers brushed past food wrappers and crumpled receipts, sliding along the deepest recesses of her purse, as if they knew she didn't actually want to find what she was looking for.

When she finally snagged her phone, she collapsed back against the foot of the bed.

There were fifteen missed calls and twenty-five unread texts. Sam was pissed. And worried.

She thumbed to his number in the log and hit the "Call" button.

"Jesus, Clarke." The layers of emotions Sam could convey with just two words never failed to impress. She squeezed her eyes against it. "You can't go AWOL on me like that again. Not in the middle of this shit."

It had been reckless, taking off like that in the middle of a case without telling her partner. It was behavior she didn't want to recognize but did. The phone. The late nights without sleep. Winding up on a plane without even realizing how she'd gotten there. When it had happened before, this dangerous slide into self-destruction, she'd been able to run away to Florida. Now, though, escape wasn't an option.

And so it played out, a pattern established long ago, an echo of a childhood she wanted so desperately to forget. She fought it, she tried, but this case was triggering every bad habit she'd thought she'd broken.

"I had a lead." It wasn't quite the apology she knew he wanted, the one she should give him.

Before, the defensiveness in her voice would have been a gauntlet thrown. An invitation to emotionally slice at each other. Sam was subtler in his technique, but he knew how to cut just right to make her bleed.

They had been getting better, though. Gentler with each other. He'd made an effort to stop treating her like a teenager, and she'd been trying not to take everything he said as a personal judgment on her life.

They hadn't had a real fight in years. Not since she'd asked for a transfer to Florida and hadn't told him.

"You don't even tell me you want to move to Florida?" Sam asked, his voice tight with anger even though he kept it pitched low. That's how they fought. Not with wild gestures and unleashed voices, but with tiny slashes and cruel jabs that hit already-bruised places so that full punches weren't necessary.

They sat in the back booth of the dive bar that was about a ten-minute walk from the FBI headquarters. It was known for its rude waitstaff and its patrons who wouldn't eavesdrop on a private conversation. Agents loved it. But it was only two in the afternoon, and the others wouldn't start filtering in until at least five. They had appearances to keep up, after all. Whereas she and Sam just didn't care.

So apart from Lola, their waitress, whom they liked because she left them alone and had a heavy hand with the pours, there was only one other person in the bar—an old woman perched on a stool, nursing a beer and flipping through a battered novel.

"You didn't tell me you were sleeping with Roger again," she countered. Even just the name of their boss sat sour on her tongue.

"And you care because . . . ?"

"Because you're stupid around him," she said.

"That's not why." Sam watched her, his eyes seeing too much. "You just don't like that I have something in my life that doesn't involve you. So selfish sometimes, I swear to God."

Saliva caught in the back of Clarke's throat. "Oh, I'm the selfish one? Real rich, Sam." There wasn't anything more to say to that. They were both selfish, both self-centered to the point of thoughtlessness at their worst times. And those times seemed to be the norm lately.

Finally Sam shifted, relented. Always the bigger person than she was. "You're angry because you think I took Roger's side over yours."

Clarke ran a hand through her hair and brought her glass to rest against her lips. She savored the burn of liquor in her nostrils before tipping it back. The smooth whiskey warmed in the heat of her mouth, and she let it sit there for a moment before swallowing it. "You did, Sam."

"He's just worried about you." He didn't argue her point, though.

"Why should I care what he's worried about?"

"Because he's your boss. And he wants what's best for you, even if you don't believe it."

"Kicking me off a case isn't what's best for me. Barring me from any other cases until I see a therapist isn't what's best for me," she said. What she'd done hadn't even warranted the extreme punishment. Did it really matter if some low-life rat had his finger broken during an interrogation? The results spoke for themselves.

He was quiet as he swirled the liquid in his glass. "You do hear yourself, right?"

Sam sighed when she didn't say anything more, and emptied his glass in one swallow. "Look, Roger was always wary about hiring you in the first place." He held up a hand. "Not because he didn't think you'd be a good agent. He just didn't want . . ."

"The liability?" she finished for him.

He shook his head. "He's not that bad, you know."

"Yeah, well, I can see past his pretty face, and you can't, so I think I'll go ahead and stick with my judgment of him."

Sam didn't defend himself, signaling for Lola instead. Clarke quickly finished her drink so when the waitress came over with the bottle, she'd be able to fill her up, too.

"You don't see clearly." Clarke continued to push.

Sam shrugged, not denying it. "But I'd never take his side over your best interest, kid."

"Like you know what my best interest is." She stared into the glass as she said it, not wanting to meet his eyes. Not wanting him to see that her own were wet for reasons she couldn't explain. That's how everything felt these days—inexplicably raw.

"I do," he said after a quick thank-you tossed at Lola, who moved off to clean tables behind them.

"No." There was an anger she needed to hold on to that the alcohol was already starting to numb. It beckoned her, that oblivion. But they'd been living in this codependent friendship for so long it had become normal, and that scared her almost more than the wildness in her eyes when she looked in the mirror in the mornings. "It's your savior complex. That's what you care about. And the fact that you've convinced yourself that you want what's in my best interest just proves how much you actually don't."

"My savior complex?" Sam asked as if they hadn't had this conversation before. They had.

"I don't really blame you." Clarke leaned forward, the wood sticky against her forearms. "As far as people in need of saving go, you hit the jackpot. That's why we're like this."

"Like what?"

Clarke looked away, her eyes flicking to the black-and-white photos hanging on every inch of the wall. Former agents, their smiles loose with alcohol or celebration or both. "Why did you talk Roger into hiring me?"

There was a pause, but Sam didn't push the question she'd dodged. "You're a great agent, kid."

"I know," she said. She was. That didn't make her a great human or a great friend. But he'd never asked that of her. Maybe he didn't think she was capable of it. Maybe she didn't think she was. "Friends tell each other things, Sam. The important things."

"Are we back to that? I would have told you about Roger and me if I thought you'd been able to handle it."

And there was the anger again. It was comforting, familiar, and it nudged through the haze of liquor. "Screw you. This is what I'm talking about. You don't trust me."

"It's not about trust, kid."

"Then what is it?"

He didn't answer. Couldn't. They'd fallen into these patterns too long ago, and now they couldn't escape. All they were doing was talking in circles, avoiding questions they didn't want to answer so that the words they did say were hollow and stripped of meaning.

"You can't save me, Sam." She rubbed her thumb over the knuckles of one hand, back and forth over the knobs of bone.

"I'll never stop trying to save you, kid," Sam said, watching her hands. "I'll never stop thinking you're worth trying to save."

It wouldn't help to argue. It wouldn't help to remind him of the thin white scars on her legs, or the early mornings he found her curled over her desk after not having gone home for the night, or the way her tongue turned too sharp at the merest provocation.

"You're not mad that I'm moving to Florida because you care about me." It was a realization she would have figured out sooner if she hadn't been caught up in her own shit. "You just don't know what you'll do with yourself if I'm not the center of your life."

He shook his head, then threw back his drink a second time, but still didn't say anything.

Clarke didn't pull the punch. "You might have to actually get your own life. No more Clarke and her messy problems for a distraction. Maybe you'll be forced to look inside your head for a change and realize you don't really like what you see there."

The words tumbled into the space between them with an abandon she recognized all too well. This was why she had to leave. Otherwise, not only would she burn in the flames, but she would take everyone with her.

He huffed out a breath. "You know what? I'm tired of stopping you from hitting the self-destruct button. You want to hide out and waste your life in a swamp, go for it. Don't expect me to clean this one up, though. I'm serious. I'm done."

"I've heard that before." Clarke smirked to break the tension.

Sam didn't smile. "I'm serious."

Something sad and desperate shifted in her. She immediately wanted to take it all back.

This is what she wanted, though. This is what she needed.

"You promised," she whispered anyway. Because this is how they were.

"Promised what?"

The words hurt her throat, catching like broken glass against the vulnerable tissue. "That you'd always be there for me."

He closed his eyes, and she knew he didn't want to remember.

There was a long pause where her heartbeats stuttered together with an anxiety the moment didn't really warrant.

Then he breathed in deep through his wide nostrils. "You're right, kid. I will be. Always."

It was that vow that somehow managed to pull her back whenever she teetered on the edge of some emotional cliff. It came back to her, just exactly where she was. Huddled on a dirty floor of a motel room in a rinky-dink town in Texas, with Sam on the other end of the line.

"You're right," she finally said. "I'm sorry. I won't do it again."

There was a pause on the other side, and she knew it was because that hadn't been the response he'd been expecting.

"I was worried about you, kid."

"I know, I . . ." She rubbed the heel of her hand against her eyes. "I couldn't sleep. Was checking the tip email, and we got one that seemed legit." They'd long ago decided to release the photos to the public in the hopes that if Clarke and Sam failed to figure it out, maybe someone out there would help. "The person recognized Gary's. It's their local convenience store. Next thing I knew I was at National, going through security."

"A note. A text. Is that too hard?"

"I wasn't thinking," she admitted.

He must have sensed something in her tone that bespoke her frayed emotional state, because he let it drop. "All right, it's done, you're safe. Where are you?"

She glanced around. "Middle of Nowhere, Texas." She paused. "I found it, Sam."

"Burying the lede, kid," Sam's voice chastised through the phone.

"We have three days."

"Goddamn it," Sam said, and Clarke finally smiled.

"My reaction, precisely."

"All right, all right. Three days. How . . ." He trailed off.

He didn't need to explain further, though, because she knew what he was thinking.

"How does he always know when to start the clock?" She voiced his unspoken question.

"How does he know?" Sam repeated.

Because she didn't have an answer that wasn't terrifying, she let the silence hang. Any way they looked at it, Cross was monitoring their movements, tracking them. He would need to know if they got to a clue early or late. And then he would have to adjust whatever timelines he kept in his own mind. The weight of his eyes, watching her from somewhere unknown, turned her skin clammy.

"So, is it any easier with this one?" Sam finally asked.

She reached for an evidence bag to slip the photo into, then peeled off the latex that always made her skin itch. The pretty little scene looked as innocuous through the ripples in the plastic as it had five minutes ago. “Maybe. I don’t know. A cabin in the woods. Looks Northeastern to my untrained eye. I’ll send you and Della a picture of it, so you guys can start working. Then I’ll get my ass on a plane back to HQ.”

“Took the words out of my mouth,” Sam said. “Any chance he’s there?”

Clarke shook her head before remembering she was on the phone. “No,” she said.

“So the hunt continues.”

“A twisted scavenger hunt that we keep losing.”

“Keep your head on straight, kid. Don’t let him get in there.” Sam’s calm voice served only to grate on her nerves.

“Yeah. I gotta go,” she said, pulling the phone away from her ear.

“Stay safe, Clarke.” Sam’s last words were tinny through the speaker. She pushed the “End Call” button.

She looked at the photo again and wished she’d bought that six-pack.

CHAPTER SIX

Bess

July 7, 2018

Sweat pooled beneath Bess's breasts and at the base of her spine as she pushed up another one of the steep, winding hills away from the mansion on the lake. Away from Jeremy and drunken gaiety she had no interest in. Her knee ached and her sports bra chafed, but she ruthlessly tamped down on the dull pain. Instead, she focused on breathing. The air was heavy with water, and her body bucked against the intrusion of it, scraping away at the particles, desperately seeking oxygen to power her bunched and straining thighs.

The steady beat of the song matched her footfalls until the pavement curved, reaching its highest point, before becoming flat again. She stumbled to a stop, and gravity pulled at her, settling like a hand on her lower back, pushing her toward the welcoming ground. But it would be a mistake to give in to it, as tired as she was, so she simply bent at the waist instead. Darkness crept in from the sides of her eyes, and she squeezed them tight.

Don't faint, don't faint, don't faint.

A rude mechanical honk brought her upright, and she stepped off the road in time to feel the air rush by her elbow as the car sailed past.

She stumbled a bit, the edge of her shoe catching on the lip where pavement met gravel. At one point in her life, she could have imagined herself screaming at the asshole, chasing after him without a care, waving her middle fingers in the air on the off chance of him glancing in the rearview mirror.

That's who she used to be.

Instead, she just stretched her arms above her head and waited for the buzzing in her ears to fade. Then she took off again. A downhill and a long stretch of flat stood between her and the small town. She'd run the route twice now, and it was beginning to feel familiar.

Once she flew through the first switchback of the descent, her mind began to probe her relationship again.

The thing was, she'd always thought she'd have known better.

Her mother's life had been a long parade of failed relationships, and Bess had vowed never to lose herself like that in someone else, to give up her identity, her thoughts, her passions, for something as fleeting as lust cleverly disguised as love.

Once upon a time, Melissa had been a wide-eyed romantic, and then Bess suspected that her father had happened. There had always been something about the way her mother's voice cracked along the edges when he was mentioned, even in the abstract, that turned her wary. She'd never pushed for any information on him, never found out if he was the drug addict who had routinely stolen from her mother, the married guy whom her mother still kept a picture of hidden under her pillow, or the one who'd rearranged her mother's pretty little nose so that it bent to the left now.

Whoever it had been that Bess could technically call father didn't matter. What mattered was he was the first in a long string of lessons that Bess should have learned from.

To her credit, Melissa tried. She tried to provide Bess with a life that didn't revolve around the shitty men who traipsed through their tiny apartment.

She'd filled Bess's brain with writing from feminists such as bell hooks and Gloria Steinem, propped her on her shoulders at rallies for local female politicians, and had her watch every horrible domestic violence PSA-type video there was, the ones filled with shadows and bruises and melodramatic tears. Bess had judged the women in them. Both the actresses and the characters they'd played.

Now it was her reality. Well, that, but without the bad lighting and cheesy dialogue.

And didn't that blow.

It hadn't always been like this. The start had been sweet enough. Textbook, probably.

He'd been the first guy to really pay her any attention. To tell her she was pretty. She'd sunk into it, like a cloyingly warm bath that left you burned if you stayed in too long but felt like golden silk at first.

The flare-ups had scared her, but she'd been lulled with soft pets and affectionate words, and the warning bells had been quieted. The first serious red flag had come when she'd ended up Jason DeSantos's beer-cup partner, a stand-in for a girlfriend who had run to the bathroom. Bess'd sunk a beauty of a shot on her first try, and they'd celebrated her beginner's luck with an impetuous hug. Jason paid for it with a sucker punch from Jeremy, who had then gripped her wrist with a hand bleeding from the knuckles and dragged her from the party.

The scariest part had been that he hadn't even said anything. Jason was sprawled on the floor, and Jeremy didn't even acknowledge what had just happened. They had never talked about it, because she'd let it go.

She picked up speed as she hit the flat stretch, letting her legs fly beneath her. The trees rose up around her, sentries guarding her as she ran. It was peaceful in their shadows.

What had proved even more insidious than the outright violence was the emotional abuse. He tested the waters with it. Tested to see how much she'd put up with. Little jabs and digs at first. The put-downs that were so neatly and precisely dressed as concern. But even when she knew it was happening, it didn't stop her from internalizing it. From accepting it as truth, as the water scalded her degree by degree until she was so used to it she didn't feel the blisters covering her skin.

Suddenly there was no ground beneath her feet. She was on all fours, with sharp pain radiating in throbbing circles from a point just below her kneecap.

The world had shifted so quickly that nothing made sense. Her brain scrambled to process what had happened, and that's when she noticed the rogue root behind her. She shifted slowly to her butt and brushed at the little pebbles that had dug into the soft flesh of her palms.

A thin line of red snaked its way down her shinbone, and she cursed the razor-edged rock that mocked her from its home beside her knee. She swiped at the blood, but there wasn't much to do about it now.

So she stood, shook out the muscles that had gone stiff from her prone position, and started toward town once more, at a more sedate pace.

She walked until she got to the intersection where her road and Main Street crossed, then hooked a left. The town had sort of a gray pallor that clung to the facades of the businesses and to the faces of the permanent residents. Tony's Pizza, closed down and boarded up, marked the start of the nonresidential section of Main Street. A caricature of Tony, fat-faced and rosy-cheeked, gave her a thumbs-up from the sign that was missing one of its *z*'s.

She swung into the little pharmacy/grocery/catchall general store, heading for the water section. It was only when she had a bottle firmly in hand that she realized she'd forgotten to stash a few dollars in her belt, like she normally did before a run.

Licking her lips, she couldn't tear her eyes from the water in her hand.

"Miss, are you all right?"

Bess swiveled toward the voice, knowing she must have looked a little rough for wear, with the blood and the sweat and just enough of a "Shit, shit" expression on her face to make a truly delightful sight for any passerby.

But she smiled at the man, a polite tug of lips upward that she had learned would keep Jeremy from making wild accusations about her flirting but satisfied her own deeply entrenched manners. "I'm fine, thank you."

With great reluctance, she put the water back and turned to head toward the door.

"Oh, wait, don't you want that?" the man called after her.

"It's okay, I changed my mind," she said, waving a hand.

He just raised an eyebrow, tossing his red Gatorade from hand to hand as he watched her.

She laughed, knowing she was busted. "Actually, I forgot my cash. But I'm okay, really. I'm not staying far from town. I can make it until I get back." She turned, starting down the row of cake-mix boxes and yellow bags of chocolate chips.

"Uh-uh," he said, and she stopped again, wishing she weren't so thirsty. He was shaking his head at her. "You are not running back in this humidity without some water. My mother would knock me senseless if I let you do that."

He reached into the cooler, nabbing her an even bigger bottle than the one she'd pulled out, and walked over to her. She took the already-sweating plastic, trying not to snatch it too eagerly. Relying on strangers made her uncomfortable, but what was ninety-nine cents, really?

"Thank you," she said, a bit embarrassed but mostly grateful.

She actually looked at him this time. He wasn't much older than she was, maybe early thirties, with shaggy brown hair that fell over deep brown eyes. Slender, but not thin, with enough muscle to add some power to his frame. The bones in his face were delicate, but it all added to his mysterious look. He had an old-world-vampire air about him, and she almost giggled at the thought. Too much Buffy fan fiction for her, apparently.

He was attractive, she realized with a start. When she'd first seen him, he'd blended in with the background, just another vague, average white man. But up close, when he smiled down at her, she felt a little tingle of awareness.

"And maybe a Band-Aid, too." His eyes had slipped from her face down to her knee, where the blood had started to pool on the edge of her sock.

"Oh no, no, I couldn't . . ." But she was talking to his back as he swung into the pharmacy aisle, and he emerged a few seconds later with a little white box. He motioned for her to join him on his way to the register.

"It's nothing. Really," he said, and she wondered if she noticed the slightest Southern drawl in the way he dragged out "really."

"Thank you." She shifted, her fingers tugging at the hem of her shirt as he tossed a few bills on the counter, waving off the cashier's offer of a plastic bag.

"Come on," he said, his hand a gentle push on the middle of her back. She grimaced at the idea of him having to touch her sweat, but he didn't seem to mind. And she felt compelled to follow him.

There was a bench just outside the doors, its green paint chipping into large flakes that fell to the ground around it. He nudged her to sit down, then ripped into the box, which it turned out was a little first-aid traveling kit.

"You're visiting around here?" he asked as he tore into the foil package of the antiseptic wipe.

"Yes, staying at a house on Brown's Lake."

He met her eyes. "That's about six miles up at the closest, isn't it?"

She nodded. "I like running."

He smiled at her, then lifted her calf, his long, pale fingers wrapping around the muscle, to bring her leg up to rest on his. Then, using the wipe, he dabbed at the cut, which was mostly scabbed over at this point.

A few stray pebbles had to be brushed from the wound before he swiped at the dried smears on her leg. She was thankful she'd shaved that morning.

"Do you live here?" she asked, remembering to pick up the conversation. She'd been so conditioned to avoid talking to strange men she sometimes forgot the proper protocol.

"Passing through," he said, laying a Band-Aid over the newly disinfected cut before releasing her leg. "There, good as new." He stood up to toss the remnants of the little package into the trash and then returned to her, holding out a hand to help her up. She took it even though she didn't need it.

"I can't thank you enough," she said.

"Don't worry about it. Where would we be in this cold, hard world if we couldn't rely on the kindness of strangers?"

They stood smiling at each other over his slightly butchered reference, until she felt it turn awkward. She sighed. It was past time to head back anyway.

"Okay, bye," she said, brushing past him to get to the sidewalk. But then she stopped. And turned. "Oh, I'm Bess, by the way. I don't think I got your name?"

He smiled at her, and at this distance he was back to being a nondescript white dude. "Simon. My name is Simon."

CHAPTER SEVEN

CLARKE

July 14, 2018

The wispy white clouds that marshmallowed the sky below the plane matched the fuzziness in Clarke's head. If she could just trace her fingertips through the bits of fluff, dip the palms of her hands into them, maybe the buzzing that hovered at the edge of her hearing would subside.

This was her life now. Plane rides. Hotel rooms. Long car trips that just led to more pictures that led to more long car trips that led to more hotel rooms that led to more planes. Would it end? Would it ever end?

In her head was Sam's quiet voice telling her yes. But too much time staring at marshmallow clouds had let the bastard slip under her defenses. Even after she'd built up her walls brick by brick, he'd still found a way in.

Her next breath met a solid wall of resistance as she tried to pull it into her lungs.

Moments later she was bent at the waist, her fingers pressed into the crease in her arm, to seek comfort from the ink that lay below the fabric of her coat.

"I'm a nervous flier, too, dear," the woman next to her said, patting Clarke's shoulder blades with a pudgy hand. "Do you know what does the trick?"

Clarke's mouth was sandpaper, and the words she tried to say caught in the roughness of it. She just shook her head instead.

She leaned closer so she could whisper to Clarke. "Pot."

The surprise of the answer was enough to reset Clarke's erratic synapses.

She laid sweaty palms on her jeans so she could push back up into a seated position, just as the plane nosed downward, and offered the woman a weak smile. "I'll keep that in mind for next time."

"First time flying?"

"Uh, no. But gets me every time." Clarke waved toward the window as if it were their descent that had her stomach trying to eat itself and not the absolute soul-sucking futility of putting one metaphorical foot in front of the other in the never-ending shit parade her life had become.

The woman nodded and patted her again, this time on her forearm. "My son is like that, too . . ."

And Clarke let herself tune out as Mrs. Claus tried to matchmake her with the very eligible, handsome, smart, wealthy doctor—"Can you believe he's single?"

While she pretended to listen to a barrage of the son's many and varied hobbies, she palmed the phone in her pocket, the silver one.

She never had to dig deep in her memory for the taunting voice that had been on the other end. It had just been more of the same, the words. The ones that were dripping with false affection on the back of the postcards and pictures he sent.

"Did you miss me?"

The way his tongue slid over vowels, though, made it different, so different from just reading them.

It made her itchy. Made her want to pick at the scars on her legs with jagged fingernails, until they opened up and let the pain seep out as the relief created champagne bubbles in her blood.

But that was her being selfish again. The want—the need—to chase the high instead of focusing on finding the girl was temptation at its hardest to resist.

There were promises to keep, and a bullet with the bastard's name on it, and if she was going to be itchy for something, it would be to help that slick piece of metal find its home.

The countdown, the one that reset with each photo, had started. It stayed with her always, a constant reminder of each second slipping into the next. The game was on, and the only chance they had at winning was to beat that clock.

A part of her realized how addictive it was. The chase, the excitement, the rush that came from outwitting the bastard.

They always had ten days for the first clue, the one that was mailed to headquarters. But it was a sticky, sweet sickness in her gut that made her want to figure it out in nine—in eight, if she could. As if it would prove something to him.

The first clues were the hardest anyway. A snapshot of a barren landscape or even a quick, shared moment caught in time. He knew it would take them longer, and it always did. The next one would be easier. They'd have nine days to figure it out. It was beautiful in its simplicity, really. A countdown they could never seem to beat. It kept them moving; it kept them on the defense; it kept them always searching desperately for a hint of the next location in a cryptic photograph instead of searching for the man behind them, the man holding the puppet strings.

And the punishment if they became distracted was swift and merciless.

They learned that with Eve McDaniel. The second girl. It was after Sam hopped on a plane to Florida to drag her into the case.

There had been nothing to even do for months. But then Eve's picture ended up on Clarke's desk, mailed without a return address. The girl's face was narrow, like a fox, her nose sharp and her eyes green. Her hair was auburn and cut into a short bob that slid just beneath her chin. Della had found her easily. A grad student at Northwestern, studying political science. She'd been missing since a week after Sam arrived at Clarke's apartment in Florida.

Clarke had gotten cocky in those early days. She thought she could challenge Cross. Hadn't realized that if she played by his rules, the girls were kept alive long enough for her to have a shot at finding them. If she didn't . . . Well. It had been too late by the time she realized he wasn't bluffing, and she paid for her defiance with Eve McDaniel's life. With at least a week left in the game before the final deadline, local police, through an anonymous tip, had found Eve's body in a hotel on the outskirts of Detroit. There had been a note pinned to her chest.

Naughty girls who break the rules don't get to play. Simon

When Clarke couldn't sleep at night, she'd run over the details of each case, wondering where they could have been faster, could have been smarter. And then when the sun crept through the curtains and she still had no answers, she simply said their names.

Lila Teasdale. Eve McDaniel. Charlotte Collins.

And now Anna Meyers.

When their names stopped being enough, she studied their pictures. The ones in which they still had sly smiles and bright eyes. And red hair. Always with the red hair.

It would be over soon, though. Patterns could be infuriating when they trapped you in their labyrinthine walls, but they also offered a sort of solace that made it almost bearable. She had to hold herself together for only a week. That was it. One week. The promise of that, the promise of not needing to be strong forever, the promise of not having to keep the molecules that made up the gossamer web of restraint from flying off into the ether—well, that was something to hold on to. She could handle one week.

The minute the wheels hit the tarmac, she turned the little silver phone on. She didn't like having it off.

It vibrated and went still as she switched airplane mode off on her own phone.

Then it beeped with an incoming text.

Play nice, Clarke.

She smiled, and she didn't need to see the way her lips stretched to know it was a bit feral as she pictured him huddled over grainy security footage of her in Gary's. Obtaining it from the CCTV camera would have been as easy as sliding a twenty across that cheap laminate countertop, and it would have been quite the prize for him. She imagined his eyes flicking over her shadowed profile, desperate to see his puppets dance. He must not have liked her flipping him off.

Perhaps she could get under his skin, too.

"Did you sleep at all?" Sam asked, not bothering to look up when Clarke walked into what she liked to think of as Sam's Command Central with two large cups of black coffee. It was one of the nicer offices in the J. Edgar Hoover FBI Building, which, to the dismay of far too many FBI recruits, tended to have more of a paper-company vibe than the high-tech labs they'd imagined in training.

But Command Central was one of the exceptions. Monitors lined the wall in front of them, and fancy, sleek computers, which she liked to avoid touching, perched on the desks. Clocks marking the time in different parts of the world hung around the room, and there was always low chatter coming from one of many police scanners Della had rigged up. It felt like home.

Sam was hunched over a little piece of free space on his desk, but he looked up when she placed the cup at his elbow.

"So did you?" he asked again. "Get any sleep."

"As if you got any, either," she countered.

He squinted at her over his computer glasses, thick salt-and-pepper caterpillar eyebrows all but obscuring his sharp blue eyes. She could see the exhaustion written so clearly there in the grooves of his face. Sometimes she forgot that he was edging ever closer to his sixtieth birthday. This was not one of those times.

Sam grabbed the coffee and sat back in his chair, taking a gulp without even testing out the temperature.

"God, that's hot," he said instead of responding to her. It didn't stop him from going back for more. He ran a hand over his eyes, drawing a sort of infinity sign with his thumb and pointer finger. They came together at the bridge of his nose, and he squeezed it tight before looking back at her.

"That's what I thought." She smiled faintly, blowing on her drink. Some days she subsisted on coffee alone. It didn't help with her insomnia, but it let her work when she'd rather crash, and for that she was grateful.

Sam and Clarke stared each other down, both trying to decide if they wanted to make an issue out of their mutual deteriorating health. It was a prickly subject for both of them. Sam looked away first.

"How was Texas?" he asked, turning the majority of his attention back to the computer nearest him, which had the blown-up picture of the cabin on the lake occupying every inch of the screen.

"Hot," she said. "And don't start with me. Please?"

"Was I starting?"

She came to stand at his shoulder. "The quiet disapproval is almost worse."

"You get results, I'll give you that, kid," he said.

A response died on her lips at the sound of heels on the slick tile. Della LaCroix. Looking far better than any human had a right to this early in the morning, all flawless dark skin and pixie-cut caramel-colored hair and smooth, endless legs.

Della's deep brown eyes scanned Clarke, starting at her flip-flops and traveling right up to her messy hair that she hadn't washed in the past four days. Polite horror settled into the corners of Della's lips, and she didn't even try to hide it.

"Don't you start, either," Clarke told her.

"Well, hello to you, too, sugar," Della said, with only a hint of New Orleans in her voice. "We thought you might have flown off to Fiji."

"I got bored of the easy life. Missed all the torture and murder," Clarke said as Della slid in behind her wall of monitors, unlocking the computer. The cabin picture jumped out on three of the five screens. The other two showed search results. Clarke squinted, trying to make out what they were of, but her tired eyes blurred.

"Well, while you were down there sipping mai tais, we actually came up with something," Della said, her long fingers flying over her keyboard. Clarke's attention sharpened.

"Already?" She'd thought the picture might be easier this time. They did tend to get easier. The clock was winding down, after all.

Clarke smacked Sam on the back. "Why didn't you say something?" She didn't give him time to answer. "Della, go."

"*No Worries* on the stern was the obvious route to take. There are twenty-one boats with that name registered in New York and Pennsylvania. I started on those two states because of the topography in the background of the picture." She pointed a short, well-manicured nail at the low, rolling mountains behind the cabin.

"Now here's where we got lucky." Della zoomed in on the corner of the picture.

"We don't get lucky," Clarke countered.

"Okay, true," Della allowed. "So, this is what he's letting us see."

Clarke leaned forward as the red smudge sharpened under Della's computer wizardry. Della smiled over her shoulder, a lethal flash of teeth. "It's a 'For Sale' sign."

"That was too easy," Clarke said, not knowing what it meant. They were supposed to be able to figure them out. But not that quickly.

He enjoyed toying with them too much. He was able to judge their ability to solve his clues with a precision that scared her and tugged at the corner of her brain. It was one of those questions to which she always came back: How did he know?

Della raised a brow before turning back to the monitors. "I can't say you're wrong there. It wasn't necessarily a walk in the park, but it wasn't hard, either. Nothing like the last one. I made out three of the numbers on the sign and ran an algorithm against them and the properties that were up for sale in the towns with boats that had registered as *No Worries*."

Della reached over at the end of her little explanation and snagged a piece of paper out from beneath Sam's coffee cup, glaring at the inanimate object and then at the man himself, before turning back to Clarke.

Clarke glanced down at what Della handed her. A map. "Staunton, New York."

"In the Poconos," Sam chimed in.

"Why do I know that name?" Clarke searched her foggy memory banks but came up dry.

It took only a hasty glance between Sam and Della for it to click for Clarke. "The missing-girl alert." Della had set them all up with an alert for when a female between the ages of fifteen and thirty was reported missing anywhere in America. It was depressing as hell, and Clarke forced herself to read every one that came in. "A couple days ago."

"It doesn't fit, though," Sam said.

It didn't. The bastard always finished with his current girl before moving on to the next. Anna. He still had Anna.

But. What were the odds? "You—Mr. Nothing Is a Coincidence himself—think it's coincidence?"

"Did I say that?" Sam asked, and Della's gaze flicked between the two, knowing enough not to interfere.

"Stop being cryptic, Sam. I'm not in the mood."

Sam turned back to the monitor, used to her sharp edges. He squinted. "The clue was too easy to figure out."

Way too easy. "A break in the pattern. Subtle but . . ."

"If he can break one rule, he can break others."

It wasn't unprecedented that there was a woman missing in the town to which they were headed. Women went missing all the time. It was far more frequent than the general public knew. They'd chased enough dead ends to realize that. But . . .

"What are you guys silently communicating over there?" Della finally broke in. "What does this all mean?"

Sam and Clarke locked grim eyes across the room.

"It means," Clarke started slowly, and Sam nodded, knowing where she was headed. "It means he may have his next victim."

CHAPTER EIGHT

Adelaide

April 1995

Adelaide held her breath as Simon crouched closer to the babbling stream that ran behind the Crosses' house, his nose almost touching the water, his knees sinking into the soft clay banks. His one hand was braced on a slick, mossy rock, and the other was held aloft, ready to strike at any moment.

Adelaide's fingertips rested against her lips as she watched. Her fiery red curls were ruthlessly pulled into two braids that hung just behind her ears. Strands had already escaped and blew across her face, but she ignored them, the entirety of her attention locked on her foster brother. Her hero.

Just as a blackbird let out a disgruntled caw from the tree above them, Simon karate-chopped his raised hand into the cool water. Adelaide couldn't contain the gasp of excitement that forced its way out of her mouth. She leaned forward, but Simon's hand had clenched into a fist, the gentle current washing over it, and she knew he'd missed his target.

She met his angry eyes. "It's okay. We can find something else for our picnic dinner," she told him, standing and brushing the dirt that clung to the bottom of her white shorts and the back of her thighs.

"We're going to have fish." His jaw was clenched, and he had two angry red spots coloring his cheeks. She knew when he got this stubborn, there was no talking to him.

"Well, I am going to have cake instead," she cried out, and with a quick bunny hop she was running along the banks, her footing precarious along the rounded edge that sloped down, back into the water. Her braids flew like little kite tails behind her. She turned her head, laughing, to see if he would come along. But she knew he would.

With a leap she went flying, weightless as she soared over what she used to think was a great divide, but what was really an easy jump if the jumper had long nine-year-old legs instead of useless seven-year-old ones. She landed and let her toes curl into the moist grass on the other side. She paused for only a moment, turning back. "Catch me if you can."

He was close enough for her to see his eyes narrow with intent, but she didn't stay to watch him cross the stream. She stuck her tongue out and then took off through the woods instead. She dipped and dodged, under rogue branches, over fallen trunks rotting their way back into the soil. She knew the way well, even if there wasn't a path. Brambles caught at her purple T-shirt and ripped into the delicate skin of her arms, drawing pinpricks of blood, but still she didn't stop running. The calloused and well-used soles of her feet, though softer from the winter hibernation, withstood the harsh, unforgiving rocks and twigs and pebbles of the woods. Only once did she cry out, but she quickly bit her lip against the pain and kept going.

She burst into the meadow seconds before Simon caught her, his forearm coming about her waist so that he could lift her up against him, spinning her in a circle. The flowers blurred into a watercolor painting before her eyes.

"Caught you," he said, still holding her.

"Nuh-uh! I beat you fair and square," she shouted into the air that was turning cooler with the setting of the sun, kicking out her legs and pushing playfully at the arm around her stomach.

He dropped her to the ground, and her feet scrambled for purchase. She tumbled into the soft bed of flowers anyway. "Whatever helps you sleep at night," he said, but the rage had burned out of his eyes, and the angry flush had left his cheeks. She smiled. All was right with her world again.

Adelaide embraced the change in altitude and flopped back against the earth, a snow angel without snow. Her fingers turned down, digging little indentations into the soil with the tips. The light had changed, turning soft and golden. The last remnants of the sunbeams clung to the blades of grass, to the leaves on the trees around them, to the soft swell of his cheek.

She didn't want to admit, even to herself, that Simon scared her sometimes. She peeked at him under one eyelid.

He'd come to sit beside her, a long blade of grass stuck between his teeth, his legs sprawled out in front of him as he leaned back against his hands. His face was upturned, and she knew he was watching and waiting. For that first star to come out. When it blinked to life in the dark blue sky, the corners of his eyes would go all crinkly with the power of his smile. She'd asked him one time why he liked it so much. He'd shrugged. "You can get away with things at night, can't you?"

She'd thought maybe that had been a lie. He was good at that. Lying.

When she'd first arrived at the Crosses', Simon had been her lifeline before she even realized she so desperately needed one. There had been so much confusion. She hadn't even realized what had happened. Or had refused to realize it.

The Crosses weren't so bad. But they were old. Old as dinosaurs, he'd said that first day and countless times afterward, often in their hearing. They'd smile at him kindly and pinch his cheeks, and he hated it.

She used to wonder why he'd kept poking at them like that. Then she watched closer. A flash of pain would spark in Mrs. Cross's eyes for the briefest moment, before her expression would turn calm and happy once more. But Simon would catch it. He was wicked sharp and had eagle eyes for that kind of stuff. There was something inside him that enjoyed hurting the Crosses. For no good reason that she could tell. She never called them dinosaurs even when he tried to goad her into it.

It wasn't that Simon was mean. He was so nice to her. Except every once in a while. But most of the time, he played with her even though he was older and must have thought her a nuisance and a tagalong, like his friends at school called her. He would always say hi to her in the cafeteria as his class filed in after hers was done with lunch. Even though it was surely suicide for a thirteen-year-old boy to acknowledge a younger sibling—especially a girl one.

He would even wait for her in front of school to walk her home. Her friend Mary Ellen had a brother in Simon's grade, and he made Mary Ellen meet him three blocks down from the school so his friends wouldn't see him with her.

And Simon played with her on these warm April days. All summer break, too. They'd been on so many adventures together. To Narnia to rule over the whole kingdom, to the South Indian Sea to hunt pirates, to China to climb over the Great Wall, just like the Huns had. True, their adventures were limited to the woods behind the Cross house, and they didn't venture out to the park or the streets where his friends could see, but he picked playing with her over playing with them. She hugged that knowledge to herself on the days when no one would talk to her because she was that weird foster kid.

No, for the most part, he wasn't mean to her. There was just a hard edge to him, like he hadn't learned how to be gentle. "Too smart for his own good," Mrs. Cross would say, something dark in her voice. It took a while for Adelaide to recognize why being smart would be a bad thing. But now she thought maybe she got it.

Simon turned, catching her one open eye. He grinned, the long piece of grass still hanging from his lips.

"Why do you call them dinosaurs?" she blurted out. Because that was what she had finally realized about Simon. He could in a heartbeat identify the thing that would make the person he wanted to hurt bleed the most. And while others would be gentle with the information, he was not. He used it. When he was mad or annoyed or just bored. He sliced into them.

His face went blank, slack now, and suddenly she felt way too vulnerable in her position. She sat up and tucked her knees under her chin. Oh, how she wished she had swallowed the words instead of letting them tumble out.

"Cuz they are," he said, and she wanted to roll her eyes at the teenager in his voice. She often sat with Mrs. Cross as she crocheted baby blankets for the women at church who were expecting. Intricate collages of pinks, blues, yellows, and greens. Adelaide enjoyed running her fingers over the fluffy strands that wove together in ways she couldn't quite comprehend. She'd watch Mrs. Cross's fingers fly through the air with the needles, and still didn't know how the final product actually came to be. But on those days, when Simon came storming in through the front door, the screen slamming against wood, cussing something fierce with sarcasm dripping from every word, Mrs. Cross would wink at Adelaide and talk about the teenager in every little boy's voice. They grew out of it, she assured Adelaide. Sometimes.

"They're so nice to us, though," she said, her voice quiet as she plucked at the head of a happy buttercup. It resisted her tugging, then gave way with a small pop. She rolled the petals, crushing them between her fingers. She didn't know why she was picking this fight. She liked the Crosses well enough, but not like she loved Simon, the brother she'd never had. Why anger him?

He glanced at her. "They're nice to you. Their little angel."

She wanted to protest. He just didn't want to admit that they treated him well. That was it. But she finally had wised up and kept the words to herself.

"Matthew called them that," Simon said when she didn't say anything. "Dinosaurs."

Every single muscle in her body clenched. Matthew. Simon had mentioned him only twice. Once on that first day, and then once again when he'd screamed at her that Matthew would never have told the Crosses about that fire he'd started in the pile of dry twigs and branches right where the backyard turned into woods. It had been a long, silent three months for Simon to get over that supposed betrayal.

She didn't even want to breathe. If she did, it could break the spell; he could yell at her and take off toward the house instead of telling her about Matthew. But he didn't stand up. He just stared off into space, his floppy dark hair falling over his eyes. All his clothes were still too big on him, and for the first time she wondered if they were Matthew's.

"He was their twenty-first foster kid. What kind of psychos take in twenty-one kids?" He paused and gave her a look. "Twenty-three."

"They didn't have any of their own," she said, defending her foster parents. Mrs. Cross had always wanted a baby. That's all she had ever wanted. It made Adelaide sad when she saw her coo over the ones at church, wrapped in the blankets her fingers had slaved over, reaching for mothers who weren't as scary as a plump old lady grabbing at chubby cheeks.

"Grow up, Addie." His voice was sharp and cutting. He called her Addie only when he wanted to annoy her. He knew she hated the nickname that she was too timid to stop her foster parents from using.

"What happened to Matthew?" she asked instead of letting him provoke her.

He looked away from her again. "He wasn't the perfect son they wanted. They got rid of him."

She found it hard to believe anyone could be as imperfect as the boy sitting next to her, but once again she held her tongue. "How?"

"Ever wonder why they have so much land behind the house?"

She felt her stomach drop as her brain caught up with the implication. No. She would not believe it. Simon was messing with her, like he always tried to do. He was making it up, just like the horror story he told her that first summer about the murderer lurking outside little girls' windows. She hadn't been able to sleep that entire summer because of his stories. Night had been an unrelenting horror-filled trauma. But then he'd stopped. Adelaide had guessed the Crosses had discovered the reason they would find her sobbing outside their bedroom door every night.

Just as she opened her mouth to dispute the claim that the Crosses had murdered Matthew, they heard it.

The sound crawled along her nerve endings, starting at her toes, running up the ligaments behind her knobby kneecaps, finding the base of her spine, and creeping up each vertebra until it reached the top. There it settled and scratched and clawed at the little jutting point of a bone at the center. Her shoulders pressed up, as if to protect her fragile ears.

Their eyes turned in unison to the far side of the meadow, where a sleek black cat stumbled from the shadows of the dense trees. She couldn't see it clearly, but she saw the outline of it take a few steps toward them, stop, and then collapse into the ground.

Adelaide's breath caught in her sternum, the same feeling she got when she tried to swallow the too-big-for-her vitamin Mrs. Cross forced on her every morning after breakfast.

Simon was already on his feet, walking with purposeful strides toward the animal.

She pushed off the ground, found her footing beneath her, and chased after him across the meadow.

They both skidded to a stop. The cat blinked up at them with one startlingly green-yellow eye. It yowled again, a quieter version of the one that had first caught their attention, then it mewed several times, its one eye pleading with them.

They both crouched next to it, and she knocked Simon's hands away when he would have touched it. "Diseases," she said, her eyes assessing the wounds.

They were deep and bloody. The fur was matted around an injury on the cat's hindquarters, and she saw dark clots around its neck as well.

"We have to get it to the vet," she said, her voice frantic over the thundering pulse echoing in her ears.

She would not let this animal die in front of her. There had to be something they could do. Her eyes darted around, trying to figure out what they could wrap it in. Would it try to scratch them if they did? Would it put up a fight? "Your shirt, your shirt," she said, almost mindless now.

He looked down at the black tee but shook his head. "We're not going to save it, Adelaide."

Her eyes locked on his face. "What? What do you mean? Of course we are. Look at it." She gestured to the cat, who was watching her. And her only. It meowed again, a pitiful protest if she had ever heard one. *Fight for yourself,* she willed the cat. Always fight. Always fight.

Simon was shaking his head, though. He got to his feet and began looking around the ground. She watched him but couldn't figure out what he was searching for. She put him out of her mind and stripped out of her own shirt.

She scooched her knees closer to the wounded animal, murmuring nonsense words to it. It dropped silent, its eerie yellow eye hot against the cool black of its fur. It lifted its head, but that was too much effort for it, and it crashed back against the ground.

She was just reaching out to wrap it in her shirt, when Simon pushed her. It was a hard shove, two hands against her shoulders. She tumbled, unprepared, her head striking the hard earth, a sad mimic of the cat's movements a moment earlier. She lay on her back, not sure what had just happened.

From there, she watched him raise the large rock above his head with both hands. There was something wrong with his face. Something about it that made her limbs go numb. But her brain was struggling to push through the fog of panic to figure out what it was.

It was only when the stone arced through the air that she realized.

He was smiling.

Her own howl rocked and reverberated through the quiet meadow, and she wondered if it echoed in Simon's chest, just like the cat's had in hers.

CHAPTER NINE

CLARKE

July 14, 2018

"Here," Sam called out, pointing a burly forearm in front of her face. She slammed on the brakes, and the seat belt caught and tightened over her chest as she spun into the little path that had been almost hidden by overgrown shrubs.

"A little warning would be nice next time."

She took in their new headquarters as the car, having lost most of its suspension what must have been years ago, bounced them along the rutted dirt path that passed as a driveway.

"Home sweet home," she singsonged, pulling to a stop and climbing out of the car. The cabin—which a generous soul might call rustic—was nestled between two hulking evergreens. The security would be nonexistent. Anyone could hide in those trees without being noticed.

The cabin itself was a few miles outside Staunton, which had turned out to be a blink-and-you'll-miss-it town, and a bit away from the place in the picture Cross sent. Since the deadline for finding the clue they'd already figured out wasn't for another couple of days, they had time to set up shop.

"We've had worse. At least there's a roof." Sam pushed by her and handled the key drop box. She followed him inside, letting her bag fall to the floor by the door and flipping on the light. It let out a low, consistent buzz but flickered to life, shining an unfortunate spotlight on the musty, dilapidated purple-flowered couch. She eyed it.

"Rock, paper, scissors?" she asked, turning to Sam.

He laughed and dropped his bag on the cushions. A puff of dust billowed out in protest.

"It's your lucky day, kid. I was just itching to sleep on a couch for the foreseeable future," he said. "It does wonders for my back."

She wasn't about to put up a fight. A tour of the bedroom could wait until later. Instead, she pulled out her MacBook and set it on the serviceable kitchen table that wobbled only slightly under the weight of it as she powered up.

Sam, who preferred old-school paper files, dug out his folder and began reading through them.

Just like the bastard had settled into patterns, so had she and Sam. Although every part of her was screaming to go out, go find Cross, tear apart each building in town, searching for him and the missing girls, she knew it would be pointless. She had made that mistake before.

Tonight would be better spent strategizing.

Clarke pulled up a picture of Anna Meyers, even though she'd memorized every detail of her face by now. The seafoam-green eyes, the red hair that curled around a face that was just a little too round for her to be called pretty. "Cute" would be the word she probably heard all her life. She had freckles, orange dots that left not even a breath of air between them. Clarke imagined they were the bane of Anna's existence. Or had been. The bane of her existence now was probably the bastard.

"Anna Meyers," she said, knowing Sam was looking at the same picture over on the couch. "She's been missing since April."

It was undeniable—the tight, pulsing guilt that lived right underneath her clavicle. There were times she suspected this was the ultimate game, not the girls, not the scavenger hunt. But the way he tortured her with every person she couldn't quite save.

"Why are we doing this?" she asked softly.

Sam watched her with quiet eyes, but he didn't seem surprised by her question. He didn't even ask her to clarify. Because he was Sam. He was her rock, and always had been. Even when she hated him, even when she wanted to forget his name and his face and the way he called her "kid," he was her rock.

There'd been only one time he had walked away from her, had let her down. One time she had thought he wasn't coming back after she pushed him away.

"So you're quitting?"

Clarke ignored the question and instead concentrated on the amber liquid that swirled so beautifully in her crystal glass. The large ice cube bounced off the edges as she rolled it between her hands.

"You realize if you don't finish your degree, that spot I got you at Quantico disappears, right?" Sam's voice was harsh and cut deeper than she wanted to admit. "Don't mess this up, kid, just because you want to go on a bender."

Irrationally, she felt her temper spark at him calling her "kid." The first time he'd done it, it had made sense and been a comfort. It had curled around her like a warm, affectionate hug. But tonight? Tonight it was a condescending uppercut right to the chin.

"Coming from the man who has yet to meet a drink he could pass up," she muttered, swallowing the rest of the whiskey. She pushed the glass forward and signaled to the bartender, who obliged. She flashed a smile in his direction, catching his eyes as she did. It might be interesting to see what that stubble felt like against her skin. It certainly added texture and depth to his baby face.

He turned his attention to Sam, who ordered a Coke.

"Didn't realize you'd turned into such a straightedge, Sam," she said, looking at him for the first time since he'd climbed onto the red vinyl bar stool next to hers.

"Didn't realize you'd turned into such a drunk, Clarke," he countered, and she felt the words lodge themselves just below her throat. She shrugged them off, though, and then did what she did best.

"You've become a stick-in-the-mud, Sam. Must be why Roger left you," she said. "Or, wait. It was that he moved on to a younger cock, wasn't that it?"

She felt his muscles tense beside her. His fingers were probably itching to hit her. One slap across the pale flesh of her cheek would make him feel better. God, it would even make her feel better if he took the swing.

But he wouldn't. He would never. The sudden, inexplicable bite of tears pushing against the ducts of her eyes caught her off guard. She blinked hard and fast to control them as he sighed a long exhalation of air, which he somehow loaded full of disappointment, hurt, anger, and love.

"You started it," she said, feeling all of thirteen. She squished her eyes tight until little stars exploded on the canvas of her eyelids.

"You can rot here for all I care," Sam finally said, and the emotion was thick in his voice. She knew she shouldn't have brought up Roger. It was a low blow. But she was nothing if not consistent.

Why did he even care about her? Why didn't he just leave her be? Wallowing in the little pity party she'd decided to throw for herself. "Great. Happy to. As soon as you leave me the hell alone."

"I vouched for you, kid," he said. The anger was gone, leaving just disappointment. That was harder to take. "I pulled strings for you. All you had to do was make it through your master's."

"Well, we all make mistakes, don't we?"

They were silent for a moment, and she wondered if he was contemplating all the ones he'd made. Just like she was doing. It was a long list.

"Do you know how many people would kill for this opportunity?"

"Well, now they'll get it."

"This is it, kid. I'm not going to come around again," he said.

"Thank God for small favors." She mock-toasted and let the liquor burn its way to her belly.

She saw him nod. "Okay. Okay." He sounded like he was coming to terms with something. She felt a sharp pain, a literal pain, in her heart. He was giving up on her. She knew it.

She had always known he would. Why wouldn't he? But now it felt real.

"Remember, you know where to find me, if you need me," Sam said, sliding off the stool and dropping a twenty on the bar, enough to cover her two drinks and his soda.

"I won't," she said, though she felt the pain gathering, a tidal force, in the back of her throat. He was giving up on her. The one person who she thought never would.

He stopped next to her, his hand raised, as if he was going to pat her shoulder. It dropped, though, and he turned.

Then he walked out of the artificially dark bar.

Blinking away the memory, she met his gaze through the moisture in her eyes. A little manic laugh escaped because she was near tears. She never cried.

He ignored both her little, desperate sob and the waterworks. He'd seen her at much worse, anyway. There was a deep crease between his brows as he considered her question: *Why are we doing this?*

"I'd like to say something along the lines of 'because we're the ones who have the best chance at saving them,'" Sam said. "But, really, it's because we're both too stubborn to let it go."

And wasn't that the sad truth. She nodded once. It was enough for her.

She returned her attention to the computer, clicking off Anna's picture. Staring into those eyes was rubbing at her exposed emotions.

The next picture that popped up was the first in what they called the "Meyers Series." She knew it by heart. She knew them all by heart. Every single photo he'd sent them. Clarke studied them. She studied them during the nights that never seemed to end. She studied them in the lulls when the silence seemed more menacing than any action would. She studied them after, when the crushing weight of guilt sat heavy on her chest. And she knew she was missing something.

This one was no different. It was all movement and blur and energy. The camera had caught a moment between the bartender of a hole-in-the-wall and a tipsy patron who had leaned over the scratched mahogany and fisted her hand in his shirt, pulling him in for a kiss. The light bounced off the mirror behind the two, obstructing the other details in the scene. It had been a pain in the ass to figure out that it was a place called Black Dove in Portland, Maine.

But something had always bothered her about the picture. It tickled at the edges of her consciousness, a face she couldn't quite place, a lyric that skipped away just as she reached out to grab it. But they'd solved it anyway, so she'd moved on.

"Ten days," Sam said, reading the simple words she knew were on the back of the photo. "We found it in nine. A box was waiting for you there. A picture of the back of a waitress's head in Tucson. Eight days. Then there was the nightclub in LA . . ."

She let his voice wash over her as he ran through the rest of the photos until he got to the one in Texas. She hunched her shoulders against any possible recriminations, but there didn't seem to be any coming. Perhaps he'd actually forgiven her for the carelessness of running off in the middle of the case by herself. It was an interesting concept—one of them actually letting go of a grudge.

"There's a deeper pattern here. We're just not seeing it," Clarke said. Her fingers tapped against the table, unable to stay still.

"He's just jerking off as he makes us jump through hoops," she finally said.

"Delightful image, thanks for that."

"Anytime," she said, smirking at his disgust. "But that's what it feels like, right? What is he getting from all this?" She waved a hand to encompass both of them and their respective files.

Sam leaned back, steepling his hands on his chest. It was a pose she'd seen countless times. "This whole thing is about power, yes? Power over us, but mostly power over you. The scavenger hunt is just an extension of that, and it serves two purposes."

She pulled her feet up, bringing her knees against her chest and resting her chin atop them. "He gets to tell me when to jump."

"And how high," Sam agreed. "This setup, this directing-your-every-move thing, it's one of his prime motivations."

She knew this. "And the second?"

Sam shifted, resting his forearms along the tops of his legs. "He wants you to think he's clever."

"They all do, though," she said. Most serial killers—especially ones who contact the authorities—want the world to know how smart they are, even if they actually aren't.

"I think it goes beyond that," Sam said. "Sometimes he comes across like he's . . . trying to impress you. Just you. Flirting, almost."

Her stomach clenched against nothing. Had she eaten today? Apparently not.

"Flirting." The word was a bitter taste on her tongue.

Sam shrugged. "It's not exactly news that he's obsessed with you. It's just . . . in a way I haven't seen in any other case. The language he uses? It all revolves around fun, playing, games. He's taunting in the way young boys act toward girls when they've yet to develop more appropriate methods of conveying their interest."

She rubbed two knuckles against her tattoo, grounding herself. "You know, it sounds really messed up when you put it that way."

He laughed at that. "It is messed up, kid."

"Okay, so he wants to impress me, not just control me," she said. "But how is he getting his rocks off if he can't even watch me when I'm discovering how clever he is?"

"We know he hacks into security when he can. He's taunted us about it in the clues enough times to guarantee that he at least gets CCTV recordings from stores and bars."

"Some grainy surveillance footage where he can probably only see the side of my face? That's it?" It couldn't be.

"Could be why he brought us here early," Sam said. "It's not enough anymore. He wants to watch you. Up close and personal."

"God, he has a slow burn, then," she muttered, even though that still didn't feel right. In her gut. It was too random a reason for a man who built his life around intricate planning. "If it's taken him this long to stick around and watch."

"Maybe . . ." Sam trailed off, his gaze on the ceiling.

"What?"

He tapped a finger against his chest where he'd rested his hands in contemplation, then dropped his eyes back to her face. "Maybe it has to do with this particular girl."

"Anna." She turned her attention back to her laptop. Nothing had jumped out about her to Clarke in their investigation so far that would be a red flag. She fit his victim profile as if she were made for it. She wasn't special. Not relatively speaking. Shaking her head, she looked over to find him lost in his own thoughts once more. "I'm not sure. So much of what gets him off on having the girls is the control he can exert upon us. They're just the means that give him that power."

"There's also the girl who's gone missing," Sam reminded her. As if she could forget. "Though we don't know he has her."

She plucked at her chapped lips with her thumb and forefinger, considering. "Probably he does."

"Yeah," Sam agreed. "The patterns are breaking."

But did that mean anything? Were they just chasing him again down the same rabbit hole? "They die anyway," she said, the frustration turning her voice harder than she'd intended. "So do we just stay in this never-ending cycle?" The darkness of what was in front of them threatened to consume her. There was no way she'd last much longer.

Sam shook his head. "He'll make a mistake, kid. They always do. We just have to be in the right place when he does."

"We never get there in time," she said, a catch in her throat making the words painful as they crawled up it.

"Yeah, well, this time he was nice enough to give us extra time," he said. "We better not waste it."

The countdown clock clicked over in her head. Wasting time. They were wasting time. They should be out there, in the night, in the darkness where he thrived. She was already pushing to her feet when Sam stopped her.

"Kid. Sit your ass back down. You're not going out there tonight. We have to figure out our next move, and you getting yourself killed is not it. We'll hit the cabin at first light, then see what the locals can tell us about the missing girl."

Shit. The urge to get out, to do something, didn't recede entirely, but she was able to tame it. To not do something stupid. Or, as stupid as that. She still eyed the powder-blue 1950s fridge tucked into the corner of the kitchen. Maybe there was wine in it.

"You know, it could be more than grainy images," Sam said, his voice tugging at her. It was on purpose. He knew what she was thinking. "He could be setting up his own equipment in advance. To watch you."

That destroyed any thought of potential numbness in the guise of alcohol. "God, that's sick."

She pictured the bastard sitting in front of a computer screen, watching her through a lens that caught her only from unnatural angles. The curve of her cheek, the stretch of shoulder under leather jacket, the baseball cap that, she imagined, frustratingly hid her eyes from his gaze. Whether he was doing it or not, just the thought of it burrowed into the paranoid part of her mind. She would forever feel the prickle of awareness at the nape of her neck now. The feeling that he was always watching her. As if she needed another layer to add to the tapestry of her screwed-up psychology.

"He's sick," Sam said. Something everyone could agree on.

She glanced at the ceiling.

"There's no way there are cameras in here, right?" She turned pleading eyes to Sam, her rational side knowing it was unlikely that Cross would have known the exact rental they were staying in before they got there, but the rest of her still caught in the grasp of the first breath of a panic attack.

He shook his head. "No way, kid. I think it's safe to say he knows we're here. He'd be watching out for us, and we're easy enough to track. But he wouldn't have been able to get cameras in here."

Her tension didn't ease, though, until she searched most of the obvious nooks and crannies she knew could be potential hiding places. Sam watched her without saying anything until she flopped onto the couch next to him.

"Always assume the worst," he said with a slight smile that completely forgave her paranoid whirlwind. "Be surprised by the best."

"You know," she said, the buzz in her ears finally subsiding, "sometimes we sound like complete cynics, you realize that, right?"

"It comes hard-won, kid. Hard-won."

She tapped a finger against the file he held loosely. "Don't I know it."

CHAPTER TEN

Bess

July 7, 2018

Bess didn't retrace her steps. Instead, she took the circuitous route back through the little quiet neighborhoods with houses that, while they may have seen better days, seemed well loved. Big Wheels and jump ropes lay where they'd fallen, discarded in a moment when the child's fleeting attention had been caught by the next shiny object.

Her sneakers smudged over chalk drawings of kitties and elephants and a fading hopscotch grid, and she smiled at an elderly couple who sat perched on a white porch swing despite the midday heat.

She continued on when they didn't wave back, and sipped her water, grateful for Simon's generosity once again as the cold liquid soothed her raw throat.

She made her way back to the main street, knowing she'd lingered long enough. Jeremy might start to wonder where she'd gone. Bad things tended to happen when he did that.

Her thoughts wandered back to Simon, though she didn't quite know why she was still thinking about him. It wasn't like he was outrageously hot or anything. He'd actually been so—her brain searched for the right word—normal.

A little rush of victory swept through her when she tossed her water bottle, and it fell into the trash can without bouncing off the rim.

"Nothing but net," she murmured. It was silly. She missed just being silly.

Despite the borderline poverty they'd struggled through when she was growing up, her mother had put an emphasis on celebrating the ridiculous, on fun, on lightness. Even when her mom was busy in the shop, Bess would simply create a sister—one of those magical creatures she'd only ever heard about—or some other imaginary friend to keep her company, and she'd turn the back rooms into pirate ships and secret forests. Even as she'd grown out of childhood adventures, the whimsy had remained. She was the girl who painted her bedroom walls with murals of wildflowers and chased the sunrise only to find herself on a random beach hours away as the day broke through the night, the surf lapping at her toes.

It had been gradual, that loss of playfulness. Just like everything else.

With a tap of the finger, she started the time on her Garmin again and took off, back toward reality. Back toward Jeremy.

There had been something familiar about Simon. It was like she'd seen him before. But that was impossible. She would have remembered him. He probably had one of those faces. He was that person who got that all the time. Strangers squinting at him, trying to place him in their cloudy memories. Once she was up close to him, he had features that stood out, but even a few feet away, they started to blend and fade into a nondescript blur.

Her pace was steady, but slower, as she left Main Street for the two-lane road that would take her back to the lake house.

She noticed the Jeep pulled to the side about a quarter mile before she got to it.

Bess was the type to help strangers when they asked for directions, but she rarely stopped for motorists. It left her far too vulnerable, and in this day and age when she often considered taking Mace on her runs, she couldn't be too careful. But there was no good way to avoid the Jeep owner, who was halfway obscured by the propped-open hood of the car. She could cross the road, but she thought of Simon buying her water. If a person in trouble couldn't rely on the kindness of strangers, what could they rely on?

She slowed to a walk, stopping her run timer. She stepped into the grass so she wouldn't be putting herself at risk of being slammed into by a passing car. Not that many had gone by. There had been maybe two in the fifteen minutes she'd been on the road.

Still. Better safe.

Wary of startling the man, she called out softly, not wanting him to bump his head. "Hello? Do you need some assistance?"

Surprise, followed by relief, followed by an emotion she didn't want to examine crashed through her when the man pulled out from the dark depths of the engine. Simon. She laughed in delight, but then sobered when she realized the difficulty he was in.

He grimaced at her. "Fancy meeting you here," he said, wiggling his eyebrows, as if he were standing in a bar feeding her a pickup line instead of next to his broken-down car on the side of the road.

She batted her lashes. "Of all the roads, in all the world, you break down on mine." She knew she was rusty at the flirting business, but she got a little buzz trying. Like the second after taking a shot of tequila when you knew it was too early to really hit you, but you felt it anyway. It made her want to smile bigger, giggle quicker.

"Actually, I'll count that as the one lucky thing that's happened all day," he said. He held up his phone. "This died on me almost immediately after the engine started smoking. Almost as if it knew."

He pushed away from the front of the car, walking closer to her. He opened the back door on the passenger side and leaned in. "My charger is back here somewhere, but of course it won't work. And there's only been one car that's gone by, and it didn't stop. If I could use your phone, you'd be my savior."

He straightened, holding a coiled white phone charger, and gave her the most pitiful look.

"Of course you can use my phone." She pulled the headphone jack out and held it out to him.

He plucked it out of her hand, looking up and down the road. "No one comes down this way, huh."

"Yeah." She turned back toward the stretch she'd just come from. "Seems pretty deserted. I'm glad I stumbled upon you and hadn't already gone back."

"Me too, dearest," he said and something in his soft voice made the tiny hairs on the nape of her neck stand up, even before the oddity of the endearment registered.

"What did you . . ." The question died on her lips as a cloth came down over them. She smelled something sweet. His other hand had wrapped around her waist, holding her against his small, compact body. She flailed and kicked out, landing a solid strike against his vulnerable shin. He grunted, but his grip did not loosen. The world was starting to go gray and blurry at the edges.

"Shhh." His voice was hot and clammy against her ear. "We're going to have so much fun." It was the last thing she heard before everything went black.

◆ ◆ ◆

Bess blinked against the throbbing pain in her shoulder that brought her to consciousness.

Why was she on the floor? It was hard, concrete. Not cool bathroom tile. So not the lake house. Where was she? What had happened? Had there been a fight?

Something was not right.

Panic clawed at the back of her throat. If she could just breathe, it would be okay. Then she could think. She could figure it out.

When Bess tried to suck in air, though, she couldn't. Her mouth was duct-taped.

Why was her mouth duct-taped?

Fear coated her tongue and made everything slow and hazy. Was she going to die? She didn't want to die. Unconsciousness beckoned her, the soothing blackness so inviting that tears of relief gathered in her eyes at the thought of it. But if she gave in, would she wake up again?

She must have shifted because the pain was back. An old friend. It was welcome, that ache of bone and flesh pressed against concrete. It was something she could understand. It helped her fight off the darkness.

There was a general soreness that had settled into her, radiating from the pressure points where her shoulder and hip took the brunt of her weight, but there was no sharpness. Nothing that would suggest she was about to bleed out from any gaping wounds.

When she tried to run her fingers over her skin in an urgent need to check, just to make sure, she realized her arms were pulled tight behind her. The cold, harsh metal of the handcuffs dug into the fragile bones at her wrists.

Her pulse was still pounding in her ears, but the roar of it was receding with each breath she took through strained nostrils.

Simon.

The quiet, kind stranger in the store with the warm eyes who had smiled at her like he'd found a kindred spirit. Then he'd been on the road, and his car had broken down. But, no. No. That wasn't right. It had been a trap. For her.

God, what did he want from her? The panic was back, barking and nipping at the solid edges of her already-shaky sanity.

Fight it. She had to fight it.

Wherever she was being held was pitch-black. She could see the thinnest sliver of light from a door that looked like it was floating in the sky but was probably just at the top of some kind of staircase.

Even as her eyes adjusted, she could make out only large, bulky shapes, inanimate thugs all ready to knock her out if she made one wrong move.

Simon didn't seem to be with her. To be sure, she stilled completely, listening, straining against the oppressive, thundering silence that pushed into the very crevices of her body. There was nothing.

Bess closed her eyes and thought back to the church basement with the hippie self-defense instructor. They'd run scenarios about what to do if they were approached on the street, what to do if a criminal broke into their apartments, even what to do if they were conscious and stuffed in the trunk of a car. They had not covered what to do if bound and gagged in a basement. Couldn't get to it all in a three-month class. A desperate giggle she couldn't contain erupted from behind the tape.

But one thing had run through the whole course. And that was to act. Don't give in to fear. Go for vulnerable points, like the eyes, the throat, the groin, the kneecap, if the circumstances allowed. And if they didn't, make it happen. She concentrated all her energy on focusing on the memory of her instructor's harsh but somehow melodic voice, telling her to strike a Superman pose at the end of class because it would make her feel powerful. Telling her to be big, be strong, use her voice, use her size to her advantage. It played like a loop in her head, and she tucked the mantra underneath her breastbone where it could live until she needed it.

She opened her eyes again.

Get to a sitting position. Assess the surroundings.

She braced herself and then rolled to her back, onto already-abused arms, so that her hands were caught in the arch of her lower back. Using her fingertips, she pressed down and rocked up until she was sitting upright. The change in position let her roll her shoulders, returning blood to at least part of her arms.

It was just as she was trying to ignore the little jagged knives that came with the renewed circulation that she was presented with her next unpleasant obstacle. A deceivingly delicate chain connected the steel band around her ankle to a loop attached to the cement floor.

It was naive to think she would be allowed to roam the room. But she was disappointed anyway. She eyed her leash—it was short.

Bess promptly consigned the kindness-of-strangers philosophy to hell. If she survived—no, when she survived—she would never be nice to another human she didn't know again. Some people might have prayed, or promised to dedicate their lives to righteous pursuits, if they found themselves in her situation. Not her. She would say screw them all. Starting with Jeremy.

The slight pressure in her bladder gave her an idea. He would have to unchain her to let her pee. Or she hoped he would. She guessed he could let her stew in her own filth, but she didn't imagine that would fit nicely into whatever fantasy his lunatic mind had concocted. That opened up so many possibilities that her head felt light for a moment considering them. She could attack him, rush him, take him out at the legs. She could try to escape, up and through that mysterious door. She didn't know what was on the other side, but it had to be better than this dank prison. She could fashion a weapon from bathroom items, or, if she was truly lucky, there would be an easy out from wherever he took her to do the deed. That didn't seem probable, considering he'd thought enough to have steel loops installed to keep her chained in the basement, but there was always a chance.

Bess felt calmer, now that she had a plan. Or, a rough outline of a plan. Her eyes had even adjusted further, and the looming shadows around her started looking less like monsters out of a child's nightmare and more like heavy machinery of some sort. Thick, heavy canvas provided dusty covers for whatever was beneath, but some metal stuck out.

Just as she tucked her free right leg under her left thigh in a fruitless effort to get within a spitting distance of comfortable, she heard it.

She froze. It had sounded like a rattle of metal against metal. Like the way her own chain jangled against the silence. But softer.

Was it him? Should she brace herself for a fight? Should she beg? Cry? Would anything get through to him? Was it worth trying?

Bess didn't move a muscle during the silence that followed. It felt like an eternity but was probably only five minutes.

And then, when she had just given up, when she had just chalked it up to her overwrought imagination, she heard it again.

She shouted a "Hello?" But the duct tape turned it into a garbled mishmash of vowels and consonants that had no meaning. She paused and then tried again.

"Shhhh." The reprimand emerged from the deepest shadows of the room. "He's coming."

And just as the voice reached Bess's ears, the door at the top of the stairs swung open.

CHAPTER ELEVEN

Clarke

July 15, 2018

All police stations looked the same on the inside. No matter if they were in Massachusetts or Florida, New Mexico or Montana.

To the left of the front desk—manned, like always, by a young officer just out of the academy—was a coffeepot, its bottom coated with something that probably used to be drinkable at one point but was now primordial sludge. If it was before dawn, the uncomfortable chairs lining the wall of the room would be filled with low-level criminals from the night before, sulking as they waited to be booked and released back on the streets. When the hour turned more respectable, good Samaritans, their bodies shivering with self-righteousness, would flock in to get a pat on the head for reporting some menial misdeed.

The worst, though, was the lighting. And it was in every goddamn precinct. Fluorescent tubes whitewashed cold, stark tiles, the artificial light sucking the soul out of everyone who pushed through the doors into the hellhole. The ambience really amplified the red-streaked eyes and the greasy strands of hair that had gone too long without shampoo. Or at least that was what it did to hers.

Because she was annoyed and sleep deprived, she glared at Sam's back as he stepped into the entrance of the Staunton Police Station. It was far easier to direct her frustration at him than to think about why she was there in the first place.

He turned, as if he could feel the bad vibes, and raised a thick, bushy eyebrow at her, silently asking, "What bug crawled up your ass?"

She shot him a look that clearly said, "Which bug do you think?"

They'd gotten to the point where they could even curse at each other without words.

There was an ease in that. Knowing someone, so well, for so long. The politeness, the caution, had long faded into something that probably had too few boundaries, but there was at least brutal honesty left in its wake, and she appreciated that far more.

They'd spent the night working until an hour that some would call uncivilized, but they deemed normal. Even when they weren't on a case, it wasn't unusual to find them parked on her couch with Indian food, watching the 1950s movies that Sam loved so much, both of them pretending it wasn't because they hated being alone when they couldn't sleep. At least this time they'd had an excuse.

This time there was no Indian food and no black-and-white Hitchcock. It was just the two of them poring over maps of the town, old photos and every single piece of information they'd ever collected on Anna. When the sun broke the horizon, Clarke felt no more prepared than she had when they'd arrived, but at least they'd been able to move. To do something.

They'd brewed the crystallized shit coffee they'd scrounged from the back of the cabinets and then piled in their rental as the sky began to lighten. The silence was comfortable between them as they made the short drive to the cabin—the one in the picture Simon sent. As expected, there had been nothing there yet; they still had days before the deadline, after all.

If he was in town, there'd be no reason to leave a clue there days in advance. Still, it made her want to dunk her head into the slick black water of the lake until the carbon dioxide dulled the frantic pacing of her thoughts. They'd lingered with nothing left to do but take pictures for Della and then make sure a surveillance detail would be set up on the location.

Clarke turned her attention to the young pup at the reception desk, who was giving them his fiercest impression of a guard dog.

After cursory greetings, they handed over their badges to the boy—Officer Mills, read the pristine name tag pinned to his uniform. He ran strangely long, elegant fingers over the raised letters on their FBI shields, almost reverent, before returning the soft leather cases.

"I'll see if the chief is in," Mills said, pushing to his feet. She watched his lanky frame disappear into the long hallway that separated the waiting room from the real action. The bull pen.

"Have you checked in with Roger?" she asked Sam, not looking at him.

"Of course," Sam said, an edge to his voice he rarely employed. He wanted to shut down the conversation before it started. "I inform him of all major developments on this case."

She slid her eyes away from his. "Wouldn't want to miss an opportunity at a press conference, would he?"

"Clarke." It was a warning. And she took it to heart, dropping the subject of their boss. It was a sensitive one for more reasons than Sam's past relationship with him. Roger Montoya had poured money and resources into their eager, open hands in the first months of the case after Sam had dragged her up to DC, as if she was going to be their savior. Then with each failure, everyone started realizing that maybe Clarke wasn't the Golden Goose to catch the sick psychopath, and murmurs calling for her to remove herself had begun to haunt her in the hallways. And Roger had done nothing to quiet them. If anything, he sowed the seeds of doubt, at one point threatening to pull her off it himself in front of several gawking agents. It was only Sam's intervention that had kept her working it. That, and Roger knew—deep down knew—that she was their best chance.

It had left an even sourer taste in her mouth for the man. The man who swooped in when there were cameras pointed at them when they had a lead but was nowhere to be found when they were catching their one hour of sleep a night on crap purple-flowered couches. Roger had an eye on a political office, and dead girls weren't really the right aesthetic for that.

Plus, he'd screwed Sam over. And nothing would ever make her forgive him for that.

"Let's just get some more proof while we can," Sam said. His gaze scoured the room, the way it always did when he went into an unfamiliar building. Searching for the exits, looking for threats. She had already performed her own sweep.

"It's him. I feel it. He took her."

Sam was saved from a response when Officer Mills came trotting back up the hallway. Such a good puppy.

He was slightly out of breath but trying to hide it when he pulled to a stop before them. "Chief Bradley will see you now."

Clarke pushed away from the desk, and she and Sam followed Mills down the hallway. It was a small town, and the bull pen reflected as much, she thought, as they weaved their way through empty desks piled high with messy files and plastic sandwich wraps. Three different phones were ringing, and they would go unanswered, as the room was all but empty. One plainclothes detective slumped back in the desk closest to the chief's office, guzzling from a small Styrofoam cup. Poor man didn't know the storm that was coming his way. He didn't look up as they passed. Maybe not such a good cop. It was hit-and-miss in small towns. Hell, it was hit-and-miss in the cities, too.

Mills gestured them into the office that had a little gold plate outside its door that read **Chief Kathleen Bradley**.

It was the woman's hair that Clarke noticed first. She wore it in a classic nineties Mom cut: all volume at the top and hair-sprayed within an inch of its life to rest just above her shoulders. She finished off the look with a blazer that was just a little too big, over a flowing flower-print blouse that was tucked into a khaki skirt, which hugged generous hips. Her badge was hooked to a loop at her waist. Any lipstick she'd put on had long worn away, and a black smudge underneath her left eye was the only sign that betrayed her effort to swipe on some mascara that morning.

She was smiling at them, though, and the warmth of her expression made the stress lines that came with the job of running a police department disappear.

They all shook hands, and then Bradley waved at them to take a seat in the metal and polyester-cushioned chairs in front of her desk. Every single precinct.

"Now," Bradley started, her palms facedown in front of her, "how can I help you folks?"

Clarke nodded for Sam to go ahead. They had perfected their spiel at this point.

"About a year and a half ago, I received a photo. Printed out and everything, not digital. On the back was the message 'Ready. Set. Go. 10 Days.' The picture itself was just a blur of colors and shapes to me. We get that kind of thing all the time, so I didn't think much of it. But I kept the photo on my desk, and a coworker happened to see it. Turns out he was born and raised on the Strip in Vegas, and the photo was of a casino on Fremont Street. I thought it might be worth the trip," Sam said.

"Did you find something there?" the chief asked, her gaze swinging between them. She didn't see yet how this led to her. But she would.

"Another photo. Taped behind this famous little slot machine, which is how the coworker recognized the spot in the first place. It sent me off on a . . . well . . ."

"Scavenger hunt," Clarke said, filling in the pause. It might sound flippant to outsiders, but it was what best described the games the bastard played.

Sam's eyebrows raised in agreement. "A scavenger hunt. And there was a countdown that led to a final clue."

"I have a feeling there was not a prize at the end of all this," the chief guessed.

"No."

She nodded.

"At the final location I found a woman named Lila Teasdale. She had been missing for two months. The two months he had me scrambling around the country," Sam said.

"She was dead?"

The chief was blunt in a way Clarke could appreciate.

"Yes." Clarke took over, knowing Sam was still seeing Lila's blank eyes. He'd walked in expecting another photo. "And then three months later we got a picture of the next victim. Her name was Eve. She was found in Michigan in an abandoned hotel on the outskirts of Detroit."

"Jesus Christ," Bradley said, her fingertips brushing against her temples before coming back to the desk. There, her hands clutched at each other, her knuckles white. "Yeah, I think I read about this. Cross, right? Simon Cross. But it kind of died down, right? That was more than a year ago?"

"Yes. And we've been chasing him ever since," Sam answered.

"How many?" Bradley asked after a beat of silence.

It was the kind of question that didn't need to be clarified. They all knew what she was talking about.

"In the past two years or so? He currently has his fourth girl," Clarke said, wondering if Bradley would catch the phrasing. It was a delicate balance they always had to strike. Give enough information to be helpful, not enough to be dangerous. It was really tiring, sometimes.

Bradley's eyes narrowed, but she didn't follow up. "So, while this is all very sad . . ."

"You want to know why we're sitting in your office right now," Sam finished for her.

"Right," Bradley said. She knew, though. Clarke could see it in the tightening of the thin skin around the corners of her eyes and lips.

"He's here." Clarke confirmed what Bradley must have been thinking.

"Yup. Okay. All right." Bradley dipped her chin in a small nod, more to herself than to them. She was already strategizing. Maybe canceling dinner plans or the weekend barbecue.

Clarke glanced over at Sam. They weren't done.

"There's also a possibility he has his next victim," Sam continued.

"More than a possibility," Clarke said, earning her a sharp look from Sam.

"Well. Goddamn it." Bradley stared at them, the desperation of the situation evident in the white-knuckle grip she had on her pen. There was resolve there, too, though.

"Can you tell us more about your missing female?" Clarke asked. "Finding out where she fits the patterns and where she deviates is crucial."

The chief shifted to her computer and tapped at her keyboard for a moment, her eyes on the bulky monitor. "Bess Stanhope was reported missing by her boyfriend, Jeremy Peterson, on July seventh around midafternoon," she started. "They were visiting here from New York—we get a lot of those, especially around the Fourth—and she never returned from her run. After a few hours, he came to us. We couldn't officially file her as a missing person until the ninth, but we took all his information. He seemed pretty torn up."

"Address for him?" Clarke asked. The chief rattled off a combination of words and numbers, and Clarke scribbled them on a piece of scrap paper she'd found in her purse.

"What was your take on him?" she asked, looking up in time to see a quick flash of emotion flicker across the chief's face.

Bradley glanced at them. "Something was off with him."

Clarke could relate to that feeling. Sometimes it was just a gut reaction that something was not quite right. Really, it came down to reading body language, decoding wording choices, even registering micro expressions that could flit across a suspect's face in a hundredth of a second. People just didn't realize they were processing all that, so they called it instinct. "Too concerned? Not concerned enough?"

"The former," Bradley said. "That's why I'm making sure you think it's this guy, this Simon Cross." She waved a hand at the folder Sam had slid toward her. "Otherwise, I would bet my lucky lotto ticket it's the boyfriend."

"There's always a chance it could be coincidence," Clarke allowed. There was a chance she was wrong here. Not likely. Possible, though. "But part of his MO is to choose women who are considering leaving abusive relationships. So if you're getting that feeling from the boyfriend, that would fit."

It was the worst part of Cross's victim methodology. He preyed on the survivors, the ones who were starting to think there was an escape from the unrelenting darkness. And then he snuffed out the light, locking them in a world of pain and fear and death just when they'd started holding on to hope. The night she and Sam put those pieces together, she'd thrown an entire bottle of wine at the wall and let the shards slice into the calloused skin of her heels as she cleaned it up. She'd barely felt the cuts.

Bradley looked between them, lost. "What do you mean?"

"It fulfills several needs for him," Sam explained further. "They're already vulnerable, usually having been isolated by their partner away from family and friends. It makes them easier to target."

"It also provides him with a way of finding his victims," Clarke said. "He's stalked self-defense classes, hacked into domestic abuse hotlines' databases, things like that."

"God, that's awful," Bradley whispered.

"It's also . . . we believe it's tied to a woman leaving him," Sam said. "His first victim. Adelaide Young. It was a domestic abuse situation that escalated."

Clarke's mouth went dry at the name. Too often she forgot to add it to the list she repeated to herself at night when she couldn't sleep. The victims. Lila Teasdale. Eve McDaniel. Charlotte Collins.

Adelaide Young.

None of them had survived Simon Cross. Anna Meyers would be next. She'd become the name that sat familiar on Clarke's lips, a penance and a prayer for forgiveness all at once. How many more girls would there be?

"The first victim was the one from a year and a half ago?" the chief asked.

"Unfortunately, no." Sam took the question, and Clarke was thankful. Dwelling on the ones she couldn't save did nothing for the case, and she needed a moment to find her footing again.

"His first victim was when he was younger," Sam continued. "Then he went quiet for years. I thought we'd lost him completely, actually. I've kept my ear to the ground, of course, but cold cases are the first to get cut when budgets need tightening. When he reemerged, I didn't realize it was Simon Cross, at first. But he wanted me to know. He started signing his work."

Clarke leaned forward. "We've never been able to fill in the missing years, despite all the information Sam and the rest of the team have been able to collect on him. In truth, there could be an untold number of victims we don't know about."

A certain grimness settled into the room with the shared knowledge of just how bad it could be.

Clarke swallowed hard, her fingers numb where they gripped the chair. "He has many of the same thought patterns as abusive partners.

We believe Cross felt deeply betrayed by Adelaide Young. She tried to leave him, which he saw as an unforgivable breach of loyalty. He seems to have transferred that rage he felt toward her onto these women, as placeholders for her. The amount of torture he inflicts on them while he holds them hostage is indicative of that."

Bradley nodded. "Okay, I get that. I don't want to, but I guess it makes a twisted kind of sense. How does he . . . ?"

The chief trailed off, waving a hand. Clarke understood the question without it needing to be voiced.

"Strangling," she said. "He strangles them. It's a particularly personal method of killing. There's no distance between the killer and the victim, no weapon to hide behind. Just hands on skin, controlling the very air they need to survive."

There was a beat of silence, and then the chief cleared her throat, shifted in her chair.

"So Bess Stanhope may fit that pattern."

She was still 90 percent sure Bess fit into their case. Maybe even 93 percent. She'd learned to listen to her instincts, especially when it came to the bastard. And now? They were screaming at her.

"Bess is a runner, right?" Clarke asked. "That's another thing he likes. Three of his other victims were runners."

Bradley glanced at her screen again. "The boyfriend said it wasn't unusual for her to go for long runs. He didn't even start to worry about her until she'd been gone for four hours."

Clarke raised a brow at that. "Either that girl is an avid runner, or something's rotten in the state of Denmark with the boyfriend."

"That's my thinking. I'd been keeping my eye on his group since they rolled into town for the Fourth."

"Rowdy?" Clarke could just picture it.

"Drunk and disorderlies just waiting to happen," Bradley affirmed. "And they're still there, long past when they were supposed to leave."

There was a beat of silence.

"So was the original . . . um . . . Adelaide Young . . . a runner?" Bradley asked.

Clarke ran her tongue along her teeth. They were fuzzy, and it was easier to concentrate on that. "Yes. But I think it has more to do with opportunity. Again, isolate the target. Easy getaway if you can get them near a road. Few witnesses. Most runners have routes they follow every day. Things like that."

"So we've got two for two with Bess," Bradley said, glancing back at the computer. "Or likely two for two. What else?"

The amount of information they could dump on the woman could fill days. Clarke debated what else to even say. How could she condense years of living inside the bastard's head, crawling around in his dirty thoughts, into any sort of useful dossier?

"He likes power," Clarke finally settled on. "And he doesn't like to lose."

Bradley waited, as if expecting more. But she soon realized that's what she was getting.

"That's something that's been bothering me," the chief said. "The logistics. You know his name and presumably his face?"

Clarke nodded.

"Okay. So how is he setting up these elaborate cross-country games? Without you guys catching him?"

It was a sore point. A wound that was infected and just kept rupturing every time she picked at it. Because at the end of the day, she just wasn't good enough to stop him.

"His IQ is off the charts," Sam added. "Which, despite popular culture, is actually not typical with serial killers. They tend to have just slightly above-average intelligence. But Cross is scary smart. There's a missing decade or so in which he went completely off the grid. We have linked that time to some offshore accounts that reroute to nowhere.

But from what we've found, he has significant funds to finance his sick little games."

"Follow the money," Bradley said.

Clarke nodded. If she'd learned nothing else in her Florida years, it was that criminals could hide a lot of things, could bleach out evidence and bribe witnesses, but they always needed funding. The bastard had turned out to be far too talented at covering his tracks, though—just as meticulous with it as he was with everything else.

"He also employs messengers," Clarke continued, relaxing her arms to her side once she realized she'd brought them up across her chest in a defensive gesture.

"They never saw the person they got instructions from," Sam picked up. "Just an email from an account that was deactivated immediately after directions were sent. And they collected the packages from PO boxes. The payment was always in cash attached to the packages. They would take them to the locations specified and drop them off with someone who worked there. They would tell that person what to do when two FBI agents came looking for the boxes, and that's it. Everyone just had their little piece of the instructions, so no link in the chain ever knew too much."

"Even the PO boxes were untraceable. And we have our own genius trying to track them down," Clarke said. "Cross is . . . I hesitate to say *perfect*, but he's yet to trip up."

"So, you're just chasing him, hoping he makes a mistake?" There was a hint of disbelief colored with disapproval there in her words, on her face, where before there had just been cautious respect.

Sam tensed beside her, possibly to hold her back or keep her in check.

"I said I wouldn't call him perfect. He's not," Clarke said, her tone leaving no room for doubt. "He has weaknesses. He has an ego. He has gaps in his carefully constructed defenses. We just haven't found them yet."

"We will, though," Sam added.

"All right," Bradley said, placing both hands flat on her desk. "What do we do now?"

"Is your best detective on Bess's case?" Clarke asked.

Perhaps they'd cleared some sort of hurdle with their united front. Going to battle with the locals wasted both time and energy in an investigation like this.

Bradley nodded. "Yeah, he's good. Hasn't had a case of this level yet, but none of us have. Good sense for people, though." She paused. "And liars."

Clarke held her gaze. "Great. Then we'd like to get him caught up. He can work the missing-girl angle. We don't want to scare our guy off. Not when we may have finally cornered him."

"Lucas," Bradley shouted past her closed door, drawing out every letter of the man's name, the last *s* sitting on her tongue for a good three seconds.

The man they'd passed earlier immediately appeared in the doorway, a lazy shoulder propped against it. Clarke watched him assess them under heavy-lidded eyes.

They all stood for the introductions, but Clarke froze when she caught a glimpse of Bradley's computer screen.

She ignored the rest of them as she walked around the desk for a better view. Everyone else had shut up, and all eyes were on her.

Looking up, she met Bradley's curious gaze. "Is this Bess?"

"Yes," Bradley confirmed, flicking a glance at the computer even though she couldn't see the screen.

"What's up, kid?" Sam asked.

They locked eyes. "She's blonde."

The air around them went thick with loaded silence.

Shit. Well, that dropped it to 85 percent certain. Or maybe 81 percent certain.

"Goddamn it," Sam said, the disappointment in his voice mirroring her thoughts. It wasn't that they were hoping the girl had been kidnapped by Cross. But it had felt like their first real break in the case since they'd started this shit-show.

Bradley looked between them. "What am I missing?"

"Remember those characteristics he goes after in his victims?" Clarke asked without looking away from Sam. "Well, there's one that's mandatory for him."

"Red hair," Sam finished for her.

CHAPTER TWELVE

Adelaide

April 1998

Adelaide wished she could block out the sound of the Crosses' sobs. But she could feel them in her heart. The muscles tightening and pulling in strange directions as if the organ were a dirty dishcloth in need of a good wringing.

Adelaide crouched in the deep shadows in the corner of the landing, her arms wrapped around her knees. Her soft pajamas were warm, but the chill of the night still bit into the flesh of her exposed arms.

The two policemen had left a few minutes ago, their stony expressions grim but sympathetic. "Ma'am," one of them had said as he tipped his cap to Mrs. Cross. He'd looked like he'd wanted to say more, from what Adelaide could see from peering through the spindle rails of the banister, but instead he had just turned to the door and his waiting partner.

The minute Mr. Cross snicked the lock closed behind them, Mrs. Cross let go of her fragile control. It wasn't just the tears that bubbled over; it was the great gasping heaves of her ample bosom, the rasping sound of the air catching and scraping the back of her throat, the raspberry splotches on her face.

Mr. Cross was stoic as always, but he went to his wife and pulled her to his chest. He patted a long-fingered hand against her fleshy back, and she buried her face in the region of his lower rib cage.

"Oh, Thomas," Mrs. Cross managed to get out between the sobs.

"There, there, Mary," Mr. Cross hummed, and nothing he could have said would have made Adelaide feel more like the eavesdropper she was. Mr. and Mrs. Cross never used their Christian names in front of the children. "We knew this day was going to come."

"We tried so hard," Mrs. Cross whimpered, and she sounded like she was trying to convince herself. "We did everything we could."

"Some souls just can't be saved," Mr. Cross intoned, and Adelaide wanted him to take it back immediately.

All souls could be saved. At least that's what Pastor Mike told them every Wednesday and Sunday at church, his gentle black robes swirling around his ankles, too short for his tall, lanky frame. It was a game she played, guessing what socks he would wear. Some had bicycles, others had plump baby elephants, and still others had broad rainbow stripes. She liked the way he smiled at her when he pressed a stale, spongy piece of bread into her hands for Communion.

And the way his voice boomed when he told them that Jesus loved them. If Jesus loved them, that meant Jesus loved Simon. If Jesus loved Simon, that meant the Crosses would let him stay.

"It's Matthew all over again," Mrs. Cross cried out and collapsed completely against Mr. Cross. Adelaide straightened. She had long gotten over her fear that Matthew had been buried in the Crosses' backyard. Simon had been trying to scare her. But no one ever seemed to want to tell her what actually happened to him.

She leaned forward, wishing she were closer so she could hear better. Mrs. Cross's voice was muffled in Mr. Cross's thick cable-knit sweater. "Why does this keep happening to us?"

"Twice only, Mary. And we have Addie to think about this time." His deep voice was a rumble that used to scare her, but she now found it reassuring.

"She'll be the last." Adelaide barely made out the words, but she saw Mr. Cross nod wordlessly even though there was no way his wife could see the gesture.

"Boo." It was a whisper, a hot breath against her earlobe, and she would have screamed into the quiet of the darkened stairway had a clammy hand not clamped immediately over her mouth. "You're such a girl."

It was a familiar refrain, and she relaxed against the body behind her. She nodded to let him know he could trust her not to make a sound if he withdrew his hand. His fingertips traced over her lips as he pulled away, and she tried not to grimace. She couldn't explain even to herself her new aversion to Simon touching her. But it was there.

He grabbed her hand, pulling her to her feet. They raced back up the stairs to his room, where he flung open the door, then crashed, face-first, onto the rumpled sheets.

She sank into the neon-blue beanbag chair that had sprung a leak a month earlier. Most of the beans remained encased in the faux leather, but a few white, round pill-like objects had escaped into the recesses of the shaggy beige carpeting.

Adelaide was rarely allowed into Simon's room, even though he had free rein in hers. She looked around now. The walls were empty, unlike her own, which were papered with the faces of Brad Pitt and Will Smith and Joey McIntyre. His bookshelf was filled with comic books and the young-adult novels he loved so much, but that was the only sign that someone lived in the room. Even his desk was free of any clutter. Her own had gel pens and rainbow Lisa Frank folders scattered over it. It was almost eerie—his undecorated room. Like there was nothing joyful or colorful or fun in his head to spill out and over onto the blank walls just waiting to be filled.

"What . . ." She paused, cleared her throat. "What happened?"

He shifted so that his ear was against the bed, his face turned to the wall, but he didn't roll off his stomach. "Everyone's overreacting."

That was doubtful.

"Simon." She nudged him, not sure she wanted to know.

The only thing she was surprised about was that he actually got caught doing something wrong; Simon could usually talk himself out of situations. And because he was both charismatic and wicked smart, he usually got away with it. He'd get himself in deep and then charm the pants off whoever had caught him. She'd seen him do it 1,004 times. But those other times—those times he couldn't sweet-talk himself out of whatever disaster he'd gotten himself into—those were the times the evil Simon reared his ugly head.

Adelaide had always wondered why adults went along with him. She loved him, and even *she* was terrified of some of the things he did. Most people, though, thought he was a lovably mischievous scoundrel.

Adelaide tried to weigh both sides of his soul. He was her brother, and she loved him beyond words. But then he would do things that rocked that foundation. Like that one time he snuck into her room and cut off all her hair because she had laughed at him at the dinner table. She cried for days, and he was so confused about why she wouldn't talk to him.

She thought of what Pastor Mike said at church, how Satan was hovering just at the edges of every action, and she knew that Satan had a strong grip on Simon. She also knew, in her heart of hearts, that Simon was strong enough to fight the fallen angel. He just needed her help doing it.

"I didn't do it on purpose," he muttered.

Which meant he did. But no one would be able to prove it.

He shrugged. "We were working with acid in chemistry today. I tripped."

No. She bit her lip to hold back her gasp. "Simon, what happened?"

"Some got on Sarah Gramble. I don't know, she had to go to the hospital."

Sarah. The pretty girl who had turned Simon down for the homecoming dance.

"Oh, Simon," she breathed.

He sat up to look at her, his eyes cold. "I told you I didn't do it on purpose. It was just a little on her arm."

He must have convinced the police of that; otherwise, why would they have let him return home? But she couldn't shake the image of the Crosses crying downstairs. He hadn't convinced them.

"You might have to go away," she ventured, and he crashed back down against the mattress.

"Maybe they'll kill me, like Matthew." His voice was muffled by the comforter, but she made out the words clearly.

"They didn't murder Matthew." She felt tight with anger. They'd had this battle before.

"So naive, Addie," he said, finally pushing up to look at her again. "Perfect little Addie."

It was a taunt, and not a new one. "Maybe if you just tried to be good . . ."

"What, be like you?" He all but spit the words at her, and she cringed against the derision in his voice. "Yeah, a bit too late for that."

"You never give them a chance."

At that, he threw his head back, his Adam's apple sharp against the long column of his pale neck. The sound that came out could have been called laughter, if laughter could freeze your blood. "You have no idea what you're talking about. You think you see everything that goes on around here? With those big eyes always looking at me. Always."

She shook her head, not even knowing what she was disagreeing with but unable to do anything else.

"That's right, you don't. You don't see any of it. Saint Addie."

There was nothing to say to that.

“I don’t need them,” he said. “I’ll be fine without them.”

“What are you going to do? Where will you go if you have to leave?” she asked, even though she guessed he didn’t know. He liked to talk a big talk, but his follow-through was a little more tenuous.

In a quick move, he pushed off the bed and fell to his knees in front of her.

His eyes had melted; they were soft again. In them, she saw her brother. It was almost as if a switch had flipped in the space between heartbeats.

He cupped her cheek, the calloused pad of his thumb pressing into her jaw to hold her gaze steady with his.

“Come with me, Adelaide.” His voice was silky but tight as a strung wire at the same time. “You’re too good for this place. For these people.”

Panic and hope clawed at her throat, a battle to the death in the little pocket of space right behind the palate of her mouth. Mr. and Mrs. Cross were nice people, kind people. But Simon was family. Could she really run away with him? They could travel the country, not tied down by anyone’s expectations or someone else’s reality. They would have their own.

Then she thought of Sarah and the acid. Maybe it had been an accident, but she had been on the receiving end of one too many similar “accidents” to actually believe that. Punishments. That’s what they should be called. Simon kept a meticulous scorecard, and no one was safe.

She shook her head, a small movement against her fingers. “I can’t, Simon,” she said, her voice a mere whisper as if she were afraid to say the words out loud, to contradict his wishes. But they had to be said.

His eyes pinched at the outside corners. Something in them made her brace herself. For what, she didn’t know. But it didn’t take long to find out.

His hand lashed out, grabbing a handful of her fiery curls, crushing the spirals in his palm as he yanked her face toward him. It was all harshness and violence and force as he brought his lips down over her sealed mouth.

She didn't even shut her eyes during the assault, just looked into his as he tried to maneuver his saliva-slicked tongue against the seam of her lips.

It was all so startling, all so sudden, that she had frozen, every cell in her body at a standstill, unwilling to listen to the screaming alarm bells ringing in her head. *Danger,* they yelled at her, as the tip of his tongue, acting like a battering ram, found its way inside. He hadn't relaxed his grip on either her face or her hair, and she felt helpless. No other part of his body touched her, but he might as well have been holding her in a vise.

Move. The voice was stronger as he licked the inside of her cheek, his eyes still open, almost eaten up entirely by the black of his pupils.

With a burst of clarity, she knew what she had to do, and she clamped down on his invading tongue with her teeth, as hard as she could. She tasted metal in her mouth.

It got him to withdraw, though. He'd cried out and then, using her hair, threw her to the floor. "Cunt," he spit at her, his hand at his mouth. "Ungrateful cunt."

Her mind recoiled at the language and what had just happened. She hugged her arms against her chest, protecting herself from both.

"Whatever." He flopped back on the bed. "Go cry in your room about it, little girl."

She was shaking now. She didn't think her legs could carry her that far, all the way down the hall, to the safety of her bed. Could she even stand?

There weren't any tears streaming down her cheeks, though. And she wanted to tell him that. To prove to him that she was stronger than he thought. But she couldn't seem to form words.

She got to her feet, slowly, and turned to the door. Her hand had closed over the knob when she heard him speak.

"Adelaide." Her name was a caress in his mouth. In the mouth of her dear older brother, the one who had driven her to the movies the day *Toy Story* had come out, and all of her friends had said she was a baby for wanting to see it; the same brother who had dressed in robes with her and waited in line at midnight to pick up the new Belinda the Brave book; the same brother who had knocked down mean Miles Tenor when he'd called her a poor nobody loser mouse, then bought her Dairy Queen instead of making her go to dreaded softball practice.

She paused, but didn't look back at him. He moved, coming up behind her, looming over her.

"Adelaide," he said again, the rage completely gone. His hands hovered over her shoulders; she could tell by the almost imperceptible disturbance of the night air around them. But he didn't touch her. "I'm sorry. I'm just . . . I don't want to . . . leave you."

His voice broke. Her tough-as-nails, never-let-them-see-you-hurt brother was about to cry. Her final defenses broke down, and she turned into his arms, blindly. She pressed her face against his heart, which was a slow, steady beat against her ear.

He buried his face in her hair, and she felt the dampness of the tears against her scalp.

But you have to go, she thought but didn't say. And she ignored the traitorous relief she felt blossoming in a far corner of her heart.

CHAPTER THIRTEEN

Clarke

July 15, 2018

"Clarke." The voice on the other end of the phone rounded the letters in her name, tasting them, savoring them, as if he were sipping a fine wine.

She closed her eyes. When the burner phone had rung, she wished she had thought twice. But she hadn't. She hated herself. She hated that she'd ducked back into the station's bathroom so there would be no chance for Sam to overhear her. She hated the way her pulse raced at the cacophony of wild notes and symphonies that bounced against the cold tiles.

She didn't say anything, just let her name hang in the air between them, the static of the silence buzzing out of the little speaker she held to her ear. She squeezed her eyes tight against it—and the thought of what she was doing.

"I saw you today," the voice continued. It was silky, tantalizing. The snake in the Garden of Eden. She never wanted the apple, though. She prayed she never would.

"Why didn't you say hi?"

There was a quiet exhale of air that might have been a laugh. "Ah, pretty girl, it's not our time yet," he drawled.

She took the bait. "When's our time, then?"

"You'll know."

She sank to the floor and let her head fall against the exposed metal pipe of the sink. She wanted it to draw blood even though she knew it wouldn't. "Where are you?"

"Where would the fun be if I told you that?" The tone was flirty, as if they were lovers exchanging banter and innuendo.

"I haven't had fun in years," she countered.

The tsking sound crackled against her ear. "Now, Clarke"—he always liked to draw out her name—"what about all the games we've played? So many games."

This was part of the game, too. Every word. Every tone. Every sound. Each a strategic move.

"I never get to win." There was a pout in her voice that she knew he would pick up on. She squeezed her thighs together, the flesh beneath her jeans a siren's call. If only she hadn't promised Sam, she would find the scissors she kept in her bag for emergencies and dig the point in, drag it along so that it left torn skin in its wake.

Instead, her fingers drifted to the crook of her elbow, her thumb pressing not so gently into the ink there.

He laughed, a soft, elegant sound that didn't suit him at all. "It's not about winning, my sweet Clarke."

"It feels like it is."

"Then you're not paying attention." His voice turned brittle. His temper was a short-fused powder keg. One minute he was petting, charming, reassuring, and the next he plunged the knife in with almost no warning.

"Tell me," she said, her voice soothing. "Tell me what I should be looking for. What am I doing wrong?"

"You know what your problem is?"

She gnawed hard on her lip. Of course she knew what her problem was. It was that she was hiding in a bathroom talking to the bastard. Something told her that was not what he was getting at, though.

"You always think it's the destination that matters," he continued.

"Is that why you have me chasing pointless clues across the freaking country?" She didn't even try to hide the bitterness.

"There you go again, my love. Remember, it's not the destination that matters." His voice was husky and affection filled. She shivered as it crawled over the sensitive skin on her back. "It's the journey. One of these days you'll understand that." With that, the phone clicked off.

What had he just said? She turned the words over in her mind, while she pushed to her feet. He was not a careless man. Everything he uttered could be imbued with meaning.

She avoided her eyes in the cracked mirror and slipped the phone back into the small pocket in the side of her purse.

Not the destination. The journey.

The door swung open and she flinched back. "What the hell, Sam?"

"You were taking too long," Sam said, his eyes on her face. She knew there was guilt there. It was too raw to hide. "What's wrong?"

"You can't just barge into the ladies' room," she deflected, moving to brush past him. He caught her upper arm, his fingers wrapping around the soft flesh just below her shoulder.

"Clarke."

She met his gaze. It would be suspicious not to.

Why couldn't she tell him? She should tell him. Something always stopped her, though. Back when she'd first found the phone, she'd had Della run every test on it she could think of, to track any incoming calls and record them in case Clarke missed an important piece of information. Nothing. That first call had come from a drop phone, picked up at any Walmart and disposed of just as easily. The phone itself had been clean. There was nothing more it could tell them. At least that's what she let herself believe. Because she wanted to.

They never talked about it, but Della had suspected. Sometimes Clarke would catch her eye and see recrimination there, but Della never reported it. Maybe it would have been better if she had.

Would she always need someone to save her from herself?

"I still think he has her," she said now to distract Sam.

He knew the diversion for what it was. She could see it in the way his mouth worked over words he didn't actually say. Finally, he dropped her arm and stepped out of her way, gesturing her into the hallway.

"Me too," he said.

And that's why they worked.

"Not sure the locals are on board anymore," she said.

Sam shrugged. "Not the first time."

"So, what now?"

"Now?" Sam touched her elbow, guiding her toward the hallways that led to the front of the building. She saw Lucas already waiting for them there. "Now we see how torn up our grief-stricken boyfriend really is."

Detective Lucas Sheffield drove like Clarke would have predicted: relaxed into the seat, one hand on the wheel. He had the air conditioner on blast, and the slight sheen of perspiration that had covered her body from her short time outside in the heat turned against her. She clenched her teeth to keep from shivering and glanced over Lucas's lanky frame.

Staunton's finest.

She'd missed the mark on him, and she was willing to admit it. If only to herself. Instead of being arrogantly territorial over his case, he'd immediately jumped on board with helping them. It hadn't been with the eagerness of the young puppy at the desk, or even the grim determination of the chief. Lucas was simply being a consummate professional, and something about it was throwing her. Small-town cops were supposed to be dicks. Especially ones who looked like Lucas, and wore dusty jeans and baseball caps.

Clarke shifted her attention to the houses that were much more McMansion than rustic-cabin retreat.

"The rich kids stay out here?" she asked.

"Yeah, we get a lot on the Fourth," Lucas said, his words clipped from a hard upstate accent.

"And this was Bess's running route?" Clarke kept her gaze on the narrow shoulder, and her imagination filled in the scene. Cross would have had a car, would have picked the best place to isolate Bess. Maybe he surprised her, or maybe he'd come up with some ruse to get her to stop. Either way, it would have been over in moments. He knew what he was doing.

"The boyfriend said she was running into town." Lucas's voice was careful, as if he didn't want to be tripped up making overbroad statements of fact.

"This is the most logical route, though, right?"

Lucas nodded. "It is, yeah. It would be hard to get into town any other way, and we know she was seen here. There was an older couple who said a woman walked past their house headed back toward the lake about an hour and a half after we know she left for her run."

"So he got her on the way back," Clarke mused.

"Seems like," Lucas agreed.

It didn't take them long to pull through faux gold-plated gates that seemed to be mostly for show. They crept through the quiet streets of the small community until they found the mansion Bess had been staying in.

The door of the rental Peterson was staying in had an eagle knocker on it that challenged the world to question its patriotism with its fierce stare and wings that were poised for flight. Or battle.

It didn't bode well for the guys who had rented the place.

A tall kid with a mop of brown curls and bloodshot eyes opened the door and spared them only a cursory glance before calling out over his shoulder, "Peterson, yo-o-o-o, it's for you." He then proceeded to walk away, leaving them standing on the stoop.

It was then that she got her first glimpse of the boyfriend, bedecked in American-flag board shorts and laughing over his shoulder at something a passing leggy blonde had said.

Peterson finally turned his attention to them and immediately sobered when he caught sight of Lucas, the smile dropping from his lips, the humor seeping from his eyes. He looked concerned. If only it hadn't taken so long for him to tear his eyes from the blonde's ass before he realized who was at the door, she might have bought the act.

There was no preamble. "Did you find her?"

Lucas cleared his throat. "Not yet." There was sympathy there that Clarke wouldn't have been able to show. "But we have had some developments in the case and would like to ask you a few questions."

Peterson nodded but didn't move, and for a second he seemed frozen. Then he shifted to let them in.

The moment she stepped into the place, the smell of sweaty sex and stale beer sent her reeling. It was all too familiar—comforting and disgusting at once.

Peterson led them out to the deck. The gut-punching view of the lake and of the gentle mountains behind it was a clear visual of the price difference between this cabin and the one she and Sam were staying in.

They all settled around the glass-topped table. Clarke picked the seat that gave her the clearest view of Peterson's face.

"Sorry about these jerks." Peterson preempted any questions with a nod toward a group of tanned, movie star–attractive twentysomethings playing what looked like football. "They didn't know Bess at all."

Past tense. Sam's eyes flicked slightly, so she knew he'd heard it, too. For the truly distraught loved ones, it often took years—if ever—to accept that they should be using the past tense. It had been mere days for Peterson.

"Mr. Peterson, I'm Clarke Sinclair and I'm with the FBI," she said, watching to see how Peterson would react to that bit of news. He was impressed and a bit taken aback.

"Call me Jeremy, please," he said.

"Jeremy," she repeated dutifully, her tone easy. "We'd like to ask a few more questions about Bess."

"Of course," he said, leaning forward, ever the eager beaver to help. His jaw was clenched, his muscles bunched. He looked like he was ready to leap into action to hunt day and night for the man who had taken his girlfriend. "Anything I can do to help you guys find Bess. Anything."

She had a sudden flash of an old John Lithgow *SNL* skit flit through her mind. *Acting! Genius!*

"When was the last time you saw her?" she started.

He was prepared for the question. "That morning. She was her normal, happy self. She ate breakfast with all of us. We had pancakes, and she made some eggs, too. And then we put on *The Hangover*, but the girls made these white cranberry mimosas, and we all decided to head down to the lake before the movie was finished. Bess wanted to run off some of the calories, though. She was a little self-conscious about her weight, to be honest. I told her she did not need to run as much as she did, but she never listened. Hardheaded."

That was . . . a lot of detail. Those who were guilty often sought comfort in minutiae. It meant the story was rehearsed; it meant the person planned out what they were going to say.

Now, they just had to figure out if it was because he was actually guilty of murdering Bess or if it was because he knew they would suspect him of it.

Either way, he rushed to fill the silence she'd let hang. People tended to talk to fill voids. If you let them sit in their own thoughts long enough, they'd often tell you what they never meant to reveal.

"Not that she wasn't amazing, also," he hastened to add. "She just definitely had a mind of her own, that's for sure."

"In other ways, too?"

He shrugged. "She was stubborn, you know?"

Was.

"Mmm," she hummed, low in her throat. "Had she been enjoying the vacation?"

"Of course. We were happy for the chance to get out of the city. She is so amazing. She makes everything fun."

"A stressful time for you two?" She prodded. "Back in New York, that is."

"At work? Sure. But when is it not?"

"And for her?"

"Bess is a little . . . more aimless in her career," he said. "She does not really get stressed out."

Clarke nodded. She wanted to convey she understood perfectly. Bitches be flighty.

"Were there . . . Did you fight because of it?" she asked.

"No. God, no. I just wanted her to be her best self, you know? She's just so amazing."

"And the stress from your job? Did she get upset about that?"

Again, a blink-and-you'd-miss-it shadow passed over his face. "Bess is the best. She is always so supportive. Like I said, she does not really get stressed out."

For the first time, Clarke had real doubts. She was good at reading people. She'd built a career on it. She'd seen people at their worst, when they'd been told a loved one had died. Everyone reacted in their own way. Some went blank. Some crumpled. Hell, some even laughed, a physiological reaction they couldn't contain. The common theme, though, was that it wasn't scripted. It wasn't controlled.

This, on the other hand, seemed like an open-and-shut case of domestic violence escalating. His body was completely closed off, tight and defensive. His arms had come up across his chest the minute she'd asked about how Bess had been enjoying the vacation. He was avoiding using contractions and self-validating his own lies by repeating the same wording multiple times, which were both clear signs of deception.

And there was the blonde hair. For all the deviations that each particular case inevitably brought, the bastard never strayed from redheads.

It was almost more to reassure herself than anything else when she pulled the well-worn piece of paper out of her purse. She hesitated. It might not prove anything either way. But, God, she didn't want to be wrong about this.

"Jeremy, do you recognize this man?" They hadn't managed to get a picture of Cross. Ever. The only one they had was from when he was a young teenager, his skinny arm tossed over the shoulder of an even younger girl with a riot of red hair and a shadow in her eyes. The original girl. It haunted her, that image. Sometimes she traced the pad of her finger over the girl's face and wished. Wished life wasn't so cruel. Wished girls with bright red hair like the sunset could grow up in a world where boys with evil minds didn't sap their fire. Wished the past wasn't set in stone—that it was malleable and that she could change it.

Wishing was for childhood, though, where that girl in the picture would forever be stuck.

But it served its purpose, that snapshot. They'd had their digital forensics guy age Cross to what he should look like now.

She slid a copy of the printout across the table to Jeremy. He took it, holding it up close to his face, his eyes darting. He lowered it with a frown, a deep crease just inside his right eyebrow.

He nodded very slowly, his gaze meeting hers.

Yes. Everything in her relaxed and slipped back into place. The world still made sense. Or as much sense as it ever did.

Jeremy, however, knew this was not good news for Bess, and for the first time she actually believed the emotion she saw on his face.

"I saw him the first time we went to town," he said, his jaw clenched. "Is this the asshole who did it?"

"Tell me about seeing him," she said, ignoring his question.

His gaze returned to the printout, his head swaying from side to side. He looked like he was trying to remember something.

"We'd just stocked up, but Bess forgot to get something from the store," he said. "I was waiting for her outside, and the rest of them were loading up the trucks." He flicked a chin at the paper. "That guy came up to me and tried to bum a smoke."

Clarke stilled. She'd been expecting him to say he'd caught a glimpse of the dude somewhere in town. But, no, Cross had actually talked to him.

"I said no and he left," he said.

"That's it? You said no, and he didn't say anything else?"

Clarke saw tension around his eyes. He was lying.

"Look, if you said something like 'piss off' and then your choice of slur word instead of just 'no,' we don't give a shit." She'd hit her mark there. "But if he said anything that would otherwise be helpful, and you continue to lie to us, I'll have you charged with obstruction." It wouldn't stick, but she wagered he wouldn't know that.

A flush of red crept up his neck, a mixture of embarrassment and rage.

"I mighta said something like that," he finally mumbled.

Exactly like that.

"Did he react?"

"He just smiled at me, real creepylike," Jeremy said, with a shiver. "Then said something about how lucky I was to have Bess, but he didn't say 'Bess.' He just said something like 'your girl.'"

"I'm guessing you didn't take that kindly," Clarke said.

His fists clenched on the table, his knuckles white. "What was he doing looking at her? I should have killed him then and there."

That would have cleaned up everything quite nicely.

"She came out just as I was about to, and when I looked back to see if he was still there, well, he'd left," Jeremy finished. "That's it. I swear. That's all of it."

"Did Bess see him?" Sam finally chimed in.

Jeremy thought for a moment. "No," he drawled the word out. "She doesn't really look at other guys when she's with me."

Clarke bit down hard on the inside flesh of her cheek. She stood up instead of smashing his head into the table. "How long are you staying here?" The other men pushed to their feet as well, but he remained seated.

He glanced around. "My buddy rented the place out for the next two weeks so that I wouldn't have to find a place. Everyone who could took off extra time. They'll leave soon, though. I guess I'll get a hotel then."

"Okay. Thank you for the help. We'll be in touch."

"*Did* I help?" The question was pitiful, not contentious. His voice had reverted to that of a little boy.

"Yes," Lucas drawled, and they all turned to the stairs.

She paused, behind the guys, one foot on the first board, the other on the porch.

"Oh, one more question, Jeremy."

He shifted toward her.

"How often did you hit your girlfriend?"

A mask dropped, quick and smooth as a guillotine over his face. The blankness there chilled her, but it was soon replaced by the perfect mix of confusion and anger.

"What are you talking about? I loved Bess."

Loved.

"I love Bess." He must have seen something in her face. He'd pushed to his feet. "And you're wasting your time if you think I'd do anything to hurt her."

A single tear escaped to trail through the stubble of his five o'clock shadow. "She's the light of my life."

And, scene.

CHAPTER FOURTEEN

Bess

July 7, 2018

The tape took a small, delicate piece of skin along with it as Simon ripped it off her mouth.

Bess used the energy from every cell in her body to let out an unholy scream that ricocheted off the closest walls and the ceiling but then seemed to fade into the nothingness of the room.

He didn't flinch, even though his face was mere inches from hers, close enough for her saliva to hit his chin.

Those eyes—those brown eyes that were deep pools in the shadows—just stared, unblinking, letting her yell. But eventually they crinkled in amusement, just as the corners of his lips tipped up.

She was gasping by the time her vocal cords gave out on her. Her throat was raw, and tears gathered along the lower rims of her eyes, threatening to spill out.

"You can keep going if you want." He said it as if he were letting a little kid take an extra turn on a pinball machine. She glared up at him. "It's okay, really, my pet. No one will ever hear it."

She felt something she hadn't felt in months. Years. It started in the right ventricle of her heart and spread like a live thing into her lungs.

It crept up that back passage of her throat that stung when ocean water went down her nostrils. And buried itself right behind her eyes, burning away all the fear that had kept her in its clutches since she'd woken up in the strange room.

Rage. It was rage.

She had spent years locked up in a glass prison, and now that she was actually chained to the floor—all her resentment, all her anger, all her damaged self-worth and broken bones concentrated on the man in front of her.

And she made a vow to herself as he waited for her to react. She would escape. And she would take him down in the process.

"I have to use the bathroom," she finally said, keeping her voice small, which wasn't hard. It was rough from the screaming, anyway, and unpracticed from the hours she'd been drugged out.

"There's the drain, pet," he said with a gesture to a hole covered by a metal grate. He laughed at the revulsion she couldn't hide. "Change your mind, then?"

He straightened and walked over to the girl in the shadows. She noticed he held a bottle of water in his hand, and she licked her dry, bleeding lip, wishing it was for her. But it wasn't.

"Ah, my love," he crooned to the girl. She was behind one of the bulking shapes, so Bess couldn't see her, but she was able to follow Simon's trajectory. "It's almost your special time."

Even Bess winced at the words. In no way could "special time" be a good thing in this circumstance.

"Do you like your replacement?" As if the words weren't already terrifying, he whispered them in a lover's caress that ratcheted it up to horrifying. "She's not as pretty as you. But she doesn't have all these cuts on her face, either."

The tips of Bess's fingers went numb at the words, but she refused to give in to the panic. Focus on the rage.

There was a moment of silence where Bess strained to hear what was happening. Was the girl going to be killed right in front of her? There was a part of her—a part of her that made her cheeks burn in shame—that didn't think she had enough energy to worry about someone else. The better part of her, the one she hoped made up the majority of her, knew she wouldn't be able to just sit and let it happen. There certainly didn't seem to be much she could do, but something was better than nothing. And that's all she could hold on to.

There was a scuff of boots against cement just as she was about to try screaming again. He walked by without glancing her way and headed up the stairs. The door closed, and she could hear heavy locks sliding into place.

"He likes you." The voice was quiet, hesitant, blank. There was no jealousy there or encouragement. Just the facts.

"I'm not sure how to take that, to be honest," Bess said.

She heard the shrug in the girl's voice when she responded. "I used to think he liked me, too."

The exchange was like sandpaper against an already-bleeding abrasion.

"I'm Bess," she tried, instead of responding. "What's your name?"

"He doesn't like when I say it."

"Well, he's not here right now," Bess coaxed, keeping her voice gentle.

Silence. Bess wondered if she'd lost her. Until finally, "A-Anna," the girl stuttered out.

"Anna. That's very pretty. Nice to meet you, Anna." Bess vowed to say the girl's name as much as possible. She deserved to remember who she was.

"Do you know how long you've been down here?" She needed information. And she needed to build up this girl's confidence enough to get her to help Bess out. *Strike that Superman pose, Anna. You can do it, girl.*

Silence again. Bess wondered if she was listening to make sure Simon wasn't coming each time before she answered. That made Bess think the punishment for talking was perhaps something she should avoid. "April. I think."

Damn. That was a long time to be held captive by a psychopath.

"That means you've been here about three months."

A little puff of air followed that. Anna hadn't known. Bess bet time became an abstract construct when you lived in darkness.

"Did he tell you his name was Simon?" Bess asked.

She was getting used to the delayed answers now. "Y-yesss."

Simon the snake. Simon the sociopath.

Now the important one. "Have you tried to escape?"

"T-twice. I—I don't know where we are. But we had to drive a long way to get here. He . . . he kept me drugged in the trunk of a car. It was wearing off. I think I'd been making noise. I can't remember now."

"It's okay."

"W-well, he stopped the car to give me more. But I heard someone else. I think he parked in the back of a lot somewhere, and someone surprised him. Simon shut the trunk door but not before I started yelling. You shouldn't yell, you know."

Noted.

"I think Simon killed him. He opened the trunk not long after, told me not to try that again, and punched me in the face. Then everything went black."

"And the second time?" Bess prompted when Anna didn't seem inclined to continue.

"It was a few days after I got here," Anna continued. "I don't think he was giving me . . ."

"Giving you what, Anna?"

"Drugs?" she said it like it was a question. "Whatever he uses to make everything fuzzy. My muscles don't want to move when he gives it to me."

That was something to digest for later.

"So this was before he started sedating you?"

"I don't know. I think so. It all blurs," Anna said, her voice growing frustrated.

"Shhh. It's okay. How did you try to escape?"

"It was stupid."

"Trying to live is not stupid, Anna," Bess said, wanting to hug her. "Whatever you did, you tried."

"It wasn't . . ." Anna trailed off. "It wasn't enough."

"Did you try to get away?"

"I ran. I ran up the stairs as fast as I could. I'm a fast runner." There was a bit of pride there. *Build on it. Hold on to it. Hold on to who you are. It was so easy to forget.* "But he caught me. He said he always catches us."

"Us?" It came out sharper than she'd intended.

"His girls."

Bess's muscles contracted in an involuntary shiver at that.

"Did you . . . Were any of the other girls here?" She forced herself to ask.

There was the longest pause yet. "Not here. No."

"How do you know about them?"

"He tells me about them. His girls."

Jesus.

"When he caught you . . ." Bess needed to know the rest. Needed to know so she could plan.

"That's when he started giving me the drugs," Anna said. That threw a wrench in her strategy.

"Does he ever unlock these?" She jangled her foot so that Anna would know what she meant.

"It seems like once a day for . . . necessities," Anna said. "I get a shower sometimes. But that's down here. And then when he takes you into the room, also."

"What happens in the room, Anna?" Bess didn't want to know. She really, really didn't want to know.

But she wasn't finding out. She'd lost Anna with the question. She waited enough time to realize she wasn't just pausing like she had before.

"Anna?" She tried the girl's name a couple of times, but she was met with silence.

So there was nothing left to do but sit in the dark and wonder when she would find out what happened in the room.

The light under the door went dark at night, Bess realized, and she was able to keep herself oriented by watching it.

Anna had stopped talking to her completely. She'd throw out the girl's name every once in a while to see if she would respond, but she hadn't yet.

Simon had come to fetch Anna several times in the—from what Bess gathered—four days she'd been held in the basement. She'd caught sight of the girl's strawberry-blonde hair around a sharp, sunken face that looked like it used to be round. She hadn't even glanced at Bess. He'd taken her toward the back, where the small bathroom was, for a good amount of time.

When she returned, there would be fresh blood on her clothes and a sick air of unwholesome excitement lingering around Simon. He'd rechain her to the floor out of Bess's sight and then leave.

Bess had tried to provoke him one time, yelling that he was a pathetic excuse for a man if he needed to keep women locked up in his basement.

He'd paused midstride, one foot hovering above the first stair. Then, in one of the most chilling movements Bess had ever witnessed in real life, he'd turned with his whole body, horror-film style. He'd stopped before her, his head tilted, studying her. Then he'd knelt down so their eyes were level. The pupils almost blacked out the brown of his irises.

And then, without warning, he'd slapped her so hard across her cheekbone she'd ended up sprawled on the floor. He'd removed the handcuffs that bound her arms days earlier, but the attack had been so sudden she hadn't been able to catch herself before her head bounced on cement.

"It's not your time yet, pet," he'd cooed as if nothing had happened. She held a shaking hand to the welt she knew had already bloomed, red and angry, across her pale skin. "You wouldn't want to rush the game now, would you?"

She'd held her tongue. She didn't want him to know she was used to getting hit. It didn't bother her as much as he probably thought it did. And, in that moment, she had realized something. Something that would help her escape.

But now it was just her and Anna again. And the ever-imposing silence of darkness. She decided to fill it, even if Anna didn't want to.

"I'm a kindergarten teacher," she said, deciding to start with the basics. "My boyfriend hates that I am, but I kind of love it. He thinks it's a waste of my time and my degree . . . that I'm just babysitting other people's kids. His words."

She gave Anna time to respond, but nothing came. "It's not, though." She told her about the kids at her school. The bad ones. The good ones. The charmers. The future nerds.

Nothing.

"I also run," she said, hoping to spark a connection. "It lets me be free, you know? Away from any expectations. Disappointment. You don't have to be perfect when you're running, you know?"

Strike two. She reached down deep. Emotional connection. They needed to work together. They needed to figure this out. Bess needed to jolt her out of her despair and dejection. Anna had given up all hope. She was a lamb being led to the slaughter. Literally.

And then, all of a sudden, Bess knew what she needed to talk about.

"The first time my boyfriend hit me, we were both so shocked, we started crying together," she started. "We were in a stupid fight, and I remember every detail about it. But you know what? The fight itself doesn't matter. Because it wasn't about the fight."

"No."

It was the first word Anna had said since Bess had asked about the room. Bess shook her shoulders in a little victory shimmy.

"You know what I've been thinking about? I'm not sitting here wondering when it all became so normal. Just so expected. One day it was just . . . that was the way it was, you know?"

"Y-yes."

"It doesn't feel like abuse even if you know it is. It feels like . . ."

"Love." Anna finished for her.

Bess nodded even though Anna couldn't see her. "Like love. Like a wildfire raging, uncontainable love. And then there are those bad times that shock you out of it, and you're absolutely sure he's going to kill you, and you call the cops, and you see it in their eyes. You see the judgment and the questions and the blame. And they ask you what you did to set him off. And they ask you if he actually hit you or just threatened to. Did he have a weapon? No, just his fists? Okay, then."

Her breathing had turned ragged, as she looked at the jagged edges of her nails that had broken off when she'd tried to pick at the locks on her chain biting into her palms. "And you see the girls who look at you when they see your black eye and silently wonder why you stay. Why I stay. Even if I ever get away from Jeremy, that's all I'll ever be asked. 'Why did you stay so long?' Fuck you, that's why."

Bess heard a little gurgle that could have been laughter.

"I was planning to leave, you know," Bess said, and she heard the defensiveness in her voice even after her bravado a few seconds earlier.

"Me too."

"Yeah?"

"I'd been collecting the change from around the house," Anna said. "A few spare dollars every time I went to the store. He usually checked the receipts, but sometimes I could . . . distract him."

Bess felt a pang. *Your replacement,* the words echoed in her head.

She realized she had let the conversation drop as she turned the similarities over. Looking for a way to use it to her advantage.

Then, for the first time, Anna asked her a question. "What were you thinking about then?"

Bess realized she'd never finished the thought. "I'm sitting here wondering if, when we escape, I'll be strong enough to actually leave him. And I'm worried I'm not."

"That's him talking," Anna said, and for once Bess heard the girl she used to be in her voice. The one who collected pennies from the couch cushions so that she could leave a bad situation. The girl before the room happened. "You're so strong."

"Well, you are, too, Anna," Bess said, her voice fierce. "And I'm going to need you to recognize that. You know why?"

Bess was going to make her ask. No more of this silence crap.

Anna gave in to her curiosity. "Why?"

"Because you're part of my plan to get us out of here."

CHAPTER FIFTEEN

Clarke

July 16, 2018

"Sleep is for wussies, huh?" Sam set a large mug of tea at Clarke's elbow before settling into the Adirondack next to her.

"Sleep is for a night when there aren't at least two young women's lives on the line," she said, before sipping from the cup.

It was past midnight, and the brutal heat of the day had long given way to the relief the darkness brought. She was burrowed in a sweatshirt and sweatpants, with her feet curled under her. She'd been too comfortable and too focused on what she'd just recently discovered to seek such creature comforts as hydration. That was Sam. Always knowing what she needed, before she knew it herself.

"I got news for ya, kid. There's always gonna be a girl's life on the line."

"Yeah, but this is different," she said, closing the MacBook on her lap so she would stop staring at the screen. Even as she rubbed the heel of her palm over her dry, tired eyes until lights popped in the darkness, she knew the pain was worth it. She was onto something.

She'd been going over every detail of the case since they'd returned to their little makeshift HQ after giving up hope of finding anything more at the cabin. Though she'd been frustrated at the lack of action, she'd been eager to get back to her files. The bastard's voice had been echoing in her mind all day.

Not the destination. The journey.

She had to ask herself, *What destination? What journey?* The one they were on?

The destination they'd been focused on was the dead girls. Maybe too focused, apparently. Logically, then, the "journey" would be the scavenger hunt. So what hadn't they been noticing? It had to be the pictures; it was all they had to work with. But she'd studied the pictures. Sam had studied the pictures. The top brains at the FBI had studied the pictures. If there was something to have been found, it would have been found.

When all the drama was swept away, they were pretty simplistic clues for someone who thought himself so clever. Or at least that's what she'd always thought. Some were near impossible to figure out, but it was not because they were complex; it was because there just hadn't been enough detail.

Simon, more than anything, wanted to show how smart he was. How he could outwit them time and again. But, taken at face value, the photos weren't a reflection of that.

Unless you didn't take them at face value.

Despite the low-level hum in her veins, the one she got when everything in a case started making sense, she didn't spill it all out to Sam yet. Instead, she watched the ripples from a jumping fish roll and crest across the otherwise smooth surface of the lake, which had turned silver in the moonlight.

This one was different, she'd said. Why had that never felt more accurate?

Sam sighed, an exhale of air that spoke volumes. "I know, kid."

"What did Roger say?" She side-eyed him so she wouldn't be so obvious about assessing his emotional state.

"He keyed in on the boyfriend until I told him that Peterson positively identified Simon. Even Roger can't ignore that. He's flying up tomorrow."

"Our white knight to save the day," she said, not even trying to hide the bitterness that coated her words. Roger had blood on his hands. He had blood on his hands for pulling resources from the Simon manhunt, and he had blood on his hands from Sam, when he'd chosen career advancement over him. Back when politicians were scared of the idea of a gay man leading the FBI, Roger had put the rumors to rest by simply making sure there was nothing for anyone to talk about. In the end, he'd gotten what he had so highly coveted, and Sam had gotten screwed over. "Do you think he'll bring his expensive suits for the cameras?"

Sam's relaxed smile always confused her when the topic came up. "It's time to forgive him, Clarke. For his crimes against me, at least. That's between him and me. And it's over."

"Fine," she bit out. "But you can't deny he's left us out to dry on this case."

"He did what he thought was best."

"He did what he thought would secure him a promotion and limit the bad press."

"You got me there. He let us keep Della."

"After you threatened to quit entirely," she said, not willing to give Roger points on that one. "No way would he have let you out of his control like that. At least we know what his weakness is."

"It was an empty threat on both sides," Sam sighed. "He wouldn't have taken Della."

The argument was old and not worth their time. "Speaking of our resident genius, I had her help me with something I've been thinking about."

Sam showed no obvious signs of relief at the change of topics, but she knew his body language well. He had been tense, and at the switch of subjects his shoulders dropped slightly, the knuckles around his glass relaxed, and the muscles of his face sagged back into his hangdog everyday expression. "Oh yeah, trying something new? What have you been thinking about?"

She ignored the teasing remark delivered to lighten the mood.

Not the destination. The journey.

"Our guy. The bastard . . ."

"Simon."

"Simon." She acquiesced. There was something about calling him by his name that made him human. Maybe that's why Sam did it. Humans could be caught. They could be brought to justice. They could be killed, if needed. Scary monsters in the night, well, not so much. At least in Clarke's experience.

"He's a planner," she continued, reopening her laptop. "He's meticulous. Everything he sends us, it means something."

Sam nodded. "Even if we don't realize it at the time."

"Precisely." She jabbed her pointer finger in his direction. "Precisely. So all these pictures, these messages, these clues for our scavenger hunt. We've been looking at them as individual pieces. Solve one, move to the next, solve that one, move to the next. Always a dead girl at the end of the line."

Sam straightened. "But what if there's a bigger message?"

She pressed her lips together in a grim line. "Yeah."

"Jesus," Sam breathed out, and she almost laughed. He'd tipped his head so that the bald spot she knew was there rested against the back of the chair. The moonlight bathed his grooved and creviced skin in silver.

"I'm going to text Della. She's got some crypto friend that can help us out, but I've been working on it, in the meantime," she said, tabbing over to her spreadsheet. "Sam. He gave us the location two or three clues out. Every time."

"How?"

"Look at Lila Teasdale. She was found in that town in West Virginia. At 147 Meadow Drive, Elkins, West Virginia, precisely."

"I remember." His voice was thick.

"Look." She flipped through the pictures that sat in the file resting on the arm of her chair. "Look." She held the one she'd been searching for up, her finger a staccato against the glossy paper. "This was his first clue. Do you see the address? It's the Chinese place next to the bar he sent us to. One four seven."

He took the photo from her and rubbed the pad of his thumb over the numbers. "How did we not see that?"

She honestly didn't know. She'd studied these pictures until they were no longer places, just blurs on glossy paper. And then she'd studied them more until they turned back into places. She hadn't seen it, though.

"Look, there's no way we could have known to look for any of this shit. And not all of them were that obvious."

She shuffled the photos again. "The second clue. There in the corner. The billboard just almost out of the shot. Forever Meadows Nursing Home. Meadow."

"Drive. Meadow Drive. What was . . ." Sam paused. And then he got it. "That old drive-in."

"Third clue." She found the photo of the dilapidated throwback to the 1960s. Weeds had overtaken the place, but the screen was still there, the speakers that piped the sound into viewers' cars. The concession stand with its barber-pole-striped awning.

"Holy Christ." Sam ran a gnarled hand through his hair, before covering his eyes with it. He pinched the bridge of his nose.

"The next one's harder. But that's what Google's for," she said. "That little town in Maryland. Look at the intersection in the background."

"Route 355?"

"Yeah, this one stumped me," she said. "I was looking up every single thing I could find in the photo. The 'three five five' was about thirty-six Google searches in. Nothing was coming up. But then . . ." She unlocked her phone and pulled up the keypad, as if to dial a number. She flipped it in her hand to hold it out to him.

He took it gingerly.

She helped him get there. "Three five five. *E L K.*"

He pushed to his feet and walked to the very edge of the water. His toes tipped into the frigid lake, but he didn't react. He just stood there, rocking back, his heels sinking into the soft sand-mud at the edge of the grass. There was nothing to see except for the trees across the way.

She stood, the soles of her feet sinking into the thick, damp grass. The wind had picked up slightly, enough to ruffle the strands of her hair that had escaped the sturdy beige rubber band that had served as her makeshift hair tie.

She was tall for a woman, so their shoulders bumped when she stopped next to him. She leaned her body weight into him, just at that one contact point on their arms. And everything that was between them narrowed to that one place where sweatshirt met sweatshirt. The years of frustration, hope, despair, laughter, crushing defeat, friendship. The memories were palpable entities, as if she could reach out and capture them. Fireflies that she would be able to hold in her palm, that she could put into a jar and watch as they lit the world. Or let fly away. He shifted, rocking forward, his toes curling into the loose pebbles that rimmed the water's edge, and the connection was broken. She missed it immediately.

"He's all but drawing an arrow for us," Sam said. His lips were drawn tight. This was a new and different Sam. One she'd rarely seen in the past two years. She had come to think of him as her own personal Yoda. Calm, centered, always having the answers. She was the one who doubted. Who turned inward with self-loathing. Who was the rain cloud on his sunny day.

His mess he had to clean up. The one he always cleaned up.

Clarke sat on the cracked porcelain of the toilet seat and traced over the graffiti decorating the stall's walls. The music from the bar drifted in under the bathroom's door. Someone had selected the entirety of ABBA's second album on the jukebox, and the impossibly cheery notes provided an ironic soundtrack to her current breakdown. Light Swedish pop music shouldn't be playing at this type of hole-in-the-wall, the one she'd chosen because the bouncer didn't glance too closely at IDs. And because people who frequented it knew how to mind their own business.

Drunken, slurred shouts of "Waterloo" crashed into her brain, but she tuned it out as best she could, instead concentrating on the words littering the cool metal beneath her fingertips.

Susanna wuz here. Mary sux cock. Screw you chris. H+L 4evah.

All the classics.

She paused at one written in gold sparkly marker. She liked the glitter, the way that it was textured beneath her thumb. But the words themselves were what stopped her. They would probably be scraped off or covered up in the next night or so. But for now, they were here.

The world breaks everyone, and afterward many are strong at the broken places. But those that will not break, it kills. It kills the very good and the very gentle and the very brave impartially.

It was signed with two x*'s. Kisses. Or hugs. She could never remember which was which. She imagined what the girl would have looked like, hunched and bent finding a blank space among the poorly spelled insults and declarations of love. Was she a poet? Why did she have a gold sparkly marker with her? Had she come in with the intent to destroy the very souls of the girls who would follow her in as they sat to pee?*

It didn't matter, Clarke told herself, shaking off the image of a Goth with a pixie cut and mischief in her eyes. As if she could predict Clarke would sit here running her thumb over the words over and over again. At the broken places.

Her breath hitched, and she dropped her head in between her legs.

What did that make her? she wondered. Strong? Had the world broken her? She didn't want it to have. But she knew the truth. It had broken her. And she wasn't strong in those broken places. She wasn't fooling anyone that she was.

She saw it in their eyes. Those around her who called themselves her friends and family but didn't act like it. Not in the way she desperately needed. She saw the hesitation, the delicacy in which they couched the words they spoke to her. The pauses where nervous breath spilled over chapped lips, and fretful tongues darted out to wet the cracks, not able to form sentences for fear she might tumble over the edge if the sentiments were wrong.

There was only one person who might get mad, who might yell, and he wasn't here. Or not enough, even though she knew she could call him and he would come.

She didn't know if she could handle that. Because, yes, maybe he'd get mad and tell her so. But far more likely he'd just be disappointed in her. It always seemed to lurk there behind his eyes, the disappointment.

"You're so smart, kid," he'd told her one time. She hated when he'd called her "kid." She wasn't a kid. She'd been through enough of life to never be a kid again. He knew it, too. But she'd warmed at the words anyway.

She couldn't remember anyone else telling her she was smart, worth something. They told her she was nice. That she was a good girl. That she was polite. But they hadn't told her she could do something with her life. He had. He wanted her to do so much with it. As if it meant something. As if it weren't already completely ruined.

She pushed the thought of him away because it was too sharp and she was too raw.

Her fingers tucked into the pocket of her jeans, searching. The bite of the sharp metal edge against her soft pads startled her more than it should. She sat up, scooching her hips down so that she could pull the razor out without causing further damage.

Clarke held the blade in her palm. It was so small, nestled into the little lined crater there. It immediately made her heart rate steady. She'd been feeling like her synapses would just not stop firing, and then she held the cool little piece of metal, and they seemed to calm immediately. The manic fire that had burned in her brain was about to be doused. And that was one real and true thing she could count on.

The fingers of her free hand worked at the button of her jeans until she was able to push the fabric down over her hips. She ran a hand over the jagged little scars that decorated her upper thigh. They were her talismans. The white ridges, the pink ones. They made the pain go away. She would lay her lips on each one of them in thanks if she could make her body bend that way.

Her breath quickened as she brought the tip of the blade against her soft, pale skin. The relief at the first burst of blood streamed through her veins, releasing the tension in her shoulders, her neck, her clavicle, her stomach, her toes. Each piece of her relaxed into the bite of the wound as she drew the razor down the length of her thigh.

She wanted to cry out, not because of the pain but from the intense rush from the high that swept through her. It was better than any of the drugs she'd tried in the past few years. And she'd chased enough highs to rate them.

Clarke pressed into the cut, which was only leaking blood now. It wasn't enough. The hand that had been holding her spine in its steel grasp all evening was back, working its way toward her throat. She clutched at the skin there now, terrified of the feeling of suffocation she knew was only a whisper away.

When she curled her hand around the razor, its sharp bits cut into her palm. She flipped her hand over so that it was resting on her freshly cut leg, wrist up. She plucked at the blue veins there with her fingers, like they were guitar strings. Her skin puckered and pulled back to its normal state when she was finished with the machinations.

Sam would be disappointed with her. But he always was. If that was her only reason not to do it, well, he'd be better off without her in his life anyway. Screwing it up. Calling him at three in the morning, sobbing.

She dug the blade into the delicate skin right below the heel of her hand. She bit her lip to keep from crying out from the relief. She went deeper than she usually did. Then switched to the other side. The deep red pulsed with each beat of her heart. Her eyes were pulled to the glittery gold words that shimmered in and out of her vision. She blinked the tears away so the words would become clear again. She needed to see them. She needed to see them.

The world breaks everyone, and afterward many are strong at the broken places.

Her breath caught on a sob, and she stood. Black dots swam in front of her, but she pushed them away. She yanked up her jeans from where they'd pooled around her knees, ignoring the bloody trail she was leaving behind. The wounds had not stopped weeping.

She managed to get the door open and rushed past a startled girl swinging into the bathroom.

"Oy." Then, "Hey, are you okay?" followed her down the poorly lit hallway. She ignored both as she steadied herself with one hand against the flyer-papered wall. She collapsed against the phone booth but was able to dig enough change out of her pocket. With shaking fingers, she slid the coins into the machine and dialed the numbers she might as well have had tattooed on the back of her eyelids.

It rang. And again. She almost hung up after the third one. But then she heard his voice.

The word caught in her throat. She panicked as she tried to make her tongue work even as it sat damp and heavy at the bottom of her mouth. He was going to hang up, her mind screamed at her. She pinched herself hard, and the little bolt of pain was enough.

"Help."

The next hours were a blur of shapes and colors and sounds. Of brusque hands reaching for her, of flickering fluorescent lights, of that familiar alcoholic burn in her nostrils, of the quiet beeping of medical equipment. She feigned sleep as long as she thought she could get away with it. Then Sam shifted in the chair beside her hospital bed. She peeked at him beneath one lowered lid.

"You scared me, kid," Sam said, and she could hear the emotion there. He didn't always let it show. Almost never, really. He was the strong constant in her life. But he was scared. Her skin was oversensitive from it.

"It got too much for a second there," she admitted.

"You're supposed to call me when that happens."

"I did call you."

They were both silent, maybe both grateful that she had.

"Kid, this can't happen again," he said, his eyes locked on hers. She wanted to look away but didn't.

"I know." Gone was every defense mechanism she usually employed. She was completely stripped down and raw and hurting, and she had messed up and she knew it.

"No." He scooted forward, his hands clasped together, forearms resting on the tops of his legs. She'd rarely seen him this intense. "That's not good enough. This can't happen again."

She couldn't promise. She tried. Even though she wanted to, she couldn't. She just looked back at him.

"It doesn't have to be forever." Sam's eyes flicked over her face, searching for something. She didn't know what. "Today. All you have to make it through is today."

She narrowed her eyes, because she knew him too well. "All the 'todays'?"

Smirking, he saluted her with his coffee cup. "When tomorrow becomes today, you'll make it through that one, too."

"In perpetuity," she said, without the bitterness the promise usually would have made her feel. Maybe it was the memory of that graffiti that was forever burned into the back of her eyelids. Strong at the broken places.

She could be strong. If only for today.

She nodded slowly, just one tip of the chin down, but Sam relaxed completely, melting back into the chair.

"This means no cutting, either, kid," he said sternly.

She hadn't. Since that day, she hadn't. And it was because of Sam. She wished now that she could hug him, but the gesture would make them both uncomfortable.

"Cross wants us to find him," she finally said, blinking back to their current case. She knew why the past kept sliding into her consciousness, nudging at the edges of her awareness, but that didn't mean she had to give in to it whenever it pressed for her attention.

"He wants me to be smart enough to catch him," she mused. "But I'm not."

That shook Sam out of the depths he had sunk into, as she knew it would. "That's bullshit, kid. You figured this out."

"Only took me three dead girls." When in doubt, fall back to self-deprecation and dark sarcasm. It was her MO.

"You know what's nuts?" Sam asked, turning back to the lake. "We know who he is. We. Know. Who. He. Is."

She didn't need further clarification to follow his thoughts. "How many other agents can say the same? How many others would we judge for their absolute failure at catching someone where they knew so much about the perp?"

"I would maybe put it differently . . ."

"Of course you would, babe. You've got a heart of gold," she said with affection. Between the two of them, Sam was the good person. The white hat with a kind, forgiving soul, who got cranky only sometimes and mostly with her.

Sam nudged her. "Not quite a heart of gold, but . . . doesn't change the fact. With everything we know about him, we should have been able to catch him. We have his victimology, we know his weakness. Jeez, now we even know where he is holding the girls, if we look hard enough. And still he's always one step ahead."

"We suck." Clarke sighed.

Sam barked out a harsh laugh. "God, we really do."

They grinned at each other with a shared humor they wouldn't be able to explain to someone who hadn't lived through this with them.

"It's different this time. Everything's different," she said, with enough optimism to startle him. She shrugged, happy to ride out the rush from the breakthrough she'd just had with the clues. "Can't you feel it?"

"I don't know what I feel anymore when it comes to Simon," Sam said, defeated once more.

They'd both given up so much because of Cross. Relationships that could have actually meant something, nights of dreamless sleep, a life without an endless parade of bodies. God, Sam was so pure these days he didn't even drink more than a glass of Chardonnay at Christmas parties. She wondered where the pain and frustration seeped out. Or if it didn't. If it just lurked in his veins like a just barely toxic venom that was slowly poisoning him.

Back when they first started working together, she'd been able to get under his skin like no one else. He'd slash at her, and she'd swing back, and while they might have emerged from the tussles a little worse for wear, it let them both deal with some issues neither wanted to admit to having.

Now, he wouldn't even do that. He knew her too well. He knew that coming from him, even a small nick to her carefully built-up self-worth and confidence would leave her destroyed like it never would have earlier. He was her best friend, her father, her confidant and shoulder to cry on.

So he held back; he held in. And he suffered in silence. Or she assumed he did. And she hated herself more for it. Not enough to change, though.

"Well, I feel it," she said, pretending she was strong enough for the both of them when he so desperately needed it. Something in the air shifted and turned cool against her neck. A cloud partially covered the moon, and shadows tangoed along the banks of the lake. If she were the type to get jumpy, she'd be ready to hop out of her skin at the briefest noise.

But the demons of the dark had nothing on Simon Cross. She should know; she'd faced them both down.

Only one continued to defeat her.

She turned from both the thought and the endless black depths of the lake. She didn't need the metaphor at the moment.

Sam followed her back, watching her as she collected her work. They started up to the little rental.

"So, you haven't addressed the most obvious question there, kid." Sam broke the silence as they slipped inside. "What are the clues telling us this time?"

"I was hoping you didn't notice," she said, grabbing the salmon-colored file with the name Anna Meyers printed on it in thick black letters. "Because I have no idea."

"Ha." Sam dropped onto the cushion of the couch next to her. He snatched the folder out of her hand.

"Have at it," she said with a wave of her hand. "I haven't been able to make any progress. He seems to have deviated from his number-based approach on this one. I've started by making a list of every single thing in each of the pictures, but that's as far as I've gotten."

"Do me a favor?" Sam's eyes were already devouring the first clue while he handed her the second. "Put a pot of coffee on. Doesn't look like either of us is getting any sleep tonight."

CHAPTER SIXTEEN

Adelaide

April 2002

Adelaide kept the box hidden in the shadows of the far corner of her small closet. She dropped to her knees to retrieve it, knocking out of the way fallen shirts and shoes that had lost their mates.

It was heavy and dragged against the carpet as she pulled it out to rest in front of her. She pried the lid open, and it caught for a moment, before lifting it free of the edges.

The latest photo was still on her pillow where she'd found it. Adelaide walked over and reached out trembling fingers to touch its white edges. The Polaroid looked like it was out of another decade, all faded black at the corners.

She held it up to her desk light. An enormous sycamore tree stood tall in the center, its thick knobby trunk the focus of the picture, its branches reaching up toward an eggshell-blue spring sky. Its leaves were fresh and lush and wild, and she could almost feel their silkiness underneath her thumb.

But what made her pulse stutter was the young girl. She had her white-stocking-clad legs tossed through a dusty tire swing, her feet kicked up to the sky. Her head was tipped back, and red curls hovered just above the ground. Joy lit her face and stretched her mouth, and Adelaide thought the tire was the only thing tethering her to the earth.

The girl was even slightly blurred, out of focus, as if she were just an idea instead of a real person.

Adelaide turned the Polaroid over with shaking hands.

You would love it here. Soon. Simon

She didn't know what "soon" meant. A day? A month? It seemed like she'd been waiting forever. Years. Four years.

She hadn't seen him in four years. Since she was twelve.

But he wrote constantly.

I miss you. I'll come back for you. Do you miss me?

Endless variations of the same idea.

Long ago, they'd made up a code name for him so that the Crosses wouldn't get suspicious by her influx of mail once he'd left. They pretended he was a pen pal from Indiana. Part of a school project that had lasted long beyond the scope of the assignment.

But sometimes she'd come home and there would be something in her room. Or in another private place. She would know, then, that he had been there. In her space. Every once in a while she thought she could still smell the musk and herbs of male cologne in the air.

He was close tonight. Was he even now watching her silhouette against the wispy white curtains? She felt his eyes on her sometimes. When she was walking home from school. When she was at the mall with her girlfriends. When she'd gone on that one date that ended so disastrously she'd wanted to bury herself in a hole in the ground for the month following it. But he never showed himself.

She shivered.

Then she dropped down next to the box once more, the more recent Polaroid still clutched in her hand.

He'd written her so many letters, hundreds. She knew if he found out she hadn't kept them all he would be livid. But she couldn't have. There was no practical way to hide that amount of paper. She'd kept all the pictures, though. Stacked and rubber-banded together in different piles. They were chronological, starting with the first one. A close-up, smiling picture that was just his eyes, his nose, and his top lip stretched wide in a grin.

So you don't miss me too much, pet.

He'd left it on her pillow the morning he'd left. She'd clutched it to her chest and cried for hours. Mrs. Cross had pulled Adelaide's head onto her lap and cooed to her. Mr. Cross had brought her brownies. They'd both reasoned and cajoled and explained. But she'd been inconsolable.

She hadn't talked to them for three days.

She plucked a different pile from the box. The top picture was of a bloodred cherry pie with a single slice missing. The lattice was a pleasant baked brown, and the cherries were plump and spilling out where the pastry had been sliced. She knew what the back of it said, by heart.

Me without you. Simon

She slipped the tree Polaroid in at the bottom of the pile, snapped the rubber band around the glossy stack, and then placed it back in the box. She shut the lid and pushed it back into the far corner of her closet.

She had to keep them. Even as they whispered to her in the darkness and sent shivers up her spine. She could almost hear them at night when the rest of the house was quiet. The worst ones were of the girls. They talked to her. They cried out sometimes in little girl voices. And she'd curl under the thick homemade quilt and stare, with eyes wide open, at the closed closet door.

She had to keep them, she knew, even though she did not want to. Someone might need them as evidence one day.

◆ ◆ ◆

The girl on the tire swing stayed with her. As Adelaide brushed her teeth, washed her face, slid beneath the quilt made from her old T-shirts, the girl stayed with her.

She dreamed of her. The red hair. The smile. The girl was running through fields of sunflowers, her fingers tracing the upturned face of each one, neither flower nor girl constrained to the reality of the evil that lurked so nearby.

It was a happy place.

The gentle pings of fingernails against glass pulled her from the meadow with the girl.

She sat up, disoriented and still caught in the delicate space between dreams and consciousness. It took a minute for the shadow on the other side of her window to form into the shape of a boy.

The air stilled, and the electricity in it had the hair at the nape of her neck standing on end.

Simon.

Joy warred with fear warred with nostalgia warred with horror. And underneath it all—pulsing and unwanted and confusing—was something that still felt like love.

She clambered off the bed, rushing to push against the stubborn, distorted wood of the white-painted window frame. His smile was a breath away from her lips when she finally got it open.

"Adelaide," he whispered, and it was hot against her cheek even as the cool spring night wrapped around her.

"Simon," she said just as quietly. "What are you doing here?"

The happiness fell from his face, just a bit. "Not really the warm welcome I was hoping for."

She just stared. What was she supposed to say?

He shook his head. "Come here." He wrapped long fingers around her wrist and tugged. She let the force of it pull her out onto the little roof. The tiles cut into the soft flesh of her calves, and she drew her legs to her chest to escape the biting pain. Resting her cheek on her knees, she watched him. He was vibrating, and she could swear there were little flares of energy in the spaces where his body blended into the night.

"Adelaide," he said again, "I came back for you."

Who asked you to?

She bit her lip so the question didn't tumble into the space between them.

"Where have you been?" she said instead.

"I know you might be mad at me for leaving you. But you got my letters, right? I told you I'd come back for you. To save you from them," he said, his voice breathless. The tone wasn't that of the confident boy who sent her letters and notes and told her she was his. There was something different about it, something that terrified her.

The night was cold, but the weather had nothing to do with why she couldn't stop shivering. She took a deep breath and lay back against the uneven slabs of the roof.

"Hey, Simon," she said and she wondered if the universe had swallowed the words, because she almost couldn't hear them. He stretched his body out next to hers and nudged her shoulder, so she thought he did hear her at least. "Why do you watch the stars come out?"

Maybe he didn't anymore. Maybe he'd stopped looking up to the night sky. Maybe she didn't even know why she'd asked that. But he tensed beside her, and she thought maybe the question was still relevant.

His chest rose and fell, enough times that she lost hope that he would answer. But then there was a quiet intake of air, the kind that came the moment before someone revealed a little secret part of themselves. "My mother told me it was all the people we loved coming out to check in on us every day."

She turned her head to look at him. He was still lying.

"I don't believe you."

There was a flash of something—anger? amusement?—when he met her eyes. But then it was gone, and he grinned, stark-white teeth bared against the dark night.

"They're like you," he said.

"The stars?"

"Yeah," he said, watching them once more. His hand rose to trace patterns in the air. "They're a puzzle, aren't they?"

"I'm a puzzle?" She didn't understand. But this time it actually felt like the truth.

"Everyone's so easy to figure out," he said. "People are so boring, aren't they? The reasons they cry. The reasons they yell. The reasons they hurt. They're all so fragile and boring. The stars aren't so easy to figure out."

He shifted so he was lying on his side, reaching to press his thumb against her cheekbone. "You're not easy to figure out."

She flinched away from the touch, shaking uncontrollably now. A mask slipped over his features. "Come with me, Adelaide. We can leave this place. We can be together. You and me. Like how it's supposed to be."

If she squinted, just a little bit, she could almost imagine this was everything she'd ever dreamed about when she was younger. She and Simon running off into the sunset, leaving behind the people who never quite loved them like parents should. They'd start a new life, go places that had always seemed unreachable, be people they'd never believed they could be. There was a part of her that ached for that future. That wanted to be able to sink into the comfort of his arms, to let him make her laugh like he always could, to challenge her, to spar, to chat, to love.

But she wasn't squinting. Her eyes were wide open.

"Did you hurt those girls, Simon? The ones in the photos?"

In a quick move, he rolled on top of her, holding most of the weight on his forearms as a leg slotted in between hers. "Why would you think that, Adelaide? Is that what you think of me?" His voice was soft, like a caress. But there was something underneath it that made her wish she'd kept her window locked.

"I can't go with you, Simon," she said, wiping her palms on the soft cotton of her shorts to get rid of the slickness that had suddenly coated them in a thin film.

He almost looked regretful as he pushed back onto his knees to free his arms. She didn't feel any less claustrophobic. "Oh, pet. It's funny that you think you have a choice in the matter."

It took her a second too long to process the words. His forearm was already pressed against her windpipe, both silencing the scream that had risen to the back of her throat and cutting off her air.

This wasn't happening. This couldn't be happening.

She slapped at him, her fingernails digging into skin where she could find it. Her hips bucked up, trying to dislodge him. But he simply batted away her hands and settled his weight more firmly onto her. "This could have been so much easier if you had just trusted me, Adelaide," he said, his voice composed. It terrified her.

But everything had started going black at the edges of her vision. She clawed at his arm, but the pressure didn't relent. There was no glorious air to save her, just dry-heaving lungs and a fuzziness that popped like bubbles in her brain.

"We're going to have so much fun together." The words came from far away, just an echo in a dark tunnel. She lifted her eyes from his face and found the fairy lights in the black sky above her. The stars blinked at her, becoming soft and golden. They were the last thing she saw before she gave in to the darkness.

Adelaide awoke with a gasp as everything slammed back into her. It was as if she were still desperately seeking air, even though Simon must have let up right after she'd passed out.

"Welcome back, Adelaide," he said. She searched for him in the shadows cast by the dull bedside lamp, but all she could make out were shifting limbs and a flash of pale skin before he moved farther away from the mattress where she was curled. There was a spring poking into her rib, and the bed was hard and flat. They were no longer at the Crosses' house.

"Where are we?" Her voice was raspy and broken. She touched her finger to her throat where there must have already been a bruise blooming. At least she wasn't bound. She sat up, looking around. The room was small and messy. Clothes were piled on every available surface, and a staleness hung in the air as if food had been left beneath one of the heaps.

Her eyes flew back to Simon when he stepped into the light. The hollows beneath his cheekbones and the deep pockets of his eyes were thrown into dark contrast where the glow touched his face.

"You'll have to excuse the mess." There was disgust on his face as he waved a careless hand. "Matthew's a slob."

The name rattled against the back of her skull, a memory that wouldn't quite form. But she silenced it, her survival instincts screaming at her to pay attention to the man in front of her instead.

"What do you want from me, Simon?" she asked, though she knew what he wanted. What he'd always wanted.

"I just want you to realize I can make you happy," Simon said, coming to kneel on the mattress. She shuffled backward until her spine came up against the wall. She tucked her knees to her chest. "So happy, Adelaide."

The intensity in the way he moved, the way he looked at her, told her everything she needed to know.

"Simon, don't do this," she said.

"Don't do what? Love you?" he asked, shifting closer.

"You don't love me."

"I do," he said, this time moving so that he hovered over her, and she flashed back to those moments on the roof. "You're the only one I ever have. You'll see."

He reached out to catch a strand of her hair. "You'll see," he said again, so quietly she didn't know if she was even supposed to hear.

He wrapped his other hand around her upper thigh and pulled her so that she was lying flat beneath him against the mattress. A spring dug into her rib, but the pain didn't register. She knew what was about to happen, and there was only one way to get through it.

Don't think. Don't think. Just breathe.

Rough, chapped lips slid over her mouth, over the tops of her cheeks, over the tip of her nose. They caught the single tear that slipped down her face. His tongue lingered as if savoring the saltiness of it. She shuddered against him.

Don't think. Don't think.

Even just those words were too much to hang on to when his teeth sank into her neck. The letters turned inward, ripping at themselves, until the only thing that remained was a vague memory of where they'd been.

There'd be more bruises tomorrow. There, at her neck, and other places, too. At her hips, where his thumbs dug into the fat that cushioned her pelvic bone. At her wrist, which he kept pinned against the comforter. On her thigh, where his knee pressed into her femur to keep her still.

He fumbled at his jeans, and she could do nothing to stop him. And it didn't matter, because then there he was, in her mouth. He had shifted so that his legs straddled her shoulders, and his hands were buried once again in her hair, tugging at it so that it pulled against her scalp. It stung and brought tears to her eyes as much as the feeling of him against the back of her throat.

Everything started fading at the edges, and she fought it.

She squeezed her eyes shut, and then all of a sudden there was air again. Blessed air.

He'd pulled away, murmuring, "So gorgeous for me," before moving lower.

Hands. She felt them everywhere. Did he have only just the two? It didn't seem like that. They were on her ankles, on her breasts, on her upper thighs, pushing them apart.

She didn't know what to do with her own, so she left them at her sides, letting the tips of her fingers take comfort in the softness of the blanket. She didn't know what to do with her eyes, so she left them to stare at the ceiling, which was blurring behind the veil of unshed tears.

But then his fingers were on her chin, making her meet his gaze. Not allowing her to look away.

There was lust there. Pure and unadulterated. But what was scarier, what made her toes clench against the bed and lifted the hairs on her forearms, was what she saw behind that.

Love.

Jesus.

Her stomach heaved, but she swallowed back against it.

It didn't take long for him to come. A few strokes and it was all over. He was collapsing into the crook of her neck, muttering endearments that felt like needles against her bruised psyche.

She shifted and he rolled off her, gathering her in his arms as he did. The movement dislodged him from her, and she wanted to cry in relief at the empty feeling he left behind.

She wouldn't close her eyes against the darkness of the room. If she slipped off, just a little, her opportunity would be totally lost. This was her window.

So she stayed there, wrapped in his arms and the smell of sex, and counted the lengths of his breath until it evened out. Even then she didn't trust it. How long was too long to wait? The red numbers on the big digital clock slid into the next hour without any acknowledgment from either of them.

It was only when he snored that she dared to act.

Smooth movements were key. Hesitation would be fatal. Keeping that in mind, she slipped from beneath his arm and rolled to the edge of the bed, pushed to her feet, then froze.

He shifted, coughed, and then resettled against the pillow.

Fear clawed at her, an angry beast holding her paralyzed.

There was no time for panic. There was no time.

Move.

Somehow her feet listened, even as her mind swam in a blind haze of terror. She grabbed her shorts from the floor, slipping them up to settle at her hips. Then somehow she was by the door. She didn't remember crossing the room.

Simon was just a lump of body in the shadows when she turned back to check. He didn't move at all, but this would be the hardest part. The door would make noise no matter how quiet she tried to be.

One more deep breath gave her the push she needed. Shaking fingers found the doorknob, and she let the cool metal beneath her palm ground her. It turned, and the hinges protested.

A rumble lifted into the air. Every muscle tensed, but she didn't look back. She just waited for the next breath. Once she heard it, she cracked the door just wide enough for her to fit through.

She was out and running down the carpeted hallway in the next heartbeat. There was someone in the kitchen, but it didn't matter. He was too far away to catch her anyway.

Two more strides and her fingers were fumbling at the gold chain lock on the door. Out. Out. Out. She wasn't trying to be quiet anymore. Didn't think she could be.

The locks finally gave, and she was on stairs.

Then she heard it.

A shout.

She was dead. He was going to kill her, and she knew it with such a sudden certainty she almost stopped right there. Halfway to the final door that signaled her freedom.

But she pushed forward, and her hand slapped against the beveled glass, slipping through into the cool night air. Her feet hit the rough sidewalk, and she had a split second to decide. He was only moments behind her, ready to wrap thick arms around her torso and drag her back into the apartment. Back to hell.

The street stretched out before her, beckoning her. She fought every instinct she had that screamed at her to just keep running and turned toward the giant plants on either side of the building's entrance.

Her toes curled into the mulch just as the swinging door slammed against wood. And there was Simon, naked and disoriented. He stopped just over the threshold, his eyes scanning the dark. Then he took off at a jog up the street. "Adelaide," she heard him call, before he stopped.

She willed every part of her to still. Her breath. Her blood. Her heart. The branches of the plant cut into her skin, but they hid her from view. Would he think to look behind them?

She could see just the very edges of him as he spun in a small circle.

"Adelaide?" He sounded like a scared little boy. He sounded like the brother she'd once known. "Why would you leave me?"

A sob was wrenched from the depths of his chest as he sank to his knees right there on the asphalt. "Why would you leave me?"

She used his distraction to slip farther back along the outer wall of the apartment building. The shrubbery had been the easiest hiding place, and he would definitely look there. She had to move.

There was a corner up ahead. Once she skirted around it, she let herself move more quickly in the narrow alleyway. There were some woods ahead of her. She just had to clear the small backyard, and she'd be able to lose herself in the protection of the thick trees.

She kept waiting for Simon to sound the alarm as she crossed the grass, completely out in the open and vulnerable, but the shout never came. Before she could even blink, the coolness of the forest swallowed her.

Once the tears came, they wouldn't stop. But she just kept running.

CHAPTER SEVENTEEN

Clarke

July 16, 2018

"They're about me," Clarke said, unable to swallow the revelation once it finally clicked into place.

Sam somehow managed to tear his bleary eyes from the back of Roger's head. Montoya was holding court in the interrogation room, having arrived not long ago with several other agents. They'd all set up camp at the police station.

Clarke watched as Sam tried to focus on what she'd said, but she could tell the words weren't making their way past the fog that had dropped over his normally nimble brain. Neither of them had slept.

"The clues," she said. "They're about me."

They'd spent the night curled up in different corners of their rental, poring over the photos Cross had sent for Anna. At points throughout the long hours, they had yelled, triumphant, only to have the theory crash down around them. By 4:00 a.m., they'd gotten nowhere and had returned to pictures he'd sent for the past victims, hoping to uncover a pattern. There was not one.

In Charlotte's case, it had turned out that the numbers in the pictures came together to produce coordinates. In Eve's, it had been rooted in the names of the people in the photos. Each one was different and maddening. They weren't meant to be solved at the time, that much was clear. The clues made sense only in retrospect. They were meant as one more way he could provoke them, one more way to prove just how clever he was.

As they chased down the path to nowhere, her mind kept flittering back to the Anna pictures. There was a niggling familiarity there. One she couldn't pinpoint but that snuck up on her in the quiet moments when she'd be trying to concentrate on one of the other victims.

It wasn't until she was watching the rest of the agents worshipping at the feet of Roger that something dislodged and then clicked into place.

"Do you know how many people would kill for this opportunity?"

The memory of Sam's voice was hazy, made so by both the years that had passed since then and the amount of alcohol she'd consumed before the conversation.

It had been a thing in those days—threatening to quit, probably to get his attention. She straightened against the wall, grasping at the thought before it slipped away back into the recesses of her mind. Why was this important? Her heart pounded as if she were sprinting instead of standing completely still as she tried to remember.

Before going to that bar to douse her liver in alcohol in the hopes of erasing the image of bloodied and broken bodies, she'd called Sam.

She'd told him she was going to drop out of the program, that she was going to run off to become . . .

Jesus.

"They're about me," she said again now to Sam.

He blinked at her, and she realized she wasn't making sense. Her thoughts were spilling out almost unchecked as incoherent phrases while her mind skittered away from her tight control. She took a breath, trying to reel it in.

"Remember—God, do you remember that night I had convinced myself I was going to drop out of grad school?" She turned to him fully, leaning in so that she could keep her voice pitched low to avoid being overheard by the small gathering on the other side of the dingy interrogation room.

"Just that one, huh." Sam poked, even as she saw his brain finally kick into action. It took a moment before it clicked. "Arizona. You were obsessed with the idea of moving there. Convinced you were going to drop out and become a waitress."

She hadn't thought of herself as a quitter back then. No, it had been pure survival. An instinct to flee and hide and pretend the sunlight would chase away all the dark in her life. "A waitress in Arizona, Sam."

The clue from Tucson. It had been the back of a waitress's head.

And just like that, she had his full, concentrated attention. Something must have shifted in the atmosphere, because she saw Roger glance over. She, as subtly as she could, pivoted slightly to block them off from the group.

"How would he know that?" Sam asked, his eyes searching her face.

The connection was subtle. The careful allusion to her past would be easy to overlook. But once the thought latched on, it was impossible to shake. She needed to see the rest of the clues again.

She caught her top lip with her teeth. "I don't know. I think I told other people." She paused. "I must have told other people."

"It's a stretch, kid," Sam said, running a hand through his hair. "Some offhand mention from years ago?"

But why a waitress in Arizona? Out of all the millions of moments and places and people he could have sent, he sent that one.

"But what if they are about me?" Clarke said. It made sense. Wasn't it what they always said? This wasn't about the girls. It was about Clarke. It was about Sam.

He watched her now. They trusted each other's instincts both because they had to and because they'd learned to. But he knew she didn't always see straight on this case.

It was then that Roger swooped.

"What's up, guys?"

In other circumstances she might have been amused by how attuned he was to Sam, but now she just wanted him out of this town, out of their investigation, far away from her partner.

But Roger Montoya would never stay away from Sam. No matter that he should. No matter that Sam would be better off without having to see him every day. And that's why she hated him. Because if he truly cared even a little about what they had used to be, Roger wouldn't have set Sam up as the head of a task force he oversaw.

Her voice was ice. "I need to go check on something, sir. I'm sure you'll be able to manage the press conference without me."

Annoyance flickered in Roger's eyes, but it was just the briefest flash. He was too much of a politician to let genuine emotion show on his face. It was just that: as much as she hated it, she knew him so goddamn well she could read him like a book.

"I would really like the special agents in charge of the investigation to be there," he said. His voice was smooth, but it wasn't a request.

"I'm sure Sam can handle that," she said. There were times she pissed Roger off just because she could, and it was fun to watch his carefully constructed blank expression pinch tight. This wasn't one of those times. This was actually real. This was actually serious.

"Agent Sinclair," Roger started, and there was a warning following. She could tell by the way his breath hitched as if he were already preparing himself for an argument.

She cut him off, the flash of temper a familiar friend. "Just think, with me not there, one less person to share the spotlight."

It was a standoff. It would be foolish to ignore that fact, just as foolish as it had been to initiate it in the first place. She was well aware she'd escalated the situation, and maybe in a different universe where the bastard didn't exist and where there weren't two girls missing and where every other thought didn't flare across her brain, painfully weakening already-compromised self-control, she would feel guilty about it.

"Roger." Sam finally cut into the thick air between them. "You know how difficult this . . . she's . . ." There was an apology there that he didn't quite mold into words. It rested on his tongue, though, and none of them needed him to finish the thought. *She's being difficult for a reason. Cut her some slack.*

Maybe it was embarrassing that once again Sam was cleaning up her mess because she could never quite do it herself. Even when she knew she was wrong.

Roger locked eyes with him, and something silent and heavy passed between them until Roger nodded. Just once.

"It's important," was all Sam said then.

A tiny muscle along Roger's jawline bunched and jumped, but then he flicked his gaze back to her. "Keep us updated."

She didn't respond, just raised her eyebrows at Sam.

"Go," he said, and she headed for the door without a backward glance. She felt every set of eyes in the room on her.

She didn't care. She broke into a light jog down the empty corridors of the police station, past the puppy at the front desk, and out into the early-morning air. Only then did she pause to slip on sunglasses and dig for the rental keys in her bag.

She wondered if Cross was watching her. She threw her middle finger in the air, just in case, and then made her way toward the piece-of-shit car. They had scanned and uploaded every piece of evidence from the case into a file on her MacBook, but she wanted the real clues in her hands. Where she could feel them and study them and imagine him picking each one with his careful deliberation, which sent chills along the blades of her shoulders.

Her burner phone jangled just when she turned left onto the road that would take her out of town. She groped for it.

"That wasn't very nice, Clarke."

"Well, I'm not very nice," she said carelessly, but her fingers gripped tight around the faded leather of the wheel. He *had* been watching.

"Rush, rush, rush." His voice was low and sensual. Amused. "Where are you off to in such a hurry, my love?"

"You tell me," she said. "Where should I be going?"

"Ah, Clarke, you may want to start answering questions when I ask them," he said. Her throat burned at his tone. It was no longer playful. His footfalls came through the line, but little else that she could pinpoint. He was on the move. But where?

He'd seen her. It had been less than ten minutes between when she'd exited the station and when the phone had rung. He would want to be someplace secure before he called her. Was he on foot or in a car? If he had been walking the whole time, he couldn't have made it far beyond the outskirts of town. If he'd been driving, he would be about the same distance as she was. She noted the next mile marker so she could map the radius when she got back to the cabin.

"Don't you want to know why you should answer my question, Clarke?"

She didn't want to know. She really didn't want to know. Every cell in her body screamed at her to just hang up the phone. She knew that tone. That silky, pretty tone that was a cloying caress.

Only when he bit out an "I'm waiting" did she realize she hadn't responded.

"Why should I answer your questions when you don't answer mine?" she asked.

She almost felt him smile through the phone.

He wanted to get in her head; that was the purpose of this. That was always the purpose. So she pushed back, kept him out, and instead listened for anything that would give him away. There was more muffled movement, his calm breathing, a little hum of discontent. And then she heard them.

The bells. They couldn't be heard all the way out by the lake, but their peals cascaded through town every hour on the hour.

She saw the sharp turn onto the cabin's road just ahead and made it before coming to a stop and cutting the engine.

Did he know she could hear them? Did he know what it confirmed? Had he planned it?

When he finally spoke again, his voice was laced with a combination of warning and amusement. He was having fun.

"Just because I can't use my knife on you yet, my love, does not mean I cannot use my knife."

The scream shattered the silence, an ice pick against her eardrum. Black curtains started to shift at the edge of her vision, and she laid her forehead against the wheel, praying she didn't pass out.

She gulped in air as quietly as she could. He'd wanted to know where she'd been going? Fine.

"I got my period and needed to go get tampons. Go fuck yourself," she said and snapped the phone shut. She threw it against the inside of the passenger side door and then slid out of her own. Her knees hit the dirt moments before her palms.

Don't kill the girl, don't kill the girl. It was a silent plea. It was useless. But it was the only thought she could form in that moment.

The sun beat down on the curve of her back, hunched as it was against all the evils in the world. Strands of hair hung limp around her face, but she didn't move to push them away. Not yet. The sounds around her were normalizing again. They had been muffled and distant for a moment there.

She gave herself thirty more precious seconds on the ground before pushing to her feet. She didn't know why, didn't want to think why, but for some reason this case was different.

He kept giving himself away.

◆ ◆ ◆

She already had her phone to her ear when she pushed through the door of the cabin. It went to voice mail. They were probably at the press conference.

"I think he's in town, Sam," she said. "Get a list of abandoned buildings from the chief. A place someone could scream and no one would hear. But within the town limits. Close to the station."

She ended the call without further explanation, then texted him the same information for good measure.

He would trust her. But he would certainly ask questions later.

Cross wouldn't have had enough time to drive somewhere and get inside the building. The timing just didn't work out. He'd been on foot. He'd seen her, walked to his lair, and then called her. Even if he'd had binoculars, he wouldn't be able to go far. She wanted to go back to the station, to try to re-create his steps.

One thing at a time, though. She shut out the memory of the girl's scream.

She grabbed the Anna Meyers file, then swept an arm over the kitchen table to clear it of the loose papers and bric-a-brac that had accumulated there.

When she was finished laying out the photos in the order she received them, she stood on a chair to get an aerial view.

The first one. Bar in Maine.

Clarke picked it up, holding it close to her eye as if that would help. Instead, it just blurred and pixelated.

She grabbed a pen, then lay stomach-down on the floor, flipping over one of the papers that had fallen to the floor earlier.

Maybe it was just coincidence that he'd picked a waitress in Arizona. The human brain liked to recognize patterns even when they didn't exist. It would create links, organizing chaos into something that resembled order just because that was more pleasing.

What if she was seeing something in nothing? What if she had just been thinking about the past too much on this case? What if the memory of that drunken vow to run away from her carefully cultivated life had been sitting at the forefront of her mind, ready to be plucked by eager hands wanting to arrange pieces in a puzzle even if they didn't really fit? What if.

But their lives were a series of what-ifs that had led them here. It wasn't something she could just dismiss.

So back to the first one. Maine. The picture had been maddening to figure out. But eventually they'd identified the logo of a ski resort on one of the patrons' beanies and followed that to a quiet town nestled in the shadow of the mountain.

But this wasn't about finding the bar. This was about her.

If this really was about her, she had to find herself in the picture.

He thought he was so clever.

So be clever. Think details.

The pad of her thumb traced over the corners of the picture. It wouldn't be obvious.

She squinted, pushing up to a seated position.

Then her hand crept to the spot just below the soft hollow of her elbow in a gesture so familiar she almost never even noticed it anymore. Her fingers pinched at the skin around the tattoo that lived there.

Scrambling to her feet, she found her phone to call Della.

It took the computer wiz only six minutes to verify that the partial label on the beer bottle at the edge of the bar was indeed from a brewery called Phoenix Rising.

"Thanks, babe," she murmured into the phone, staring at the empty wall of the rental.

"Stay safe, Clarke," Della said, before disconnecting.

Phoenix Rising.

The dots and lines of the ink on her arm burned. She'd had the constellation etched permanently on her skin years earlier when she'd first discovered the little grouping of stars that came together to make the Phoenix. It was an oft-overlooked constellation, just a small gathering in the Southern sky.

But once she read about it, an itchy feeling had started, at first at the soft spot behind her ears. Then it slowly crept out to her neck, in between her shoulder blades, down her spine. It had relented only with the first brush of needle and ink against skin.

Simon Cross was a man of details; the brain saw patterns it wanted to see. It could go either way.

Still, she wrote down "Phoenix constellation" on the paper, before moving on to the next photo.

It was a busy scene. A nightclub caught in the flash of a camera, which had turned the exposed skin of the closest dancers a blinding white. Blue and green filtered through at the edges, and in the smudge of shadows was the drum kit for an underground band that played only in one seedy club in downtown LA. It had taken them precisely seven days to find the location.

She ignored the familiar taunt on the back, the reminder of the ticking clock, and concentrated on the figures that had been captured by the lens instead. The main focus was on three teenage girls. Their limbs, long and slim and smooth, tangled together in wild abandon, clearly buzzed on alcohol or drugs or each other or just the danger of sneaking into a club with fake IDs. She studied them, finding nothing of herself there.

Then a lone figure just off to the side caught her eye. The girl was dressed similarly to the three dancing, but she wasn't joining in. Her hands were at her sides, her body stiff. Clarke could see the sharp cut of her jaw by the way her head was tilted just enough to watch the group.

There was something familiar in her profile. Clarke ran her fingers over her own chin. Even the girl's haircut was similar to the one Clarke had when she'd worn it short, cut close to her head. She dropped her gaze to the girl's shoulders, which were only covered by the thin straps of a camisole. The delicate white lines on her skin wouldn't be noticeable except that the flash had sharpened everything, had laid secrets bare.

Patterns. The brain sought patterns to ease the chaos.

She wrote "scars" on the paper.

Shifting the waitress photo into the pile with the Maine and LA ones, she turned her attention to the remaining five. It took twenty minutes of poring over them to dismiss four. The fifth was a church, with the main focus of the shot on the elaborate crucifix that hung over the altar. There was nothing obvious about the picture, but there was an itch along her spine when she tried to move it into the pile that she hadn't figured out.

The priest stood slightly off to the side, dressed in severe black, his arms widespread. With his head tipped down, he was a small echo of the tableau above him. But that wasn't what caught her eye. It was the gray hair, the thick caterpillar eyebrows, the stocky boxer's body that couldn't be hidden beneath his robes.

Her pen hovered over the paper. Then she jotted down "Sam?" The black letters were harsh against the white, and she immediately scratched them out.

Just as she was about to push to her feet, her phone rang.

Finally.

She snatched it.

"What the hell was your message about?" Sam said before she could say anything.

Patterns or details? Chaos or clues? She breathed deep.

"Come to the cabin," she said. "Bring Roger."

"Tell me what's going on. We've lit a fire under the locals' asses about the abandoned buildings, but we need more to go on. Come to us."

This needed to be in private. Or at least not in front of half of Roger's agents and all the local cops.

"Please, Sam."

He must have heard the desperation in her voice. "You're scaring me, kid. But we'll be there in a few."

"Okay," she said, dropping her forehead toward the floor so she was crouched in a fetal position. "And, Sam? Fair warning. You're not going to like it."

CHAPTER EIGHTEEN

Bess

July 13, 2018

Simon was excited. Bess could tell now. She didn't particularly like that she could read his moods, but here they were. She could. And he was excited.

Bess didn't know if Anna was ready. They'd practiced. They'd practiced over and over again in the dark. They'd talked through the whole scenario. Even when Anna had come back from her trips to the room and her voice was broken and her spirit was broken and her very being was broken, they practiced. Bess would chatter on endlessly until Anna eventually responded. And when the words came out finally, Bess would always feel something in her relax. Because as much as Simon wanted to strip Anna of everything she was, everything she could hold on to, Bess wouldn't let him. Anna wouldn't let him.

And somewhere in the process, being strong for Anna had let Bess reclaim the girl she used to be. The one who fought back when she was pushed, whose backbone hadn't been ground down to mere dust, who had a toughness in her that didn't flinch and cower when it met resistance. It was heady and rusty and . . . powerful.

She didn't know if Anna was ready. However, when opportunity knocked, you opened the door. Ready or not.

"So close, my love," he cooed to Anna. Bess could see only the hunched outline of his back, but she imagined him petting Anna's cheek as he said it, and she had to swallow hard against the ball of rage and disgust that lodged itself in her throat.

She heard him unlocking the chain. Bess shifted to her knees and hoped Anna would understand what was happening.

Bess hadn't talked much to Simon after he'd slapped her. And for some reason he'd paid almost no attention to her. He'd take her to the bathroom after giving her something that made her limbs pliable and her body lethargic. Then he'd lock her back on the floor without so much as an inappropriate grope. She pretended to be cowed whenever he came for Anna, even though she wanted so desperately to kick him so hard his testicles would lodge in his throat every time he laid a finger on the girl.

"Restraint" had been her mantra. Lull him into thinking she didn't pose a threat. It would make him all the more surprised.

She locked eyes with Anna and dipped her head in a tiny nod. Even in the dark she saw the girl flinch in recognition.

Simon was careful. He wouldn't have gotten away with his sick fantasies for so long if he weren't. The act alone of keeping two girls in a basement, one for more than three months, meant he was a meticulous planner. Sloppy mistakes did not seem to be his style.

That's where Anna came in.

He'd stopped drugging the girl. She could barely walk at this point anyway, let alone put up a fight. They subsisted on mostly chicken broth and stale Wonder Bread. After the first few days of the diet, Bess had found herself dragging her tongue over the smooth surface of the plastic bowls, searching in vain for any remnants that might be clinging to it. *Just one more grain of salt would make all the difference,* her starved brain told her.

Then she'd lost her appetite completely. That was after the blinding headaches, though. She was still light-headed at all times, and the blackness hovered on the edge of her vision as a constant and inevitable threat that accompanied every movement. She wondered what three months of it would do to her.

Bess had faith, though. She had faith that Anna would find whatever strength was left in her, that animalistic instinct that bared its teeth when it was hurt and bleeding and facing down certain death. Because if she didn't have faith in Anna, she had nothing.

And here it was. The moment of truth. She drew in a shattered breath she hoped he didn't hear.

Then it happened.

Anna stumbled against Simon, her body a deadweight crashing into his. If he'd been expecting it, her slight frame wouldn't have done much to jolt him, but they had the element of surprise on their side, and he shuffled a few steps. That was all Bess needed.

She used the momentum that came from launching herself to her feet to drive the heel of her hand into his nose. Her palm connected with bone, and she felt sick and victorious when it gave way and cracked.

He let go of Anna, who bolted for the hook by the stairs where he hung the keys to the door. Meanwhile, Bess went for his eyes. He was recovering from the shock but still managed to block her, and she knew she had maybe only one more good strike left.

She didn't have much room to maneuver, since she was still chained to the floor. She knew what she needed to do; years of practice had prepared her. Instead of moving back away from the blow she saw coming, she shifted closer. She wrapped her arms around his rib cage, burying her head against his neck. She felt the shock of it roll through his body like a wave. His arm paused midair; his entire body froze for an instant. And in that moment, she brought her knee up into the V of his legs. She drove her leg directly into his balls, lifting him, just slightly—ever so slightly—off the floor.

The air left his lungs in a hot rush of breath against her face, and he bent slightly in an aborted attempt to get into the fetal position. She didn't relinquish her hold.

He recovered too quickly, though. He brought the sharp point of his elbow down on her upper arm, and the pain of it broke her grip on him. Then he shoved her to the floor, his eyes on Anna, who was on the stairs, heading for the door, keys in hand.

His roar of rage and desperation sank into the marrow of her bones. He crossed the basement floor in three strides and made it up five steps in two. Bess cringed when he managed to grab a handful of Anna's hair, his fingers tangling in the limp locks that hung down her back. He pulled hard, and she didn't stand a chance.

Anna's body slammed into Simon's, but instead of catching her, he let the girl's momentum carry her backward until she ended up crumpled on the floor. He stood over her, his boots bracketing her slim waist, before yanking the keys out of her hand. He had to dig his fingers under hers to get to them. Anna was sobbing—deep, gut-wrenching, sloppy sobs that pierced Bess's heart.

Be strong, be strong, she silently told the girl.

Keep the faith, she silently told herself.

Simon still hadn't said anything since the incident started. It seemed to her that it had gone on for hours, but probably it had lasted less than a minute. His silence in the face of their defiance made her skin tingle.

Bess was huddled on the floor; Anna was sprawled on her back several feet away. And Simon loomed between them. He walked over to the ring where he hung the keys and returned them to their place. A power move to show that he was not concerned about their attempts at freedom. Then he crossed back to Anna.

He shifted his body weight onto one foot, and it was clear he was about to kick her directly in the ribs. And she was going to lie there and take it.

"Hey, Simon," Bess called out. She kept her voice casual, with the same intention she had when she'd wrapped her arms around him. Do the unexpected. It was the only weapon they had. "How're your balls doing?"

He pivoted in that way of his. The unnatural stillness of his body at odds with the tension vibrating in the air around him. She thought of that fleeting moment when they'd first met and she'd found him attractive. All she saw now was a monster.

"You might want to get your sperm count checked after that kind of blow," she said, chewing on her lower lip as if she were concerned, when the actual thought of him attempting to procreate made her want to break out in hives.

He stepped closer to her. If there was anything in life that was predictable, it was the rage men felt when women mocked them. It hadn't been just Jeremy who had taught her that. It was an infallible truth, and this time she would exploit, use it, twist it to her own advantage instead of it being used against her.

"Actually, do you think you'll even be able to get it up after that?" Again, with the faux concern. Another step. She could tell he didn't want to leave Anna there without the comforting knowledge that she was chained. *Keep going,* she told both herself and him. "Hmmm. I'm guessing you had issues in that department anyway, long before I arrived. Am I right?"

One more step and he was in front of her, and then they were eye to eye. He was studying her, and she didn't like the gleam she saw lurking there. Because behind the controlled rage that was simmering, there was curiosity. He was wondering what her game was. Their efforts had failed, so why was she provoking him?

She needed him to stop thinking. She needed to push him over the edge. She tilted her head back and brought it forward to slam into his face, the hard point of her forehead striking his already-injured nose. He staggered back, almost landing on his tailbone, which she thought might be what actually set him off. Looking foolish was far deadlier to his soul than a little blood from a broken nose.

And finally he struck out at her. It was his fist first. Then, when he'd regained his balance, it was the heavy metal tips of his boots digging into her soft hips and the flesh that couldn't protect the vulnerable organs beneath. She curled into a ball, knowing she had to get her arms up and around her head. That left the broad target of her back available to him, and he took full advantage. She cried out when his boot caught the edge of her shoulder blade, but she was able to bite back the rest of her screams.

She was used to pain. She lived through pain. She loved through pain. She survived through pain.

He landed one final, glancing blow but then seemed to gain control of himself enough to realize Anna was still free.

She was huddled against the wall, watching the scene with wide, wild eyes. She'd wrapped her arms around her knees and was rocking like she'd seen a ghost, letting out little whimpers with each kick Bess took.

Simon crossed over to her, digging fingers into Anna's soft upper arm. He wasn't gentle as he dragged her half-walking, half-limp form back over to her chain.

He didn't spare Anna another glance. But he came back to Bess. He looked alert as he squatted down in front of her, clearly braced for any more attacks.

Reaching down, he drew her to a seated position, his hands on her bruised shoulders. She winced at the pressure. Her lip was cracked, and blood dribbled down her chin unchecked. She wondered if her black eye had formed yet, or if that would come later in a bloom of purple and sickly green.

Would she even still be alive for it to matter?

She cradled her arms defensively against her stomach, but she met his gaze. He was wearing that same expression he'd had earlier. The one that seemed to cut into her brain, searching for answers to questions he hadn't even asked.

"I underestimated you," he said. "You have her fire."

She froze. "Whose fire?"

His eyes crinkled just at the corners. "I didn't think you would, you know," he said instead of answering her. He reached out and tucked a piece of her hair behind her ear. "You don't really look like her."

She swallowed hard. None of this sounded promising. It sounded creepy.

"Why would I look like her?" she attempted.

His eyes flicked over her face, tracing her features, before landing back on her hair. He pulled a lock of it in between his forefinger and thumb, rubbing the strands in between the pads of them. He closed his eyes in pleasure, and she tried not to gag.

"That one is weak." He tilted his head back in the direction of Anna, and she wanted to scream in the girl's defense. She bit her tongue instead. "You're not weak, though, are you, pet? You're strong."

"I'm not," she said, almost reflexively. She hadn't even meant to say it. In fact, as the words came out, she wished she could have sawed off her tongue instead of uttering them. And he saw that she had revealed something she hadn't wanted to.

He swiped at his own bleeding nose before thumbing at her chin. Their bloods mixed on his finger. He stared at the red smear before bringing it to his mouth. He sucked on it as if he savored the taste, watching her as he did it. "I beg to disagree, pet."

This time she couldn't stop the dry heaves. There was nothing in her stomach, but it was like her body wanted to purge itself of the image. They wrenched through her, and it was as if someone were putting pressure on every one of her bruised places.

He was smiling at her after she had finished. "So strong," he said again. "I wonder if this changes the game?"

Delightful.

"Or maybe not." He seemed to laugh to himself. He chucked her chin with affection he would show a little sister, before standing.

"Sweet dreams, girls. Oh, and don't think you've been fully punished for that little stunt."

She was so taken aback by the whole exchange that she didn't breathe as he made his way up the stairs. She heard the lock click, then waited. And waited.

When she was absolutely sure they were safe, she shifted toward Anna's shape in the darkness.

"Anna," Bess said softly. She didn't want to hope. But she couldn't help it. "Did you get it?"

She saw a flash of teeth in the darkness and heard the smile in the girl's voice.

"Yes."

CHAPTER NINETEEN

Clarke

July 16, 2018

"Do you know what the problem is?" Clarke broke the silence.

"That you've been talking to Simon Cross and neglected to inform your partner, your supervisor, or the bureau?" Roger's voice was ice.

"No," she said, keeping her eyes on him. She couldn't quite meet Sam's gaze yet. "It's that he's been calling the shots this whole time. And we're left scrambling after him."

"Hate to state the obvious here, kid, but that's the point of taking hostages." It was the first thing Sam had said since she'd told them about the phone calls.

"Right." She drew out the word, her mind leaping in different directions. "If we don't follow his game, the girls die. He's proven it's not an empty threat." She met Sam's eyes.

"But, they die every time," Roger commented.

"They die anyway," she said.

"But do you know what . . ." Sam trailed off, a look on his face she'd long come to recognize.

"What?" she prodded.

"The photos," Sam said, locking eyes with her. "Even at their most obscure, we always end up figuring them out."

"In time," she said, her thoughts turning inward, scouring over the past year. He was right. Of course he was right. They'd missed only one deadline ever, out of dozens of clues.

"It shouldn't be possible," Roger said.

"Every time we got stuck . . . ," Sam started.

"We got lucky," she said, snapping back to attention.

Sam raised his brows. "But . . ."

"We don't get lucky." It was an echo of what she'd told Della days earlier.

"So that means he's playing you even then," Roger said. "How do you guys always get to the right spot within twenty-four hours of his deadline? Always?"

How? How? How was he orchestrating even that?

"The tip line," Clarke said, her voice soft.

Sam rocked back on his heels. It wasn't a new idea—for killers to reach out to authorities through the very lines of communication created to stop them. But they hadn't thought of it. It seemed too simple for Cross, even if his goal was to help them meet his imposed deadlines.

"It wouldn't be hard to track our movements. Plane information, hotel rooms," Sam said. "If we weren't moving on a clue quick enough, all he had to do was shoot us an email or call in to give us a nudge in the right direction."

Roger looked between them. "And you hadn't thought of that? Is this your first day on the job? Jesus."

Clarke's cheeks flushed with actual shame. It was rare for her to care about Roger's criticism. But they'd messed up. It was careless and stupid and could cost them Anna. Bess.

The silence was heavy. Roger was the one to break it. "The phone. Please tell me you had it checked."

"Della," Clarke said before thinking.

"She knew about it?" Of course he picked up on that.

"Don't blame her." Clarke would never beg for herself. But Della had only been doing her a favor. "Blame me."

"Oh, I do," Roger said. It didn't matter, though. Clarke had crossed too many lines for any of them to think she'd come out of this unscathed. What mattered was that Della wasn't taken down with her.

Sam shifted, and she remembered he was there. Sam. He would protect Della. He was good at that. And cleaning up her messes.

"He's tracking us, he's playing us, he's plotted out this entire thing," Clarke said. Her screwups were inconsequential at this point. "God, he's running the whole table."

"He's running the whole casino," Sam corrected. "Scratch that—he's running whole fucking Vegas."

They watched each other, wary and assessing. The room was tense, far more than it should have been for a simple conversation. Cross was putting them on edge, and she thought again about just how much power he held over them.

"Why the hell are we still playing his game, by his rules?" she asked, frustrated and exhausted and tired of feeling like the fibers of her body were being stretched to the breaking point.

"The girls," Sam murmured.

"We're always too late," Clarke said, her voice loud in the small confines of the cabin. It bounced against the walls and sounded far too desperate to her ears when it came back to her. She took a breath. "We keep thinking that if we just catch the right break, we'll get a step ahead of him. But we can't. We can't."

"You just want to, what, ignore the clues, then?" Sam asked, and it was a genuine question. He was asking her.

She pressed the heel of her hand into her forehead. "No. We just . . . I want us to be smarter. I want us to be able to make our own rules."

"If wishes were horses, kid," Sam said, but his voice was kind instead of mocking.

Roger glanced at Sam, then back at her. "Cross said something to you to make you look at the pictures differently, right?"

"Yes."

"So he wants you to look at the clues differently. Anything you get from them is because he prompted you to find it," Sam said.

She took a beat. "Shit. Everything is . . . shit."

The air in the cabin grew heavy around her, like she could feel the particles of it pushing against her skin. Soft, gentle, but ever present. Wanting to slip between her lips, into her nostrils, in an effort to fill her up until there was nothing left of her. She closed her eyes and gathered the frustration and hopelessness and panic and let it seep out with the breath she exhaled. *Focus.* She just had to focus. She exhaled again.

And then there it was.

"It's not an escalation," she said, dropping to her knees before the men could respond. Her fingers found the file she'd tossed aside earlier. "Every other time it's been the same thing, right? Same pattern every time. This time it's different. Everything's different."

She opened the file marked "Bess Stanhope" and met the woman's eyes. His patterns were falling apart.

"He wanted us here," Sam said.

"The question is why."

She didn't need to say what they were thinking. If they knew the why of anything that man did, they wouldn't be here.

But then Sam surprised her. "He wants you to know where he is."

"That's what we've been saying," she said.

He shook his head. "No, he wanted you to know exactly where he is. So what does he do?"

Her mind spun. "He called me.

"He called you," Sam said.

"He called me when he knew I would be able to calculate his location. He wanted me in town long enough to get the opportunity to do it."

"He's setting us up," Roger said.

She glanced at him. "He knows you guys have had enough time to assemble backup. He knows that now that I have a radius, it's just a matter of time before we storm the castle."

"So what does he have there waiting for us?" Sam wondered out loud.

Again, none of them had an answer.

"What did you mean it's not an escalation?" Roger asked instead.

Their eyes focused on Clarke.

She pushed to her feet, feeling decidedly vulnerable on the floor, then held the file open against her chest so that Bess Stanhope looked back at them all.

"Well, what if it's not an escalation?" she asked, meeting Sam's eyes. "What if it's a finale?"

Clarke needed time she knew she didn't have. She rubbed her sweaty palms against the black fabric of her jeans, the toughness of it wicking away the moisture. She didn't want to be in this room, talking so many words and not doing anything.

There were so many strings unraveling. And they all led back to something she couldn't quite see yet.

The pictures.

The pictures were meant for her. They had a secret message that she'd only started to decode. But even if she did figure them out, would they really tell her anything? Or would they lead her directly into his waiting clutches?

His lair.

He was nearby. She knew it. He'd given it away. But why? Did he want her to find him? He must. He'd lured them to this town, this place. Set them up so nicely. What was his endgame?

The girl. Bess.

She was blonde. It broke the biggest pattern there was. So why would he take her? He only ever kidnapped redheads. Not once had he deviated from that. So why had he taken Bess? What was it about the girl that was so compelling to make him break the strictest of his patterns? The thing that got him off the most. That's where the answer was. Once she figured that out, the rest would come.

Cross.

She knew what he wanted. She knew what he'd always wanted. And it was in her power to give it to him. Doing so would be the ultimate defeat, though.

She pushed the thought away as she always did and focused on the players in Chief Bradley's office.

Roger and Sam mirrored each other in the chairs in front of Bradley's desk while Lucas propped a shoulder on the far wall. Clarke was hitched up against the windowsill. They had all fallen quiet after filling in the chief on their theories.

"Well, I've already provided my officers with a list of buildings to scout," the chief said, breaking the silence. "We only have three other guys on staff apart from Lucas, so I'm not sure how much ground they'll be able to cover. We're a small station." She said the last bit with an apologetic shrug.

"We're in full manhunt mode," Roger cut in smoothly. "Now that we know how serious the situation is, it's all hands on deck."

Bradley nodded, grateful.

"Can we see the list?" Clarke said, instead of the snide comment that lurked in the dark corners of her mind.

"Of course." Bradley held out a piece of paper. "Keep it, it's a copy." Clarke took it and scanned it, but nothing jumped out at her immediately. "There are a lot of buildings on here." Searching them all would take longer than she wanted it to, even with the help of the extra agents.

Bradley shrugged. "The recession."

Clarke tucked the list into the pocket of her jeans.

"We need to talk to the boyfriend again," she said to the room at large. "We need more information about Bess."

"In case you've forgotten, today's the deadline for the last picture," Roger said, issuing a little slap on the wrist. Often because Cross arranged the drop-offs ahead of time, the packages were waiting at the locations whenever they figured them out. But this time there hadn't been anything at the cabin when they'd first checked. And when they'd checked each day since, they'd turned up nothing. It would have to be there today if Cross was sticking to his own deadlines.

"Oh, is it?" she asked, the false sweetness coating a thick layer of sarcasm. "Thanks so much. It had slipped my mind."

"Clarke." This time it was Sam reeling her back in. She wondered how much longer she could take this, this walking on the edge, this feeling that she was always one comment away from slipping over.

"Sorry," she said after an indrawn breath, almost as if she were trying to hold the apology inside herself so that Roger couldn't take it. Couldn't have it.

It was a piss-poor one, anyway, and Roger knew that. His fingers slipped into the pockets of his trousers, and she wondered if he did it to hide the way they bunched into fists.

The chief's eyes were darting between them, and Clarke could tell she favored Roger's side in the battle of wills by how she rocked just a half step closer to the man. To her, Clarke must appear erratic, insubordinate. Maybe she was.

Sometimes she wondered why he put up with her. Mostly she thought it was for Sam.

Now, he deliberately checked the heavy silver watch on his wrist, refusing to break the tension that she'd provoked.

Only after another thirty seconds did he look back up. "So you two will head to the cabin for the next photo," he said. There was no room for negotiation in the command. "Meanwhile, my team will take the lead on the buildings search."

"I'll bring in Peterson. He'll be here when you get back," Bradley said, and Clarke appreciated the bravery it took to join in the conversation at just that point.

But Clarke couldn't trust herself to say anything, so she just swiveled and headed for the door, knowing Sam was close behind.

Her eyes met his for a brief moment when they turned into the hallway. Her lips parted, the words catching in her throat.

"Don't," he said, holding up a hand. "I don't even want to look at you right now."

The words were the slap she'd braced for, but knowing it was coming didn't make it sting any less.

What made her feel like a caged animal was that she knew she'd messed up. She should have told him about the phone calls. Each time she'd answered was another little betrayal. It made her want to lash out at him instead of herself. To tell him that it was his fault. To remind him she'd known something like this would happen. To rage that she'd never wanted to be part of the case. Never thought she should be. But he'd convinced her.

Instead of giving in to the need, though, she just nodded her head once. So that he would know she wouldn't fight it.

They continued the rest of the way to the car in heavy silence.

There was fear in the back of her throat. There almost always was. That this was the time she'd gone too far; this was the time she succeeded in driving the only person she truly cared about out of her life. That other time, the time he left her in the bar, drunk off her ass, about to self-destruct, hadn't even lasted a day.

She'd been so scared, not that she would have admitted it at the time. But him dropping that twenty on the bar, walking out without looking back. It had been a blow to the solar plexus. Instead of chasing him out, begging him to not give up on her, she'd grabbed the bartender and let him screw her in the dank alleyway feet away from a bin of rotting garbage. She'd dragged herself home, only then letting herself cry.

The tile was blessedly cool against Clarke's cheek, where the black-mascara tears had dried. The tiny bathroom reeked of the alcohol that had been the only thing for her stomach to rebel against. She prayed she wouldn't start heaving, dreading throwing up bile. The burn alone as the yellow poison scorched her esophagus almost had her swearing off drinking completely.

Her head pounded, and the room tilted and shifted and swirled, and she wondered if she could possibly be hungover already.

She reached up to the door handle of her shower stall, managed to pry it open, and then dragged herself over the little lip. Somehow, with great amounts of fumbling, she got the water on.

By the time she slipped between the cool sheets of her bed, she felt almost human again.

Sleep, however, proved elusive. As if she should be shocked.

The file mocked her even though she refused to look at it where it sat on the makeshift desk that was really an old folding table she'd found in the alley three days after she moved into her shithole apartment. Grad-school students couldn't be choosers. Especially scholarship kids such as herself.

Or former grad-school kids. Was she ready to throw it away? She hated that she was tempted to. She hated Sam. Hated his disappointment. His hurt-puppy-dog eyes. It was her life. She didn't owe him anything.

Except she did. Sometimes she thought maybe she owed him everything.

She sat up and waited for the room to steady. Then she padded over to the cheap plastic chair that matched the decor perfectly.

Clarke curled her legs under herself and grabbed the file that had started it all. She rested her palm on the unassuming front and took a deep breath in from the nose.

Screw this. Two minutes later she was resettled with a comforting, cool IPA clenched in shaking fingers. She brought the bottle to her lips and savored the bite of hops and how it clashed with the mint of the mouthwash, then erased the sick that had been lurking in her throat.

She opened the file.

Florence Shute's empty eyes met hers. Her pale, bloodless hand clenched her husband's. His was just as lifeless.

This case had hit her hard. But the worst of it was that she'd been so unprepared for it. There had been so many other cases she'd sailed through, to the point where she was starting to think she might have a reputation for being cold-blooded. But this one. This one made her rage-dial Sam and tell him she was done. Done with this life he'd planned out for her. Done with the murders. Done with the dark places. But, mostly, done with him.

Maybe he would have actually believed her if she hadn't told him about the bar she was headed to after she finished the bottle of wine. So he could find her.

She looked at the picture again.

If she had called Sam, begging him to come over, to hold her while she cried, to tell her everything was going to be okay, he would have been there. But that wasn't her style.

When she hurt, she wanted those around her to hurt. To feel the cuts and bruises as deeply as she did. When she'd skinned her knee, falling off a bike, she wanted her best friend to fall off his so they could share in the pain and cry together. That was the only way it felt real. Valid.

She forced herself to read the details now. To not let her eyes pull back to the damp, red mattress, heavy with their collective blood. Or to their faces that didn't look frightened in their death masks, but peaceful, accepting. Even though she knew the process had not been gentle or kind.

It wasn't a serial killer. This was personal. Seventeen stabs to the chest were nothing if not personal.

Rage. That's what she saw when she looked at the picture. The couple had recently won a court case to gain custody of their two-year-old grandson from their son. There had been no serious outward signs of psychosis in the son, but there were several police reports of domestic violence against him before the child came along. The wife died giving birth.

There were some other red herrings thrown in. But it was the son. She knew it—with the same certainty that she knew she'd be a good FBI agent. But that didn't mean she was actually cut out to survive that life.

She drew the pad of her finger over the murdered woman's white hair, loose around her shoulders. The grandson had found their bodies. And had screamed for two hours before a neighbor walking his dog had heard. Then the kid had stopped making sounds altogether.

She wondered how old the case was, and where the kid was now. In the system? That rarely worked out.

She swallowed the dregs of the beer and then walked the three steps it took to get to her kitchen. The only clean thing to drink out of was a flower vase that she never filled with flowers. She ran the tap, then drank three-fourths of it, the water dribbling down her chin when she couldn't keep up with the flow.

She unlocked her phone and flipped to recent calls. She hit the first name on the list.

"I hate you sometimes," she said when the groggy voice answered.

"Back atcha, kid."

She felt perverse pleasure in knowing she'd woken Sam up. It never seemed like he would make himself so vulnerable as to sleep like the rest of the mortals.

She refilled the vase. "I may have spiraled," she admitted. It was as much of an apology as he was going to get.

"I noticed."

She rolled her eyes in her empty apartment. "I'm going to be a good agent, Sam. Damn good."

"I've been telling you that for years. As long as you get out of your own way," he said. She heard a comforter rustle, and she imagined he was pushing himself into a seated position, to lean against the headboard.

"What if I can't, though?" she asked. She had all the classic signs of someone who was self-sabotaging. It was the closest thing to a call for help as she could manage.

The static that wasn't really static anymore in this day and age crackled over the line. She knew he wouldn't bullshit her, and found herself holding her breath for his response.

"You think your two options are waitress or special agent, Clarke," he said, his voice surprisingly gentle. "You'd be great at either, despite your astonishing lack of people skills. You'd be great at anything, if you let yourself be. But your job path isn't the problem."

"Oh yeah? And you know what my problem is, then." It came out more a plea than the challenge she'd been intending.

"Honey, you don't need me to tell you what your problem is. That's the point."

She sank to the floor, resting the vase in the valley between her tummy and her thighs.

"Will I ever stop wondering? Will I ever stop feeling guilty?" she asked, her voice catching on the sob she couldn't contain.

"Wondering what, kid?"

"Why I survived."

There was that nonstatic again. The tears had already started flowing once more, and she didn't even try to stave them off. She was sloppy drunk and exhausted. What else could she expect?

She counted the seconds as she pictured him debating the merits of telling the truth versus making her feel better at four in the morning after she'd drunk enough for her liver to be crying for mercy.

The answer she'd been expecting came simply and in true Sam fashion. "No."

She watched Sam as they crossed the parking lot. Forgiveness was always there, just waiting for her to reach out and ask for it. It always had been. At the end of the day, she knew he loved her like the daughter he never had. Wanted what was best for her even if he missed the mark on what that was some of the time. Wanted to forgive her. Always wanted to forgive her.

He slid behind the wheel, and she opted for the passenger seat and still said nothing more. Instead, she flipped open Bess's file.

"You think because she's different, she's the key to this?" Sam asked, apparently willing to talk to her about the case itself. He kept his eyes on the road as he peeled out of the station, but he knew what she was looking at.

"What do we know about him?" she asked. "He's all about patterns. It's always the same. Always. Except with her."

She tapped a finger against the picture's forehead. "What is it about you?" she whispered, almost to herself. She caught Sam's sharp glance, but she didn't look up. There was something about the girl. Around the nose and the mouth that looked almost familiar. But not like the other girls. There was the hair, too, of course. Straight as an arrow and the color of burnt honey. Not red.

"She was in an abusive relationship," Sam commented.

"One in three women are," she said with an absentminded wave. Sam knew the statistics. "Doesn't mean it fits the pattern."

He nodded. "Then she's why we're here."

"I think so." Clarke looked up to the road, not even seeing it. "He set the stage around her."

"Anna was just to get us here," he said, and she heard the grimness in his voice. Which meant Anna was no longer useful. But as painful as it might be to admit, this wasn't about Anna. Thinking about her wouldn't help them solve the case. Her being a person to Clarke would not help solve the case.

Clarke was as bad as Cross on that front, in being able to see the girls as pawns when she needed. It was also the reason she was going to be the one to catch him.

Anna wasn't going to help her do that. Bess was.

The file in her lap gave her so little, though. Who was Bess? How did she think? What were her hopes. What were her fears? Was she even still alive?

Why her, Simon? Why her?

CHAPTER TWENTY

Adelaide

April 2002

Adelaide didn't know where she was. All she knew was she couldn't let him catch her.

The fear turned branches into angry arms, ready to lash out at her as she tripped over roots and rocks in her mad scramble to get away. Just get away. As far as she could, as fast as she could.

Hours or minutes or seconds later, she finally stopped when her legs threatened to give out from beneath her completely. She crouched behind the trunk of the nearest tree, her back pressed up against the bark. Her thighs burned even as the cold air sliced at her skin. Panting, she tried to listen for a pursuer, but even as she struggled to control her breath again, she didn't hear anything. Just the sounds of the woods at night.

It took another eternity for her to relax enough to sit down. There was an ache there. She dipped her fingers inside her shorts, and they came away with blood. She closed her eyes against the sight of it in the thin sliver of moonlight and wiped her hand against the hem of her shirt.

The tears started falling again, thick drops against her upturned kneecaps. Before she knew it, she was blinded by them. She finally let herself go. Deep, gasping, shaky sobs. The kind that came directly from the gut. The heart. The lungs. That burned at the back of her throat and had snot running down her face unchecked.

Time became irrelevant. Adelaide had no idea how long she sat with her back pressed up against the tree. She didn't even know how long she'd been running to get to where she'd stopped.

At some point she would have to move. But right now, everything hurt too much. So she let herself sink into the floaty place. The one that didn't have any pain in it.

The place where Simon was still that little, rebellious boy. The one who maybe wasn't always nice. Was maybe a little mischievous. Especially when he was bored or, worse, feeling attacked. When he lashed out because he was cornered.

He wasn't intrinsically bad. He couldn't be. He'd loved her so much. So fiercely. In a way that may have warped and bent and disintegrated into something twisted and dark. But it hadn't always been like that. Sometimes it had been sunshine. Sometimes it had been the only thing that kept the molecules in her body grounded, kept them from flying off in every direction.

There had been times when he'd held her as she wept for parents she barely even remembered. For the empty feeling she carried around with her. For missing the idea of something more than the thing itself.

He'd never judged her for it, either. He'd rocked her and told her everything would be okay. Even though they both knew it wouldn't.

He had his own demons that crawled out of the shadows of the night and clawed and bit at him. One time he'd screamed out, waking her. She'd climbed into his bed and wrapped her arms around his shivering, bony body.

What hurt her the most wasn't the rape. It wasn't.

It was that he'd completely ruined her memories. The good ones, the ones touched with shimmering molten gold.

She'd been so young when her parents had died that she didn't know who she was before that time. Her personality must have been formed, but when she thought of her core memories, the ones that shaped her, well, they involved Simon. But now—now what was she? Without those?

The floaty place wasn't working. It was becoming dark, burning and curling at the corners like charred paper.

Pull out of it. Before it consumes you.

Somehow she managed to shake off the tendrils of panic that coiled at the base of her spine. *Find something to focus on. Anything.*

She glanced up toward the moon. Home. It was a thought. Something to latch onto. She needed to get home.

But how?

There was no way to tell where she was. Had they crossed over state lines? How long had she been unconscious? How far could he have taken her?

Get up. Move.

Those were the first steps. Find civilization again. That was the next.

There was a numbness in her bones, though. A lethargic hand on her shoulder keeping her in place.

Some part of her realized it came from both shock and the cold that was inch by inch slipping beneath her exposed skin. But another part wanted to burrow into the nook of the tree and succumb to the sleep that whispered to her in the quiet of the night.

Move.

It was only a thought. Only a quiet voice in the recesses of her mind. But she let it drive her to her feet.

Move.

She couldn't go back the way she'd come. That's where Simon was. But maybe if she ran parallel to the edge of the woods.

It was slow going, picking her way through the undergrowth. Maybe her feet were bleeding. Maybe her arms were. Moving forward was the only thing that was important at the moment, though.

Her mind wanted to fly off in too many directions, but she kept a tenuous control over it. There was no room for anything other than what it would take to get her home.

The moonlight kissed her skin whenever the trees would thin out, but she wasn't skilled enough to use it to help her guess the time.

So she just kept walking. And not thinking. And not feeling.

Moments away from giving up, from collapsing to the ground, she heard it. The purr and rumble that could mean only one thing. Cars.

It must have been a highway for there to be enough traffic for her to hear in the waning moments of the night.

She walked toward the sound. It was salvation. It was hope. It was the only thing that made her put one foot in front of the other.

When she finally saw the beam of headlights cutting through the darkness, relief, sweet and heady, crashed into her, almost taking her out at the knees. But still she kept moving. Forward. Always forward.

It didn't take much longer for her hands to meet steel. The guardrail. She swung a leg over it, not even flinching as the loose gravel cut into the soles of her feet.

She was on the road.

But no one was stopping. Three cars flew by her without even slowing. Desperation licked at the edges of her brain.

Maybe they couldn't see her.

She stepped, just a little bit, over the line painted on the blacktop. The oncoming minivan jerked and swerved, and she felt the air brush by her arm.

As she turned to watch it, she realized it was pulling off into the shoulder. A woman, about midthirties, threw open the passenger side door, all Mom haircut and worried eyes and frantic limbs.

"Honey, are you okay?" she was already asking as she made her way toward Adelaide. Then hands were on her. Petting, stroking, comforting.

Someone had found her. That's all that was important.

Her body seemed distant now. She let the woman shepherd her into the back of the minivan. Let her pull the seat belt over her chest. Let the hot air send prickles of agony along her skin. But she didn't seem to be a part of it.

Everything was detached. She knew she gave her an address; she knew that was where they were headed. But along the way, there was a blur of colors and shapes and rain-splashed windows. Had it been raining in the woods? She hadn't thought so.

It wasn't until she began to recognize the houses that the spell broke. Everything that had happened sat heavy on her bones.

"Everything will be okay, love," the lady said, trying to comfort her, seeming to recognize that Adelaide was back with her. Somewhat present.

It grated on her, though. The words slipped like little knives along her skin, trying to comfort but failing all the same. The empty promise hung in the air as damning as anything that had been said before or since.

Adelaide simply shook her head. "No, it won't."

Adelaide collapsed into her foster mother's chest and immediately felt all of seven again. The musky cloud of her White Diamonds perfume was as soft and welcoming as the doughy arms that came around Adelaide's waist.

The moisture on her cheeks wasn't hers, she realized. It was from lips slicked wet with salty tears, finding the sharp bones of her face and pressing there.

"Oh, Addie, oh, Addie, we thought you'd left us," Mrs. Cross kept murmuring over and over again. Even though she must have been missing for only a few hours.

Adelaide shook her head but couldn't force words out. She wouldn't have done that to them, she tried to say silently.

It wasn't until she was three cups of tea deep that she found her voice again. "It was Simon."

The name had the desired effect. They'd already been watching her, but their attention sharpened at that, their eyes tightening in unison. Then they exchanged a glance that bespoke their decades of marriage. Of being able to have a conversation with a single look.

"It's all right," Mrs. Cross said, her stubby fingers patting against Adelaide's cold hand. "You don't have to explain just now."

They didn't get it. They didn't understand. How could they? Even after the worst times, how could they even begin to comprehend what he had become?

She slammed her cup down, suddenly angry. At their assumptions, at her own inability to make them get the urgency. Did they not see the bruise that must be on her throat?

But mostly she was angry at the fact that they didn't have to feel what she was feeling in that moment. That the horrors of what had happened to her hadn't touched them yet. That they were still pure and naive and living in a world where a floaty place existed for them.

Layered over that was fury at herself for thinking such things.

"No," she said, flipping her palm up so that she could clasp Mrs. Cross's hand in hers. Her fingernails dug into the skin, and Mrs. Cross flinched, but Adelaide didn't let go. "No. You need to listen. It was Simon. He took me. He hurt me."

Mrs. Cross cocked her head, like a dog not quite sure what the noise it heard meant.

Adelaide dragged her eyes up to Mr. Cross. His knuckles were white where his fingers gripped each other in front of his belt buckle. He didn't want to hear what she was saying. She could see it in his face. They were stubborn, the Crosses. She knew this. She knew this from years of making them try to see reason. If they didn't have solid proof for themselves, they wouldn't believe anything anyone said.

"I think he's going to come back," Adelaide said. She needed to make them understand. "This isn't over."

"What are you saying?" Mrs. Cross's voice was a whisper caught in her throat.

Adelaide's teeth sank into her lip. "He's dangerous. I escaped, but he's not going to just let me go. And if I'm here, there's a chance he'll come after you as well."

"Why . . ." Mrs. Cross stopped herself, clearly biting back something she was ashamed to ask.

"Why did I come back, then?" Adelaide didn't care. She didn't care if their love wasn't quite as unconditional as they would like to believe. She didn't care if they would throw her to the wolves if it meant saving themselves. It didn't matter that she didn't expect anything else. "Because I had nowhere else to go."

Mrs. Cross's tongue darted over her thin lips, and she nodded. "We always knew . . ." Mr. Cross nodded twice, his face a grim mask.

They'd always known Simon would be trouble. Part of her wanted to ask if that's why they hadn't tried harder. They had realized he was a lost cause. A lost soul. But maybe if they'd tried, a persistent, traitorous little voice whispered. Maybe if they'd tried, it wouldn't have turned out like it had. Maybe if they'd given him one more hug, paid attention when he'd thrown fits, given him love instead of conditional expectations. Maybe then she wouldn't have been kidnapped in the middle of the night.

But no. That wasn't fair. She thought of Simon's eyes when he'd looked at her legs, there on the roof. She thought of his eyes when he'd kissed her that first time. Maybe he wasn't intrinsically bad. That didn't mean he had ever been good.

What did that make her? Because she'd loved him. Because at one point he was her whole world. Did that make her bad? Dirty? Wrong? What did the Crosses think when they looked at her? Did they see the summers spent barefoot and wild, running and laughing with Simon? Or did they realize that she'd long given up her dreams of a perfect brother? Around the same time that he'd started sending her pictures of girls with curly red hair.

But what was important now was that Simon could be heading toward the house at this very moment. If he'd tried to search her out and been unsuccessful, the obvious choice was to return to the Cross house.

"Right," she said, at once frustrated, sad, and impatient. "I think we should leave."

"Leave." Mrs. Cross turned to her husband. "No, we couldn't do that."

"No," Mr. Cross agreed.

Adelaide just blinked at them. "Are you not listening to me?"

"There's no need to raise your voice, dear," Mrs. Cross said as if she couldn't resist her instinct to scold and correct.

The urge to scream roiled in Adelaide's belly, and she kept her jaw tight, fearing if she relaxed, it would all come spilling out. And now wasn't the time for that.

"You're right. But there is a need for us to leave here." Adelaide paused. She had to say it but didn't want to. Didn't want to form the thoughts into vocalized words. When she did, it would be real and true, and there would no escaping it. But if it was what she needed to say to get them to move, then she had to do it. "He raped me. And then I escaped, and I don't think he's going to be happy about it."

"Oh, baby," Mrs. Cross breathed, but she did that wordless communication with Mr. Cross again, and Adelaide didn't know what to think. The look was filled with something. Doubt?

Mr. Cross cleared his throat. "We should call the police, Addie."

Adelaide nodded. "Yes, yes," she said, seizing on an idea. "Let's go to the station. Let's go."

Adelaide even stood, tugging at Mrs. Cross's forearm. She didn't budge.

"No need for that, dear. They'll come out," Mrs. Cross said, watching her behind a shuttered gaze.

"Listen, I don't know how far behind me Simon is. I was a little . . . out of it. But he could be close."

"You listen, girl." Mr. Cross straightened from where he'd been leaning against the counter. The air crackled around him. It was a rare thing for him to be pushed beyond his patience. "We're not going to let some punk kid scare us out of our home. We didn't let him do it before. We're not going to let him do it now."

"Oh, I don't need you going anywhere, Thomas," Simon said, stepping into the kitchen from the shadows just beyond the doorway. "You're actually right where I want you."

CHAPTER TWENTY-ONE

Clarke

July 16, 2018

The little cabin with the boat at the end of the dock was quaint. It seemed like a place you could forget you had nightmares that made you want to numb the pain with any substance that would alter reality. Even the motorboat promised an escape, the *No Worries* stamped across its stern a sweet promise that could lull a girl into imagining that was actually possible.

The chief had set up a constant surveillance on the place since Sam and Clarke had checked it out the day before. There had been nothing in the cabin. No furniture, no dust, no wild, scavenging mice. Nothing. The patrol reported that no one had approached it, either.

Still, she wasn't surprised when there was a box waiting for them. It was in the middle of the room, a ray of light catching just a corner from where it streamed in from the window.

Her name was scrawled across the cardboard, the slashes and lines almost angry in their abruptness. *New location, same goddamn box,* was all she could think. She ran a hand over her eyes. She was so tired of it. She imagined a year from now, squatting in a whole new location and staring down at that same handwriting. How many girls would die between now and then?

Finale, she reminded herself, instead of letting herself sink into the melancholy. It felt different. This one was different. She just had to make it through to the end without falling apart.

Once there, at the end, she didn't care what happened after.

After. The word had lost so much of its meaning in the endless chase that she no longer believed such a thing even existed. When he was dead—and he would be, that was for sure—what would happen? What would that life, her life, look like without him in it, without him driving it? She couldn't even imagine.

Sam was a steadying presence behind her, and she leaned back, just a little, until her shoulder pressed against the solidness of his thigh. He wouldn't move away, she knew. Even if he was livid with her. That was Sam.

They knew they shouldn't be opening the box yet. Not before the CSI team did its thing. But she'd already thrown procedure to the wolves over and over again on this case. There wouldn't be anything to find anyway, so there was no point in wasting time.

If it went to court, they'd have problems.

But maybe she knew it would never go to court.

Still, she slipped on latex gloves before she slid the box closer. Training was hard to overcome. The flaps were held down by a feeble strip of basic Scotch tape, and they gave easily when she tugged at them.

Her breath hitched for a moment, before steadying. It was a picture of a child. A boy with a mop of brown hair that fell over green eyes. His face was split wide in a grin, and there was a gap in the upper row of his teeth where one was missing. The angle was tight, but she could see a bit of his blue shirt and most of something that was pinned there. It was blurred a bit, though, so she'd need Della to enhance it before she could tell what it was.

She flipped the photo over.

One day.

"It's all out of focus, but the background looks like it might be a restaurant," she said, handing the picture to Sam.

He hummed his agreement. "He changed the timeline."

She'd noticed. They should have had two days to find the next clue.

"Are you thinking it?" she asked. She didn't always want to be the one to jump to the worst conclusion, but she didn't know any other way.

"One day means the next location is the last one," Sam said.

"Which means Anna might already be dead," Clarke said, finishing the thought.

"We don't know that yet," he countered.

"Yeah," she said for the sake of agreeing.

"Hey, kid." He reached down, hooking his beefy fingers under her armpits to drag her up to eye level. He grasped her chin in his palm, holding her gaze steady. "Remember what I said last time. Don't let him get in your head. He does this to you every time."

"What else am I supposed to think, Sam? What are you thinking? Do you honestly believe there's any hope for that girl? We have, what, twenty-four hours, tops."

"Does thinking she's dead already change anything?" he asked, his voice gentle where hers had turned ragged.

"No. Or maybe a little."

"You already thought she was dead," he said, seeing into parts of her dark soul she wished were completely hidden. It made her feel naked and exposed.

"So what if I did?"

"I'm not saying it's wrong to expect the worst, Clarke," he soothed. "It hurts less when you expect the worst."

A gurgle bubbled up from her throat that might have sounded like a laugh but wasn't a laugh. "Does it ever hurt less?"

She must have looked as pitiful as she felt, because he finally pulled her into his chest, wrapping his thick arms around her. Always forgiving her.

Her hands found each other at the small of his back, and she buried her forehead in the dip of his shoulder, pressing hard against him. He felt like everything that was steady and true in the world.

"No," he said. "Or maybe a little. When you're braced for the piano to fall, maybe you can avoid being crushed. But you can't spend your life looking up like that."

"You can when you have pianos falling on you all the time. Some would say it's smart," she said into his shirt.

"You have had your fair share," he acknowledged. "But this one hasn't dropped yet."

She pulled away, swiping the loose strands of hair out of her face.

"You're right. Everything is different this time," she said. "Which means Anna might still be alive."

"That's my girl," Sam said.

"But even so, we only have a day. And I have no idea what this means." She snatched the photo back from Sam and waved it in front of his face.

"It's Staunton. It has to be," Sam said, his eyes on it again. "He wouldn't have us go to another town when he's here. Not now, when he can watch you so easily."

She agreed. "Well. Good thing we've made friendly with the locals."

She wasn't surprised when Lucas shook his head after she had him look at the photo, but she was disappointed. It would have been nice to catch a break.

"I'll ask the chief when she gets back," he promised, but he didn't look hopeful. "I've only been here for about three years, so maybe she'll know something I don't."

Dwelling on it would not be productive, so she shifted her attention.

"You said Peterson's here?" She already started walking toward the interrogation room. Lucas and Sam fell in step behind her. "What's his mood?"

"Seems distraught, still."

Peterson certainly looked the part of Worried Boyfriend. Deep shadows smudged the skin beneath bloodshot eyes. His whole face, really, had taken on an unhealthy, sallow look that stripped him of the youthful handsomeness she'd seen only a day earlier. She wondered idly if he was hungover.

"Jeremy," she said, a little louder than was necessary. His wince confirmed her hypothesis. "Thanks for coming in."

"Course," he muttered. "Have you found anything yet? Have you found that guy?"

"We're working a few leads on that," she said, sliding into the chair across from his.

His face flushed with color. "So you've got nothing." He slammed a fist against the cheap tabletop, so quick to anger. "She's been missing for more than a week, and you guys are sitting around here with your thumbs up your asses."

Lucas shifted behind her when Jeremy brought his fist down again. She shook her head, just a quick movement, to signal that she had it under control.

"Tell me about Bess," she said, completely ignoring his outburst.

Confusion overtook the rage, and he squinted at her, the question taking a moment to work its way through the dense circuits of his brain. He rubbed a hand over the back of his neck. "What?"

"We need to know more about her. Presumably you can give us more than the basic facts, yes?"

He was caught off guard with that. "Course I can," he muttered, but then didn't continue.

"Anything you can tell us, Jeremy—really anything—will be helpful," she prodded. She'd wanted to redirect his rage, not shut him down completely.

"She's a teacher. Kindergarten."

"In New York?"

"Brooklyn," he corrected.

"You've lived there long?" she asked.

"A few years. Since we graduated. Penn State," he said, answering her next question.

She paused at that. "She's from Pennsylvania?"

"Yeah, Philly," he said.

Her heart stuttered against her chest. "I thought she was born in New Jersey?" She'd read the file twenty times over by now. Birth city was listed in New Jersey.

"Yeah," he said, as if talking to someone who was not very bright. "She was born in New Jersey. Her mom's family is from Jersey, but once she had Bess, they moved into the city. They lived there until her mom got married, when she was, like, eleven or something."

Clarke's mind raced. The most important thing first. She latched onto one of the whirling particles. The picture from the cabin.

She shifted, grabbing the file in Sam's hands. She found the photo and held it up to her face. She laid it on the table, smoothing a thumb over the corner. Her breath caught in her esophagus. *There.*

She stood up, holding out a hand. "Stay there," she said to the room at large.

Clarke sprinted toward Lucas's desk where she'd dropped her bag earlier. She hooked a hand around the strap, without breaking stride, and turned back to the interrogation room. When she burst back in, all three sets of eyes were on her.

She dropped the bag on the seat and dug in for what she needed, pulling the Meyers set of photos from its depths. She snagged a pen and a legal pad as well, then dumped everything on the table.

She slid each of the eight previous pictures in front of Peterson, in order, then slapped her hand above the photos. "Look at these, Jeremy. Look at them closely. Does anything about them relate to Bess in any way?"

Both Lucas and Sam tensed behind Clarke at the question, but she didn't take her eyes off Peterson.

He blinked at her for four seconds longer than her patience held out, but just as she was about to slam her hand against the table in an echo of his earlier frustration, he turned his attention to the pictures.

The silence in the room throbbed.

"I mean . . . ," Jeremy finally said. He trailed off. But then he nodded to himself and pushed two of the pictures toward her. He glanced up. "These two, maybe. Well, this one definitely. This one's probably a stretch." He tapped them separately.

"I'll take a stretch," she muttered. She pulled that picture closer. "Why this one?"

It was a close-up of a bouquet of pink-and-yellow roses, filled out with wispy baby's breath. It was tied with a lavender bow.

"I don't know, it might not mean anything," he warned again.

"Maybe it will help," she coaxed.

She was about to drag it out of him forcibly, when he finally shrugged. "Her mom was a florist."

It wasn't the groundbreaking revelation she would have liked, but it was something.

"And this one?" she asked, tapping the other photo.

He looked at it upside down now. It was the weathered sign for carryout that had taken her to Gary's in Sweetwater, Texas. A lifetime ago. But really only a few days.

His gaze flicked up and over her shoulder at the two men, before looking at her again. "Well, that was her mom's last name. Before she married Doug. Melissa Gary."

Clarke felt like she was on the edge of a cliff, and the pebbles beneath her feet had begun to slide off into the crashing waves below. "Was that her maiden name?"

"Um." His eyes rolled to the ceiling in thought. "No. She'd been married before, but it wasn't to Bess's dad. Then they all took Stanhope as their last name."

"Did Bess have a relationship with her biological father?"

He huffed out a breath. "Ah, no."

"Why?"

He fidgeted, his thumbs smoothing over the bones of his wrist, shifting his weight in the chair. "He died when she was little. Like when she was a baby. She doesn't talk about him at all. But . . ."

"But what?" She tried to temper the sharpness in her voice.

"I don't know, her mom made a comment one time. Like Bess wasn't in the room, and I never brought it up. But I think the dude, well . . . I think he was married."

Clarke studied the pictures she'd taped to the mirrored window of the interrogation room.

She chewed on the cap of her Sharpie while ignoring the handful of agents and locals behind her. Bradley was MIA, and the rest of the cops didn't know what the last picture meant.

She walked over to the makeshift board. "The first, a bar in Maine, is to me. A message that this time it's going to be personal." She glanced over her shoulder at Sam, the only person she cared about, following along. She tapped the marker against where she'd just scrawled her own name.

Sam nodded, eyebrows knit.

She slid over to the two photos Peterson had called out. She drew arrows off each of them and wrote "Bess" in big, bold letters underneath.

She wrote her own name beneath the club and the church. "Scars." "Sam." "Maybe."

Then the last one. The one with the little boy. She wrote "Bess" and a little plus sign, then added her own name.

Then she stepped back. It was a message. She just couldn't see the end yet. She tapped the recapped marker against her lips.

"Why is the last one both of you?" Lucas asked. She didn't look back, as she walked up to the picture, her finger finding the spot on the far corner of it.

"It's a Liberty Bell pin," she said. Della had confirmed it via text only a few minutes earlier, but Clarke hadn't needed it. She'd been positive.

"Bess is from Philadelphia," Lucas said slowly. "But how's that relate to you?"

She'd already moved back to the table to take in the whole scope of it.

"I am, too," she tossed over her shoulder, and the room went still. They were catching up.

"So it's not just about me," she said, once again directing her attention to Sam. "It's about both of us."

"Well." Roger's voice cut through her tunnel vision. "It's about her mother, not her."

She shifted, focusing on him. "What?"

"The clues." He nodded his head toward the board. "They're not about Bess, really. It's her mother's name, her mother's home, her mother's profession."

She nibbled the inside of her cheek. "They all affect Bess, too, but I see what you mean."

"Have you ever heard of either of them before?" Lucas asked the obvious question. "Even in passing? Ever gone to a florist in Philadelphia?"

She bit out a laugh. "No, I was only in Philly when I was younger. I wasn't buying anyone flowers at that age. I haven't been back since."

"So maybe it doesn't have anything to do with you," Lucas countered.

"It does," she said softly. But what did it have to do with Bess?

"What do they mean, then?" someone called out. She sighed, turning around to the crowd, debating if she had enough authority to boot them all out. Even if she didn't, she knew someone who did. She slid her eyes to Roger, who simply stared back. He wasn't going to do it. She sighed again and opened her mouth to answer when the chief came in.

"Sorry, all," she said, closing the door behind her.

Clarke shifted her attention without hesitation. "Can you come look at this picture?"

"Of course." Bradley edged around the room until she was bent slightly at the waist, her face close to the picture. "Is that . . . ?"

She trailed off. Straightened. Frowned and leaned back down. Clarke's pulse fluttered.

"I think . . . hey, Evans," she called to someone behind her. A beefy man with a thick, gray handlebar mustache pushed his way through the crowd. He was flushed, clearly pleased to be called upon during what was the most action he'd probably seen in his entire life.

"Yeah, Chief?" His voice was a deep rumble, and he couldn't quite keep the pride out of it.

"Is that . . . Tony's nephew?" She turned and stepped out of the way for him to repeat the movements she'd gone through only moments earlier.

He hummed, leaning in. "Now that you mention it . . ."

Clarke dug half moons into her palms, and the small muscle near her eyelid fluttered.

"Yeah, that's definitely Tony's nephew."

Bradley nodded. "Looks like him at least, yeah." She turned toward Clarke. "Tony used to live in town. He had a pizza place. You may have seen it."

Clarke tried to call up the image. She vaguely remembered driving past a weathered building at the edge of Main Street.

"Yes, well, he owned it for . . . what . . . maybe twenty years, but then the recession hit, and he had to close up. The bank got the building, but they've never been able to unload it. It's just sitting there. It's on the list."

Clarke dug in her pocket for the paper she'd nabbed earlier. And there it was, about three-quarters of the way down. Tony's Pizza.

"Have we checked there?"

Both Roger and the chief swiveled to the agents and officers in the room, who were glancing sideways at one another and shaking heads.

"We just really started searches, ma'am," one called out.

Throwing the marker against the wall would do nothing. Except it would feel really, really good. Jesus Christ, process was going to get these girls killed.

"What are you all standing around for, then?" she asked, and ignored the way Roger's face tightened. There was a rumble of disquiet behind her, as well. Perhaps they didn't appreciate the implication, but she didn't appreciate them sitting around when they should be doing their jobs. Turning away from them all in disgust, she looked at the chief. "This kid . . . you said you recognized him?"

"Yeah, he came up a couple summers in a row for maybe a week at a time," she said slowly. The entire room was on edge because of Clarke, and the chief could read it. "He stopped when he got older. But, yeah, I'm pretty sure that's him."

"And the background, does that look like the pizza place?" she asked. "I know it's blurred."

"Looks like."

"Holy hell," Clarke muttered, locking eyes with Sam.

She was halfway to the door when Roger dropped a heavy hand on her shoulder.

"What are you . . ." She whirled on him, unable to process much more than the *Run, go, find him* that had taken over every space in her mind.

"You can't just tear out of here half-assed," Roger said. "We need a plan."

"No, we need to go." What was he even saying?

"Agent Sinclair, watch yourself." It was a quiet warning, for her ears only.

"No. Screw protocol and procedure, Roger." She didn't bother to grant him the same courtesy. Let him fire her. She didn't care. Cross was blocks away. The girls were blocks away. "Because to me it looks like your 'planning' has gotten you jackshit so far." She waved a hand to encompass the agents who should have been out scouting the buildings.

Roger's jaw tightened.

"Agent Sinclair, you are out of line. Either control yourself or you're off the case."

"Your answer for everything." There was a buzz in her head she couldn't quite think past. "For God's sake, Roger. For once in your life, do something right because it's the right thing to do. Stop thinking about the press or how it's going to affect your next promotion."

"Out." Roger pointed to the door. His voice was calm and controlled. Ice to her fire. Tears welled in her eyes, but she refused to let them fall. She turned without a fight.

"No, Sam," she heard behind her as she slammed through the door.

She collapsed against the wall just outside the room, her body crashing from the high brought on from the adrenaline. So stupid. She was so ridiculously stupid. And she couldn't control it, not when it came to the bastard.

"We aren't going to do this with an audience." Roger's voice interrupted her self-flagellation.

Her eyes flew open. The shock of him standing there, watching her with something that looked suspiciously like understanding on his face, had her pushing off the wall.

"I already got the message, Roger," she said, cautious now.

He shook his head. "You're not off the case, Clarke."

When she started to speak, he held up a hand. "No. That's not all of it. You're going to listen to me now. I know you don't respect me, for a lot of reasons, some valid, some not. But I am your boss, and if you ever speak to me like that again in a room full of agents, it's not just a case you'll be thrown off of."

She nodded once.

"Look." He sighed, running a hand over his thick black hair. Regret hung heavy in his shoulders. "I'm willing to overlook this outburst because I know what this case means to you. What getting him means to you. But, Clarke, you were about to get not only yourself but the hostages killed. What were you thinking?"

She hadn't been. He knew that.

"Don't you think he's ready for you? It could be a trap. Hell, even if it isn't, storming in there with no plan with guns and hostages involved? You'd be lucky if anyone survived that. So here's what we're going to do. We're going to take ten more minutes"—he paused to let it sink in how much time she'd already wasted with her outburst—"and then we're going to go in with an actual strategy."

Shame burned in her throat. There was nothing to say, so she just nodded again.

"Take a minute to collect yourself, and then you can come back in," Roger said. "But if you slip like this again, I'm pulling you. I can't have you jeopardizing this. It's too important."

He turned, ready to step back into the interrogation room.

"Hey, Roger," she called. He stopped but didn't look at her. "Are you doing this for Sam?"

His back went taut, and he glanced at her over her shoulder. "You always forget I was there, too," he said softly. "So, no, Clarke, I'm not doing this because of Sam. I'm doing it because, believe it or not, I actually care about you."

He smiled at her stunned expression before pushing through the door.

"Tell me about the building." Roger had taken control of the room by the time she slunk in the back. Sam's eyes sought hers immediately, but all she could do was shrug one shoulder and hope he got the message.

They both turned their attention to the chief, who had flicked a glance toward Clarke when she'd come back in but had returned to speaking to Roger.

"Two entry points. One is the front doors. There's lots of windows, though. They wrap around the whole part along the street." She was all no-nonsense. "The back door. It opens into the alleyway."

"And the floor plan?"

"Big and open in the front. No walls breaking it up. Then the kitchen running along the back. It has a basement where they keep some of Tony's old machinery. It's unfinished, with no windows." She paused. "It always creeped me out to go down there."

"A place where no one could hear you scream," Clarke said.

Bradley looked over, eyes wide. "Yeah."

"This is it," Clarke said, and every single person in the room turned toward her, but she kept her gaze on Roger. "Sir."

He blinked, and something passed between them, across the distance of the room and across the years of simmering animosity. It was something that edged close to respect.

"I agree," he finally said. And then the spell broke, and everyone started moving, and there were more sketches made on the mirror, and somehow Sam was beside her, nudging her shoulder.

"Are we all going to join hands and sing 'Kumbaya' now?" he asked with a little smirk.

"Oh, fuck off."

He shifted so he was standing in front of her, blocking the rest of the room from seeing the moment. His eyes traced over her face. "Are you okay, kid?"

It was so familiar, the question. She reached out, squeezing his forearm. "I am. Really. I'm sorry."

"I get it."

"Yeah, I'm just surprised Roger did," she said.

There was a smile at the corner of his lips. "I keep telling you he's not as bad as you make him out to be."

The man in question turned to them in that moment. "Hey, you two, I need you."

And then finally after way too much talking, he clapped his hands to get everyone's attention.

"All right. Let's move, people."

And then they were off, moving through the station en masse, bursting out onto the sidewalk. The restaurant was only a few blocks away, so cars weren't needed.

Their feet pounding against the sidewalk was a perfect echo of the pulse in her ears. So close. They were so close.

They slowed to a stop around the corner of the pizza place, as they'd planned. She, Roger, and Sam were going to lead the way around the back. Bradley would take the front.

Clarke bounced on the balls of her feet, loosening up her muscles as she did, then rolled the crick out of her neck before nodding to Sam, who was going through his own routine.

But he stopped and took two strides so that he was in front of her. His eyes wouldn't let hers shift away as he gripped the nape of her neck.

"Listen to me, kid, listen to me." His voice was low and calm, where she'd expected it to be tight and urgent. "Remember what I told you."

She matched his breathing to get hers to even out. "Don't let him get in my head."

He nodded once, not releasing her gaze. "I'm serious. This isn't the *Clarke Show*."

She bristled. It was never the *Clarke Show*. Her life. It was the *Sam Show* sometimes. But mostly, these days, it was the *Simon Cross Show*. She couldn't remember the last time she'd thought solely about herself. Which might be his point. "I got it."

He studied her, his eyes flicking over her face. "You better be sure. And if you're not, get there. Our lives depend on it."

That's what she had to keep tucked into the rational part of her brain—Sam's life depended on her not losing it. She didn't much care about her own, but his—his must be protected at all costs.

"Okay," she promised. Even though the fire from her palm where her gun lay was seeping into her forearm, up past her elbow into her shoulder and niggling at her brain stem. That fire was casting a haze on everything around her. All she saw was Simon. All she saw was her gun against Simon's head.

All she saw was the end.

CHAPTER TWENTY-TWO

Bess

July 16, 2018

Bess didn't know how long it had been since they'd managed to get the ticket to their freedom. She didn't know how much longer they could wait.

Anna had taken the brunt of the punishment. Her visits to the room had increased with a frequency that chilled Bess. How much blood could someone lose? The girl had completely stopped communicating after what seemed like a particularly brutal session. That had been hours—if not days—ago. Time was no longer measured the way it had been on the outside. Now it was measured in Anna's torture sessions. In drugged trips to the bathroom.

Simon seemed to vary his pattern, though, so she could never quite hold on to a solid reality. It was a good strategy on his part. Keep them off balance as much as possible in the tiniest of ways.

She tried to maintain near-constant chatter to Anna when she could, even though the girl was no longer responding. Anna. She'd say her name over and over again. *Hold on to yourself,* she willed the girl.

From what she could tell, Simon hadn't found the jagged piece of metal that Anna had grabbed. She needed Anna to be ready.

"Anna," Bess whispered. "Anna, we have to try."

A shuffle. Just the smallest shift of clothing against cement. But she'd heard.

"Today," she said, just in case that wasn't clear.

Silence.

You can't last much longer was on the tip of her tongue. That wasn't what Anna needed to hear, though. "He's moving toward a deadline, babe. We need to beat him with our own."

More shuffling. That was promising. Or at least it was the most reaction she'd managed to get out of her since she'd stopped talking.

"Here's the thing," she said. "I need you to go for his jugular. Dig the metal in as hard as you can right in the soft spot of his neck." The words sat familiar in her mouth, as they'd gone over this many times before. She repeated them anyway.

Nothing.

"There will be a lot of blood, but once you do that, he's going to go down. He'll be distracted at the very least. If you need to stab him again, do it. Throat, eyes, groin. Those are the most vulnerable points. Go for them. That piece of metal in his eyes—he's not going to be able to function after that."

Still silence. She pressed on.

"Then you go for the keys." He still kept them there. Taunting them. A power play that was going to cost him his most precious keepsakes. "Come unlock me, and then we'll head for the door. He'll still be down, but if he's not, it'll be both of us against him. We can take him. Anna."

She waited. And then waited longer.

"Anna," she finally said again. "We can take him."

"What if we can't?" Finally. Bess's breath caught in her throat. She wanted to cry but bit back the rush of emotion that pressed at her tear ducts. This she could handle. Even doubt was preferable to silence.

“You almost could have gotten away last time, babes, and you weren’t even trying,” she said, keeping her voice light, positive. “You got the weapon. You got our key to freedom. You beat him already. We just have to do it again.”

“We beat him.” It was quiet, but Bess wanted to pump her fist in the air. Confidence mattered. And the entire plan hinged on Anna being confident.

“You won, babe,” Bess said. “You tricked him. You outsmarted him. You can do it again.”

She closed her eyes waiting for the response.

“Okay.”

The footsteps. Bess could never quite get the sound of them out of her head. The heavy drum of boots on wood, then on concrete. When she closed her eyes, she heard them. When she tried to sleep, they were the pulse that echoed in her eardrums.

But now, now they were the start of something. Something that could mean freedom. Or death. Either way it was forward movement. And she didn’t know if she cared which way the outcome shifted.

But as soon as she had the thought, she realized it wasn’t true. She wanted to live. Maybe there had been times in the past that she hadn’t wanted to, where the ease of sinking into the oblivion had called to her, a siren’s song that had been hard to resist.

But, when faced with the very real possibility of that abyss, she didn’t find it as inviting. What did seem inviting was fighting. Fighting for life.

So if they were going to go down—which it seemed like his only plan for them—they were going to do it in a blaze of glory. So help her.

The footsteps bypassed her huddled form, as per usual, and headed straight for Anna.

"I have a treat for you, pet." Simon's voice was silk. It never failed to raise the hackles along Bess's back. "You're going to get to go on an adventure."

Shit. This changed their plan. Or maybe it wouldn't. He still had to unlock Anna. He still had to make himself vulnerable.

"Do you want to go on an adventure?" he prodded, and Bess heard the jangle of keys against metal.

"Yes," Anna said in the softest voice that could still manage to be a voice.

"Good girl," he said.

There was some shuffling, and Anna let out a whimper.

Then they were up. Moving toward Bess, but she knew Simon wouldn't get too close. He'd learned his lesson. She didn't need him close, though. She just needed Anna to hold her shit together.

He shuffle-dragged her three more steps. Only about four more to the stairs.

Come on, girl.

It was only because she was watching so closely that she saw it. A tensing of Anna's shoulders that hadn't been there. It was only because she was listening so closely that she heard it. A catch in Anna's breath.

And then she struck. She'd tucked the jagged little piece of metal between her pointer and middle finger. It was a quick flash of movement, her hand shooting up to his unprotected neck.

Bess didn't even have a chance to yell "Again" as Anna sank the metal back into the flesh. Three more times.

There was blood. Everywhere. His fingers were slick with it as they grasped at the metal Anna had left in on her final thrust. A high, thin keening note was humming out of his gaping mouth.

"Keys, Anna." Bess's voice was sharp, to cut through the haze she was sure had descended on the girl.

But it was in that moment Simon turned on Bess. It wasn't his attention that bothered her—anything that could distract from Anna was a win in her book—but the look in those wide, soulless eyes. It was panic.

He stumbled toward Bess, his movements uncoordinated and jerky, but his target was deliberate. Bess flicked her gaze over his right shoulder and realized Anna had the keys.

Something bloomed in her chest that felt suspiciously like hope.

It was a dangerous feeling, though, and she immediately quashed it. First, they had to finish Simon off. He was weakened, but she knew all too well the rush of adrenaline in his current state could make him strong. Wild. Unpredictably dangerous.

She waited until he was almost too close, one blood-slicked hand reaching for her upper arm, when she lashed out with her foot, directly into his upper thigh. She'd been aiming for his groin, but he'd sensed her movement and shifted just in time. The blow still hurt, though. As much as it could with all of his pain sensors blitzing from the open wounds in his neck.

He went down to his knees, and she kicked out again. She connected with the soft flesh of his hips. Not effective. He barely reacted.

And his attention was no longer focused on her, no matter how many times she lashed out at him. His entire being was zeroed in on Anna.

Anna. Anna, who stood at the foot of the stairs, keys clenched in her hands, eyes huge in her gaunt face. Frozen. Even though she held her freedom in her thin, weak fingers.

"Anna," Bess said. Not knowing what she was urging. Movement of some kind. To tell her to run or to fight for Bess? The selfish part of her, the one that wanted to live, the animal in her that gnawed at her belly and told her that her own survival was all that mattered, almost begged Anna to come closer. The better part, the one she knew she should listen to, urged her to tell Anna to run as fast as she could.

In the end, Anna shifted. Closer. But then Simon lunged.

"Anna, run." Bess had never screamed so loud in her life. Her voice filled every space in the room. It became a hand placed in the dent between Anna's shoulder blades, pushing her away. "Go!"

They locked eyes. And then Simon pushed to his feet. Unsteady, but the blood was no longer gushing.

"Go," Bess yelled, and it finally worked.

Anna fled. Up the stairs on her weak, spindly, once-upon-a-time runner legs. Bess closed her eyes, listening for the sound of keys in the lock.

She opened them in time to see Simon sink back to the floor, when they both heard the door slam shut.

"Fuck," he said, but it didn't have any heat to it.

"Agreed, dude," Bess said. She wasn't trying to be flippant. It was just that she couldn't care anymore. Every last bit of hope just walked through the door. Either Anna would magically stumble upon a cop who just happened to be waiting outside whatever hellhole lair Simon had kept them in, or Simon would immediately take Bess to some other secluded location and kill her.

It was up to fate now.

They sat in tense silence, and she was wondering if he was picturing a rescue team bursting through the door. When no one came, he managed to get himself upright once more. His shirt was soaked with blood, so he stripped out of it as he made his way to the bathroom. He came back a few minutes later with a bandage around his throat. He didn't look good.

Maybe he'd lost enough blood. He was quite pale. And he didn't seem ready to finish her off on the spot. Which meant she had time. She had potential opportunities. There was a chance. There would always be a chance until she was dead. And then she wouldn't care, she guessed.

Too many times in her life, she'd stopped believing there would be a chance. A chance to survive. She'd given up before, but she wouldn't this time. Every time she failed, she would just fight harder. And maybe she could fight harder than he could. Maybe she could win.

"We have to go," he muttered, more to himself than to her. She raised an eyebrow, glancing at her chain. The key to unlock her was on the ring Anna now had.

For the first time since Anna had brought that metal up into his throat, he smiled. It was horrifying. "A little lesson from me to you, pet?" He reached into the front pocket of his tight, light-wash jeans and withdrew a tiny, delicate key. "Always carry a spare."

CHAPTER TWENTY-THREE

Clarke

July 16, 2018

It was a whimper. Just a whimper.

Was she imagining it? But no. There it was again.

Clarke held up her hand, and everyone drew to a sharp stop. They were three steps inside the pizza shop.

There was a hush that hung heavy in the air, the kind that lingered in empty places. She'd already convinced herself they'd been wrong about the location when she heard it.

She glanced at Sam and then inched forward. Her pulse pounded, and she felt it everywhere. In her fingertips, behind her knees, in the cradle of her stomach. One deep breath helped quiet it in her ears. She needed her ears.

Working her way through the tables was an arduous process. As she cleared each one, she let the boys know.

By the time she made her way to the pinball machines in the back of the restaurant, she half wondered if she'd imagined that little sound.

It was only when she was about to turn around that her flashlight caught on the dark drops. They looked like pennies. She bent closer.

Blood.

She shifted around the last of the machines. There in the crack between it and the wall was a crumpled figure.

"Shit." Clarke crouched down to the unconscious girl. *Anna,* some distant part of her mind supplied, even though she was nearly unrecognizable underneath the blood and grime. But it was that same sweet face that she'd studied for hours, days, months.

Clarke managed to get her fingers around the thin wrist and feel for a pulse. Once she'd located it, she shot back to her feet, waving in Sam's direction.

He was at her side immediately.

"Watch her."

The warning in his eyes was clear. She nodded to acknowledge it and took off toward the door she figured led to the basement. Something was off. The girl shouldn't have been up in the restaurant. And she certainly shouldn't be alive. Not if everything had gone according to Cross's plan.

Perhaps it hadn't, though. For the first time in a very long time.

Roger had her back as she made her way down the creaky stairs. She didn't think twice about how much trust she was granting him.

They cleared the room and the smaller one in the back. Next to it was a small, tidy bathroom, but it was empty as well.

Whoever had been there was gone.

She walked in slow circles around the space as Roger knelt by the sturdy chains bolted to the floor.

"Two chains," he said, his fingers running over the metal.

Her mouth was already open to reply when the glint of color caught her eye. The picture wasn't even hidden this time. Or in a box, or a book, or some unusual package. It was just sitting atop a simple wooden chair slightly off to the side.

Everything around her went quiet. Roger was saying something. Boots started sounding overhead as the rest of the team rushed in. There were sirens somewhere in the distance.

But none of that registered. She just let her feet carry her over. Each step like a march toward fate. Toward life. Toward death. Toward some inevitability in which she and Simon were forever tangled together as they hurtled toward infinity.

It was supposed to be different this time.

It was all she could think. Different. They were going to catch him. They were wise. They were practiced. They knew his tricks. They knew what made him tick.

The only difference, though, was this time the girl was alive. For now.

Maybe it was a victory. But as the picture sharpened as she got closer, it didn't feel like one.

She stopped when her shins came flush up against the chair, and she dropped her head. The girl was supposed to have been tied to it, she realized. If Cross had had his way.

Now the picture just floated there.

Clarke knelt down so she wouldn't have to touch the evidence, and at first nothing about it made sense. It was a simple photo—a picture of a man and a woman, with a little blonde child nestled in the space left by their sides. Then everything sharpened. And she wished she were still stuck in the moment only seconds earlier. In the in-between, when she hadn't realized what she'd been about to look at.

Never again would she live in that moment. Or the millions of moments before that when she hadn't known.

She didn't recognize the small cry that shattered the silence as her own.

"We spend too much time in hospitals together, Sam," Clarke said, nudging his arm with the cup of coffee she'd brought for him. He reached up to take it but let his hand linger over hers before giving it a squeeze.

"But we saved one, kid," he said, keeping his voice low so as not to disturb the sleeping girl hooked up to the machinery.

Clarke shook her head, sinking into the chair next to his. "We didn't, though. She saved herself. Or he let us find her."

"Was trying to look at the bright side," Sam muttered into his cup. He took a swig, grimacing at the quality. It was shit.

"She's alive, that is a bright side," Clarke said, relenting.

He gaped at her in turn. "Who are you? What have you done with my partner?"

She wrinkled her nose at him but resisted the urge to stick out her tongue. She was an adult, after all. "I have to focus on something other than the big question."

"Where's Bess?" Sam ventured. "Or the other big question?"

The other one. She wasn't even ready to formulate that into an actual question, let alone have a discussion about it. "Where's Bess."

"Don't you want to talk about the pho—" He stopped when her panicked eyes flew to his. "Okay. Shh. It's okay. I mean we're going to have to soon."

She knew that. But it didn't have to be this second. Or the one after that. And if she kept thinking like that, she might be able to stop herself from falling apart.

"I know. It means something. And it's going to help us find her," she said. All truths. "But so can Anna." Clarke turned her attention back to the girl. She looked so small, swallowed up by the cold, harsh room.

Sam paused, then drew a breath. Let it out.

"Say it," she demanded, not looking at him.

"Roger's going to push. Once he knows . . ."

She cut her eyes to him once more. "Does he know?"

"Not yet, but it's only a matter of time, Clarke," he said, voice gentle. It was something about the way he said it, or the use of her name that stripped her down to a twelve-year-old who had just slightly disappointed someone with her weakness. Maybe even a year ago the feeling would have turned her mean.

Now she just tipped her head against his shoulder. "Thank you," she whispered. For not pushing her. For letting her be just for a tiny moment so she could process. For so many things.

She felt him nod, but he didn't move further to dislodge her.

The gratitude she rarely let herself acknowledge pressed against the back of her eyes.

The champagne had long ago gone flat, but Clarke sipped at it anyway. Not in desperation, but because she wanted to chase the happiness that lurked in its sweetness to amplify her own.

"You did good, kid." Sam moved a half-eaten slice of cake off the chair across from hers and sat down, propping his feet on the desk.

The office was a mess from their mini celebration, but everyone else who would have cared about its state had buggered off for the night. She looked away from the empty Solo cups and back at Sam.

"Seriously, kid." He stretched his arms up to rest his hands on his head. "I'm proud of you."

Clarke blinked and studied a disturbing brown spot on the floor. It didn't stop the chemicals from flooding her brain, demanding a trigger response of tears to dispose of the excess emotions. "Teamwork," she managed to stutter out. The company line.

"Nah. Most of the time it's teamwork," Sam countered, easy and low. "This time it was you. I don't say that enough, you know."

"That I'm amazing?"

"Yeah," he said, all humor stripped from his voice.

"Stop."

"You should know that, you know." Sam cleared his throat, awkward but pushing forward anyway. "That I'm proud of you. That I haven't done that many things right in my life. And you might not think I did this right, either. Hell, I don't even know. But whatever happens, you should know that."

"You're proud of me because I caught the serial killer," she whispered, not recognizing the smallness of her own voice. Where had the confident, snarky, tough-as-nails agent gone?

"Nah," he said again, that same simple rebuttal. "It's not about earning it, kid."

Was it really that simple?

He nodded as if he'd read her mind, or maybe she'd said it aloud.

"It's really that simple."

The concept was still frightening, years later, still a challenge to wrap her brain around. They fought like wildcats sometimes, clawing at each other until they were bleeding on the floor, emotionally speaking. And in those moments it was hard to remember. In the chaotic moments, in the terrifying ones, in the ones that left her wanting to palm a razor blade, but one promise stilled her hand; it was hard to remember. Then he stayed anyway. He always stayed anyway.

"I'm never going to be normal, Sam," she said, though if nothing had done the trick to push him away up until now, this wouldn't be it. "In the alleyway, before we went into the restaurant . . ." She paused, glancing back at Anna. She was still sleeping. "I needed it to end, and I didn't care what that looked like."

"Did you not care? Or did you want one ending a little too much?" Sam asked.

"You would be sad." *If I died,* she finished the thought silently.

He rumbled a low chuckle. "Yeah, kid. I would be sad. But that's not enough, you know."

"If I die, he wins."

"Yup, that's good, too. Gives you the fighting edge," Sam said. "But you can't keep living your life to spite other people."

"Is that what I'm doing?" It wasn't a challenge. She really wanted to know. Is that what she had been doing? For years?

"Christ. No." Sam shifted toward her. "No, kid. That was . . . inelegantly phrased. I just sometimes want you to live because you want to live. Not for me. Not for him. Not for anyone else. Just you. You want it. That's what I want to see."

She was saved from answering by Anna's soft moan as she shifted on the bed. Clarke shot to her feet.

"Anna," she said as softly as she could, not wanting to wake her if she wasn't up. The girl looked so delicate, so small. She was all bones and bruises and crusted blood. Fresh, angry slashes crisscrossed ones that were starting to heal. On her face. On her arms. On skin that was now covered by clothes and blankets. No longer was she the girl in their picture with the glossy hair and full cheeks. She would never be that girl again.

Clarke tried calling her name once more. "Anna."

The girl's eyes flicked open, and horror gripped her features. She didn't know where she was. She didn't know she was safe.

"It's okay, it's okay, it's okay," Clarke said. "You're safe. You're in a hospital. I'm with the FBI. It's okay."

Clarke continued murmuring reassurances until she saw the fear seep out of the girl's muscles.

Sam held back, knowing the sight of a burly man might not be what Anna needed at the moment, so Clarke took the lead in questioning. The nurses would be here any second to push them away.

"Hi, Anna. My name is Clarke. I work with the FBI," she told her again, making sure comprehension lit her eyes before continuing. "I need to ask you a few questions, okay?"

Anna's hand shot out, her fingers digging into Clarke's forearm with a strength that was surprising, given her frail state. She half lifted off the bed, her mouth gasping out one word: "Bess."

"Bess. Is she alive? Anna, is she alive?" The electronic beeps were going nuts, and she heard the rush of footsteps just outside the door. "Anna. Is she alive?"

"Bess." But it was swallowed by the push and swirl of scrubs-clad nurses, a phalanx of soft blue nudging Clarke out of the way so they could tend to their patient.

"Shit." Clarke couldn't bite it back, and it earned her a sharp glare from a particularly stout woman who looked like she wanted to take Clarke out at the knees—and was capable of doing it. Clarke held up her hands to show she was backing down.

She snagged Sam's arm on her way out of the room, tugging him along behind. "We lost our window."

"It was never going to be more than a crack anyway," Sam said. And she knew he was right. For some reason, though, she'd hoped when Anna opened her eyes, she'd hold all the answers. And would willingly spill them at Clarke's feet.

Sam bumped her shoulder. "Coffee."

They hadn't even finished their first cups, but she liked the idea of having something to do with her hands.

The fluorescent lights were harsh against the black speckles in the tile, and the underlying buzz of the hospital at night became white noise to her scattered thoughts. It let her piece them together. Make a straight line out of them, when all they wanted to do was creep away into the dark places. She was stronger than that, though. She could handle this.

The cafeteria was empty, and they set up camp in the far corner.

Sam just let her sit. Let her be quiet and take some time. He'd pushed in his own way in Anna's room. And now he knew Clarke well enough to know she was on the verge of giving in. Of accepting what needed to be done. And he would be there at the bottom when she finally fell into the abyss.

She'd never been good at facing her problems head-on. When it came to assholes and killers and the big bads that went bump in the night, she was ruthless. They didn't scare her, because she wasn't scared of dying.

Dealing with emotions was different, though. It hurt in a way that a knife to the gut couldn't replicate. They were tiny lashes to vulnerable skin that never quite healed before being ripped open again.

So she had gotten really good at numbing the pain with a bottle of Jack. Or the edge of a razor blade. Or even the look on Sam's face when she lashed out and the strike landed on an already-bruised spot.

It was how she functioned. Block feelings. Redirect. Lash out. Rinse and repeat, as needed.

She felt it now, though. After seeing the last picture, after realizing what it meant. When she blinked, she saw the man's face on the back of her lids, the woman's smile in the moments before she opened her eyes again.

And she wanted to ignore it. Or make someone else hurt so that she wasn't alone, so that she wasn't the only one living with this throb beneath her breastbone that just wouldn't go away.

There was little she held on to from her past. She knew that for some people, memories from childhood became rose tinted. They became snippets that told a story of a life reimagined in the kindest light possible.

For Clarke, memories were dangerous things. Even when they didn't lie, they rarely told the truth. And worst of all, they were endless in their ability to deliver the pain that she was so eager to escape.

But there was a time she'd always hung on to. A brief period of light that never really formed into conscious thought. Instead, it came in flashes. The warmth of someone's arms. A cascading giggle forced out by tickling fingers. The sunlight catching red hair.

A man's smile. The same smile in that picture.

But the woman wasn't in any of those fractured memories. The woman with her child and her loving gaze that tore holes in the only foundation Clarke had ever presumed to have.

The baby. The girl cradled in gentle arms. This chase kept coming down to that, didn't it? *Why her, Cross?* The blonde curls on the toddler that didn't even hint at red.

The clues. The patterns—the ones that had been broken and the ones that had been created just for her to see. Like delicate scars that traced over white skin. The past. The pictures that were about Clarke and, at the same time, not about Clarke.

Why her, Cross? she'd asked while studying Bess's face. One that seemed too familiar. *Why her?*

It was no longer a question that needed answering. She pulled the phone from her pocket and thumbed to one of the most recent calls.

A hand settled over hers, warm and sure. She glanced up, meeting Sam's eyes.

He didn't say anything, but there was an echo there. Of that earlier conversation that he probably didn't even remember. *I'm proud of you.*

It was something to hold on to, and she needed that even if he didn't say the words.

She nodded and hit the number.

"Lucas. Is there any property on your list that has a connection with the name Brodie?" she asked without any preamble when he answered after two rings. Her eyes didn't waver from Sam's as Lucas asked the inevitable follow-up question. "It was my father's name."

CHAPTER TWENTY-FOUR

Adelaide

April 2002

The shadows clung to Simon's body even as he stepped into the kitchen light. He didn't look like a kid anymore. Just last night, on the roof, Adelaide had seen a hint of softness in the slight pudge under his jaw, seen the limbs that hadn't quite grown in yet, the stubble that was trying and failing to be a beard.

But there was a new edge to him. A confidence, a smoothness in his movements that made her think he'd grown up in the moment he'd realized she'd left him.

It didn't bode well for her. Boys threw tantrums. Men killed.

You're actually right where I want you. Their little tableau had frozen the moment Simon had spoken those words. The air was suffocating, and she didn't know what would break the tension, but she couldn't hold out against it for much longer. It lapped at her skin, her nerve endings.

Breathe.

He was blocking their access to the phone. There was the back door, but it was a good ten feet across the entire room. In theory, between Mr. Cross and herself, they could overwhelm him. She caught Mr. Cross's eye and saw the same thought there.

But just as he shifted, Simon moved. Quick—so that she didn't even realize what was happening until it was too late—he had his forearm wrapped around Adelaide's windpipe. *Air. Air. Air. Not again.* She clawed desperately at him, her fingernails drawing blood. He didn't relax his hold.

"Uh, uh, uh," he said, waving a blade that had materialized from somewhere. Had he had it the whole time? "Easy, easy. No one needs to be a hero here."

Sparkling stars popped at the edges of her vision. *Air. Air. Limp. Go limp.* It went against all her instincts, but she let herself become boneless, and the weight of her body concentrated into the sharp point of his elbow beneath her chin.

"Umf," he grunted, readjusting his hold so that he didn't stumble. He didn't let her go, but his arm came around her shoulders instead, pressing her unresponsive frame against his own to steady her. And there it was. Air. Glorious air. She drank it up in big gulps.

"What do you want, Simon?" Mr. Cross finally asked, his voice tight, rippling with fury and contempt. His eyes were locked on Simon's.

"What do I want? What do I want?" Adelaide heard the smirk there even if she couldn't see it. He wasn't intimidated at all. That meant something. But there was still fuzziness in her brain. The soft clouds had settled in and weren't clearing easily, even with the return of the blessed oxygen.

Think. Why wasn't he intimidated? He had a hostage. But he was still outnumbered.

"I want you to suck a cock, to be honest," Simon said, and Adelaide blanched even though out of everything she'd been through, that wasn't really the thing that should have shocked her. "Preferably your own."

If possible, Mr. Cross's face flushed a deeper red.

"Simon," Mrs. Cross chastised, unable to help herself. Would she ever? None of them spared her a glance, though. This was where the main action was. There was something deep and rough and broken between the two men, Adelaide realized.

"Actually, I'd prefer it if you sucked mine," Simon mused. "Imagine that. The great and powerful Thomas Cross down on his knees in front of the kid he threw away. Might make that happen, actually."

It was then Mr. Cross lunged—a flash of rage and movement. But in his focus he missed the thought that had kept hovering at the edge of Adelaide's mind.

Simon wasn't scared.

The tip of the blade dug into the vulnerable skin of her neck when a sharp, loud crack ripped through the fabric of the air, and Mr. Cross fell to the kitchen floor. Mrs. Cross screamed.

Adelaide's brain lagged, struggling to understand. What had happened?

Only when the other man stepped through the doorway, gun still raised like they held them in gangster movies, did everything click. The man's skin had an unhealthy pallor, pouched out by pockets of fat, and his hairline was creeping toward the back of his head, but there was still something there, a hint of the boy who came before them. The one who scowled out of a picture the Crosses kept on the bookshelf. Matthew.

Simon had brought reinforcements. And who better than the man who had been thrown away first?

"You better not have killed him," Simon said, and the knife pressed in further, right on the verge of breaking skin. Her pulse fluttered underneath the steel.

"Hey! Some thanks would be nice," Matthew muttered, crossing over to the fallen man. He kicked him. Hard. Once to the kidneys. Once to the rib cage. Mrs. Cross sobbed at each blow.

Mr. Cross groaned, a slurred, painful mewl against the abuse.

"He's alive," Matthew confirmed, glancing up at Simon. As if they hadn't all heard the pitiful noise Mr. Cross had made.

"All right, I'm tired of this foreplay. Let's go," Simon said, and finally the knife pulled away from her throat. She thought she might be on the verge of passing out again. But there was no time for that. Simon relaxed his grip around her shoulders and bumped her forward with his body. He directed her over to an empty kitchen chair, making quick work of securing her there with rope he'd drawn from his pocket.

"You," Simon said, ignoring her now that she was tied up to his satisfaction and pointing at Mrs. Cross. "On your feet, you cow."

There was a weak protest from the floor, where Mr. Cross lay crumpled in the middle of a growing puddle of blood slipping into the little cracks in the tiles, staining them red.

But Mr. Cross was in no shape to defend his wife. Simon pulled Mrs. Cross sharply, and she stumbled, her face a horrible mess of tears and snot. She met Adelaide's eyes, and Adelaide didn't even know what to do. She tried to soften her features, offer some sort of comfort. They all knew where this was headed, though. Who was she to offer false hope?

"Grab him," Simon called to Matthew as he dragged Mrs. Cross from the room. Matthew studied the lump of a body in front of him, disgust a mask over his features. He bent down, grunted, and heaved Mr. Cross over his shoulder. Then he followed Simon out of the kitchen without once glancing at Adelaide.

"Oh, pet." Simon's voice was silk again when he came back to the kitchen. Adelaide had been working at the ropes, but they didn't give. She'd thought of just standing up and crab-walking, but with her feet bound to the chair legs, it had turned out harder than she'd thought, and she'd almost toppled onto the tile. He'd walked in on her throwing her body weight toward the phone in the hopes of scooching the chair close enough.

Adelaide's stomach tightened as he stroked a finger down her cheek and then buried his face in her hair. Breathing in deep, he let his hands tangle in the strands. "Why did you leave me? Why would you leave me?"

She had to lie. Had, at least, to try.

"I'm sorry. I didn't . . . I didn't mean to. I just was overwhelmed by my feelings," she said softly, as if shy. Her lips were almost pressed up against his throat, and she was sure he felt the warmth there. She tilted her head up, forcing him to let go of her curls, making him meet her gaze. If she could reach him . . . well, if anyone could, it was her, right? Maybe she could convince him. She just needed to say the right things. "I was a little scared by how much I felt."

His eyes warmed, just a degree, a smile tugging at the corners of his lips. He leaned down so that their mouths were a hairsbreadth from being pressed together. Just sharing each other's air. It was more intimate than if he'd kissed her. He held himself there, still, so she moved, nudging forward so their lips touched. She felt his smile and relaxed into it.

A second later her world exploded into white as his hand cracked against her cheek.

"Oh, pet," he said, and she knew something was off. He wasn't angry. He was calm. Her face was on fire, tears running down her abused cheek, and he just kept that same expression of humor and affection. "When will you learn not to lie to me?"

She sank back against the unrelenting wood of the chair. Fear threatened, a dark shadow ready to roll in over her brain. If she gave in to it, maybe her mind would go all fuzzy again. Maybe giving in to the fear was the only way to make it bearable.

No. No. She wouldn't go out a coward. She wouldn't go quietly. She'd fight him tooth and nail.

"Fuck off," she said, the words braver than she felt. But it was a step in the right direction.

"No, I don't think I will, pet," he said, sliding one of the other chairs over, its back to her, his legs spread wide, straddling the seat. "I'm not going anywhere at the moment. You and I. Well, we have some unfinished business to discuss before we move on to the more entertaining portions of the schedule."

She shuddered at that. "We have nothing to talk about."

"Why did you leave me?" he asked again, his eyes intense on her face. It was the first time she'd heard uncertainty. He really didn't know why. "The truth this time, please."

"Because you kidnapped and raped me," she finally answered. He wanted honesty? Honesty he would get. "And I thought you were going to kill me."

"I wasn't going to kill you."

Wasn't. Her mind stuttered over the past tense. "But you admit you kidnapped me. And then . . . ?"

"We made love, pet," he slurred, his eyes hooded.

Her muscles were shaking, and she couldn't seem to control the chattering of her teeth. She tried to keep herself focused, but the shivers in her bones seemed to wiggle into her brain, and her thoughts were jumping and scattered. "You're delusional," she said, at a loss for anything else.

Faint smile lines crinkled at the corners of his eyes. "You're just not seeing clearly."

"I am seeing clearly." Anger sharpened the blurred edges. "And you want to know what I see? I see a psychopath, who, when dealt a bad hand in life, let himself turn into a monster instead of fighting to become something better."

"A bad hand? A bad hand?" His own rage was an answering crackle in the air. "Do you know how much they used to beat me? How they wouldn't give me food for days? How they'd hold me down on my knees on the concrete in the basement and make me pray for hours until I couldn't walk? All to get the demons out. A bad hand, Addie?"

It was just his ragged breathing that filled the kitchen then.

But no, she couldn't believe him. The Crosses were strict, but nothing like that. They wouldn't have done those things. She would have known. She would have known.

"Precious Saint Adelaide never saw those things." He kept going, and there was pure hatred in his eyes. She swallowed hard, and his eyes dipped to her throat. A deep breath and he had himself under control again. "You know what they did when you would tattle on me? Those were the worst times, because I was being a bad influence on their little angel."

He stood up and turned without waiting for an answer. Lifted his shirt. A gasp escaped. His back was a map of raised white ridges. Scars from being lashed.

"No," she whispered, her fingers begging to trace over the puckered skin.

"A bad hand?" He quirked an eyebrow at her as he sat back down.

"How did I not know?" she asked, her voice just a quiet breath of exhaled air, and she felt a sharp shard of glass cut into her heart for the boy he'd been. Maybe he was lying. There was a good chance he was. The scars could have come from his time before the Crosses, a time she knew little about. But someone had put them on his body. That's what hurt.

A careless shoulder lifted, then dropped. "They did a good job of hiding it from you. I wasn't going to tell you."

She closed her eyes against it all, wishing she could shut it out. Shut out the undeniable proof. Shut out the words. Shut out the fact that everything she'd ever known in her life was crashing into pieces around her.

"It doesn't . . . you can't. You can't kidnap people," she said. He had been abused. But that didn't mean he had a free pass.

"I was saving you, pet," he said, as if confused by why she'd think anything else. "I made a promise to come back and get you as soon as I could. I needed money, though. To give you the things you want."

"You could have told me what happened, then. I would have come with you."

He shook his head. "No."

They both knew why it wouldn't have worked. She wouldn't have gone with him. The photos. Those photos of the other girls, the ones who looked like her.

They sat in silence after that, and it was broken only by the slow and steady click of the clock's second hand counting down her fate.

"You left me, though," he said finally, his voice quiet. "We could have been great together. Our love burns so bright." His eyes flicked to her hair. "So bright. Like the stars."

"I never loved you, you sick excuse for a man," she bit off.

"You don't mean that."

"I never loved you. You make me sick." She didn't know where it was coming from. The words seemed to spill from her lips unbidden. Rising from the bile that roiled in her belly.

"Take that back." His voice was hard again. And he stood, pushing the chair out of the way.

She wanted to take it back. She wanted to soothe and comfort and tell him that if he just didn't kill her, she'd let him show her how great they could be. But all she could see was him thrusting into her as tears ran down her cheeks into the pillows. She'd rather die than live that future.

And she wanted to lash out and strike him the way he hurt her. Ruin any remaining bond that was left between them from years of shared secrets and sweet summer nights.

"You're just a sad, pathetic excuse for a man. I used to laugh at you," she said mockingly. "I would laugh at you. You think we would ever be together? I would never be with someone like you."

His jaw worked, the muscles there clenching and bunching. And then he slapped her again. Fast and hard. She licked out and tasted the blood from her cut lip as he bent to release her from her restraints.

He wasn't gentle as he dragged her from the kitchen, up the stairs. When she stumbled, he simply kept going so that she was half scrambling to keep up with him.

"Took you long enough," Matthew said when Simon pushed her into the room in front of him. She took it in at a glance. Matthew leaned against the windowsill, the gun held loosely in his hand. The Crosses were on the bed, which was saturated with blood. It looked like it was just from Mr. Cross's gunshot wound, but she couldn't tell. There was so much of it everywhere.

"It'll be worth the wait," Simon said, not looking at him. He manhandled Adelaide over to the old radiator where a pair of cuffs was already waiting for her. He forced her down, locking her to it. "Front row seat for my girl."

She kicked out and managed to catch his shin. But it was just a glancing blow, and it earned her another slap in return. At least now she could hold a soothing hand to her abused cheek.

He grabbed her chin in his fingers, forcing her to meet his eyes. "Remember that time you said you wanted to marry me? It was the Fourth of July, and you had been here only a couple months. And you fell down and some kids laughed at you and your knee bled. And I chased them off and cleaned you up. And when I put the Band-Aid on, you told me you wanted to marry me."

She didn't remember that. That year had been a blur. But she remembered so many moments that were just like that. She didn't say anything.

He smiled. "We won't be kept apart, Adelaide. One of these days you'll finally realize that. We're meant to be. You knew it enough for both of us then. And I know it enough for both of us now. I love you, Adelaide."

It was the last thing he said to her that evening. The last time he looked at her.

By the time the police arrived, it was too late for the Crosses; Simon and Matthew had disappeared, and Adelaide couldn't stop screaming.

CHAPTER TWENTY-FIVE

Clarke

July 17, 2018

It was one minute past midnight, and Clarke couldn't remember the last time she'd slept. The low level of adrenaline pulsing through her, though, was enough to guarantee she wouldn't be able to, even if she tried.

Not that she'd be trying anytime soon.

She watched now as the chief studied the picture in her hands.

"Let me get this straight," Bradley said, looking up to meet Clarke's eyes. "This is your father."

"Yes," Clarke said even though they'd gone over this at least two times now. And it hadn't been a question. They sat huddled in the chief's office. She'd called in Lucas and Roger as well for this little briefing, and Clarke had explained the photo when each newcomer had arrived.

The chief wiped a hand over her mouth, as if to collect herself. "But this isn't you."

She flipped the photo to Clarke, pointing to the toddler in the picture. She was a little blonde angel, smiling up at the big, burly man who was gazing at her like she hung the moon.

"No."

"And this isn't your mother." She tapped the picture again where a waiflike woman perched next to the man, her hand caressing the nape of his neck, her expression one of pure love. Clarke turned away from it.

"No."

The chief flipped the picture back around to study it once more, but Clarke wasn't sure what new thing she thought she'd see there.

"So what does this mean?"

The room, which had been filled with the low buzz of shifting limbs and breathing, dropped dead silent.

"I think it's fairly obvious what he's implying," Clarke finally said, not trying to keep the bite out of her voice. If they were offended, they could leave. "He's trying to show that my father had a child with another woman."

"And this couldn't be another relative, right?" Roger asked.

She glanced at him. "I guess there's always the possibility. But, no, I don't recognize them. And the woman doesn't look anything like anyone in my family. Plus . . ."

"Plus, what?" Roger prompted when she didn't finish her thought.

"Look at their faces," she said quietly, tipping her chin toward the picture she couldn't even see anymore. "That's not . . . that's love."

"He knew you'd know immediately," Sam said, speaking for the first time.

She nodded once. "The clues. They're all meant for me and Bess."

It hung there in the air. A live wire rippling between them.

"So you think . . ." Roger made a vague gesture as if afraid to finish the thought.

"That Bess is the girl in the picture, yes," Clarke said for him. "It's possible it's not. Maybe he's just messing with me. You could probably explain it away if you tried. But taken in the full context of everything else that's happened, I think that—at the very least—he wants me to think Bess is my sister."

"It's a trap," Sam said.

"Yeah," Clarke agreed. "It's the first time in a long time he's had anything over me. Anything I've cared about or wanted to keep safe. I've made sure not to give him any ammo on that front."

"How would he know you wouldn't hate the girl?" Lucas asked.

Sam bit off a little laugh, and Clarke glanced over at him before answering. "Let's just say I have a certain weakness when it comes to family, and he knows it. And has used it in the past."

"What happened?"

"It makes sense, though, doesn't it?" she asked, ignoring Lucas's question. "It's why he broke all his patterns with this one. It's because he had a very specific target in mind."

"Bess," the chief murmured, her gaze returning to the picture she still held.

"No," Sam said, and Clarke shifted to look at him. "It's Clarke. It's been Clarke all along."

"How does he think this is going to end?" It was Lucas who broke the silence in the room. They'd all been poring over maps, real estate contracts, and town documents for the past three hours, looking for any reference to a Brodie. It was inching toward 4:00 a.m.

"What do you mean?" the chief asked.

"Well. Let's say his main target is Clarke here," he started, in his slow, thoughtful cadence. "He just gave her the biggest clue possible about where to find him."

"And once she figured out what the clue means, she would tell us, and we would descend upon him," the chief finished.

"Okay, so Clarke"—he waved in her direction and she tipped her head in acknowledgment that she was listening—"Clarke comes to us, we go in with our full manpower, including our lovely FBI agent guests. We take him down immediately."

"He does have a hostage," Roger reminded them, his voice raspy from not talking in hours.

"Right," Lucas conceded. "But he's not a hostage taker. He's a serial killer. The rules are different. I'm guessing the average hostage taker has to be willing to kill the hostage, but this one would do it with pleasure."

"And his target is Clarke, not Bess," Sam said. "He wouldn't even have to follow any rituals with Bess, because she's not important to him outside of how he can use her to manipulate Clarke."

"You've lost me, sorry," Lucas said.

Clarke shifted. "When serial murderers kill, there are very specific patterns they have to follow to fulfill the urges that are telling them to do it in the first place. Cross's involve strangling and torture, among other things. If he ended up having to kill a girl in a way that didn't fit his rituals, he would be enraged. It matters to him to maintain that, because otherwise it doesn't—for lack of a better way of putting it—scratch his itch. And, for a serial killer, that's the worst itch you can imagine, times about four billion. So he wouldn't be happy."

"Understatement," Sam said.

Clarke nodded. "But. But since he's not using Bess to scratch that itch, not only does he not care if she lives or dies—he does not care *how* she dies."

"The same with Anna, I think, at this point," Sam ventured.

"Yeah."

"Jesus," Lucas drawled, running his fingers through his tangled hair. "But why go through this at all? He knows where you are. You're highly trained, sure, but wouldn't it just be easier to come after you directly? Instead of this elaborate scheme?"

Clarke laughed. "Do you know how many times I've wished he would just come after me? No, if he's planning on ending it, he would never let there be any variable he couldn't control. The amount of effort he's put into this? And to have his grand finale—presumably killing me—be anything short of perfection? No, he couldn't stand that."

"Okay." Lucas processed the information. "So that leaves us with the original question. What is his endgame here?"

From across the room, Sam caught her eye. Held it. She tried not to blink.

"I think you all are working on a false assumption," Sam said, and she willed him to shut his mouth. *Don't make it hard, Sam.* There was a way this had to end. And it would be easier if the locals didn't have their guard up to try to stop her.

"What's that?" the chief asked, her gaze slipping between Sam and Clarke.

"You think Clarke will tell us when she figures out where he's hiding," Sam said. "And you know what the truly funny—and by 'funny,' I mean messed-up—thing is here? Simon knows her better than that."

◆ ◆ ◆

Clarke hated proving Sam right.

They'd put her under guard. Not with so many words, but in the hour since Sam had dropped his little insight on the group, she'd felt at least one pair of eyes on her at all times. About twenty minutes ago she tested her theory by standing up to stretch. The minute she shifted to move, everyone turned to her, and by the time she got to her feet, both Roger and Lucas had come slightly out of their seats.

As if they would, what, tackle her to the floor? *Fucking Sam.*

She was already annoyed with him for giving her up, but when her finger dragged over the line on the paper in front of her, she cursed him with every swear word she knew, including ones in different languages.

This was it. She'd found it.

The chief had pulled old articles about some of the buildings they were looking at and included them in the folders for each property. This one was an old house on the edge of town, if Clarke remembered the streets correctly.

It was vacant now, but the previous occupant had been a John Davenport. Before that it was owned by a Kathryn Blight. There was an article—printed out from the local paper's archives—slipped in behind the paperwork. Kathryn had been a prominent member of the community, and it had been notable at the time that she was selling her beloved family's house. Which apparently she could no longer bear to live in after the tragic death of her fiancé.

Brody Jackson.

The words almost blurred under her tired eyes. She rubbed the heels of her hands into them and blinked fast to clear away the sleepiness. Then she looked again. Different spelling. Just different enough, really. It made sense. She couldn't be sure, but if she checked it against a map, she'd alert whoever was her current watcher. Even though she'd promised them she wouldn't run off by herself, she was a liar. She knew it and they knew it, and she wasn't even insulted about it. Because it was true. She would cross every ethical and moral boundary set by society in her efforts to stop Cross.

For good.

So she couldn't check it against the map, which was spread out carefully over the chief's desk, with little makeshift paperweights holding down the corners.

Muscle by muscle she consciously relaxed into the seat. If she looked tense and alert when she glanced up, they would sense it. Sam, at least. She had a tell, and he knew it.

"I have to go to the bathroom," she said, and four pairs of eyes were on her in an instant. She simply smirked at the room at large. "Who's coming with me?"

Don't be Roger. Don't be Roger.

They all glanced at each other. It wouldn't be Sam. They couldn't trust him to keep her in check. He was on her side. Little did they know he would have been their best hope.

Lucas stood up. "I'll go."

Jackpot.

She didn't look back at Sam when she left the room.

Lucas's long legs kept easy pace with her stride.

Her eyes swept the dimly lit hallway, looking for the right opportunity. She found it in the vending machine near the bathroom. It would be perfect.

When they got close, she stopped.

"I'm starving, actually. I'm going to . . ." She waved vaguely at the rows of chips in front of her. Lucas stuttered, a few steps ahead of her already, and then maneuvered himself so that he was standing next to her, his body blocking the exit.

He tilted his head in the universal gesture to get on with it, and she slipped a hand in her pocket as if digging for change. "Shit," she said. "Can I bum a dollar?"

The corners of his lips tipped down, suspicion written in every tense muscle of his body. She schooled her expression into something hopeful and neutral, needing him to relax for even a second. He grumbled, but then dropped his guard, reaching for his wallet. With his eyes off her, finally, she could move.

In one swift, brutal strike, she brought the edge of her hand down right into the crease of his neck. He shouted, more in surprise than pain, she knew, and she ignored it. Instead, she stepped closer, digging her heel into the instep of his foot hard enough to get him to bend in an instinctual move to protect himself. It was exactly what she'd hoped he would do. Now his neck was unprotected and exposed. She found his carotid artery with her fingers and pinched. He was down ten seconds later.

She took off running, knowing that she had, at most, thirty seconds before Sam and the others got suspicious. She'd tucked away the folder she'd been looking at under a few other documents, but Sam would find it. And know.

She'd bought herself a good twenty-minute head start, though. That was if she managed to get out of the building.

She slowed to a stroll through the lobby.

"Morning," she tossed at the officer pushing through the door. It wasn't quite 5:00 a.m. yet. He was getting an early start. But he only returned her greeting and kept on his way.

When her feet hit the stairs outside, she picked up her pace, heading for the rental car conveniently parked three spots down.

She slid in behind the wheel, and no one had come out chasing her yet. She might just make a clean escape, after all.

It's going to end now, Simon.

One way or another. She was either going to send him to hell or take him there with her.

CHAPTER TWENTY-SIX

Bess

July 17, 2018

Another basement. *Jesus Christ.* If Bess got out of this mess, she'd never go in a basement again.

This time she was tied to a chair, not locked to the floor. She didn't know why that mattered. But it did.

Simon had been pissed after Anna escaped, and Bess had the new bruises to show for it. He hadn't killed her yet, though. She'd thought he was going to, thought that she wouldn't wake up after the world started going hazy and black around her while he dragged her up the stairs. At least she'd told herself that she would have gone down fighting.

But she'd blinked back into consciousness, the pain in her jaw welcome because it meant she was still alive. If she was still alive, she still had a chance.

When Bess tried to call out, her voice cracked, a rasp against her dry throat. She coughed, then screamed as loud as she could, ignoring the way her tired vocal cords burned, rubbing themselves raw.

"Stop," Simon said from the top of the stairs. It was habit more than anything that had her mouth snapping shut.

Don't lose it, she told herself. Don't lose the fight. Don't retreat and cower and become the girl who shut up just because someone told you to.

"No," she forced out past chapped lips that wanted to hold the word inside her mouth. "No."

Simon started down the stairs, and she couldn't quite remember how to swallow. Instead of watching him draw closer, Bess closed her eyes. It was black and velvet behind her lids, and she thought not about Simon and his fists and his feet and the power in his limbs but of Jeremy.

This whole time she thought she'd been weak with him, for him. When he told her to stop, she stopped; when he hit her, she apologized; when he humiliated her, she accepted it as fact. He'd broken down her personality and told her he loved her while doing it.

But maybe she was wrong. Maybe she hadn't been weak. It took strength to survive. If she could take nothing else from what she was going through, she could take that.

It took strength to survive.

It wasn't about who could break fragile capillaries beneath even more delicate skin; it wasn't about who could twist arms so ligaments stretched and tore; it wasn't about who could snap bones with angry hands. It was about who woke up every day in a world that made that decision a painful one, but did it anyway. It was about who made the choice to live when giving up would be so much easier.

Yes, maybe she was broken because of Jeremy. But that had made her strong.

And that's why she would survive Simon.

She opened her eyes to find him studying her, his expression curious, watching her in a way he'd done only a handful of times before. As if she were the only thing in the world he could see.

Her tongue darted out to wet her lower lip. He followed the movement.

"What are you going to do with me now?"

His mouth pressed into a thin line. "You'll find out soon enough."

"Can you . . ." She stopped. Cleared her throat. Her voice was stronger when she started again. "Look, just let me go. I won't tell anyone what happened."

He shifted back, propping a hip against the wall across from where she was tied. "Don't beg. It's beneath you."

"How do you know that? You don't know anything about me."

"Do you really think that?"

No. Yes. She didn't know anymore.

"You think just because you've watched me, you know me?" Despite the bravado, the idea of it, of his eyes on her when she hadn't known, left a sick, twisting feeling in her stomach.

"I know on Wednesdays you take the long route home to walk through the park," Simon said, his voice an intimate caress.

Don't lose the fight. Don't let the fear take hold. "You know my walking route. That makes you a stalker. That doesn't mean you know me," she shot back.

He hummed, deep in his throat. "I know why you do it."

Not even Jeremy knew that. "You don't."

He smiled. "It reminds you of the park near your mother's apartment. You used to play there when you were younger."

"What?" Her tongue tripped over the word, and black flecks floated into her vision.

The corner of his lip tipped even higher. "I know a lot about you, my dear. Do you still think it was an accident that we met? That it was the simple bad luck of being in the wrong place at the wrong time?"

Of course she did. Who let themselves imagine they'd been stalked? Hunted? Studied so meticulously.

He walked over to her and curled a strand of her hair around his finger. "So naive." He was laughing at her.

"But that doesn't make sense. You never even paid attention to me. You always talked to Anna."

That came out wrong.

"Were you jealous, pet?" he asked softly.

If she denied it, something told her he would only laugh. "Why me?"

When he let go of his hold on her hair, he didn't look annoyed. Instead, it was almost as if he were debating with himself. There was a shrug in his voice when he answered, as if he couldn't see why not to tell her. "You, my dear, are bait."

Bait.

The answer ricocheted off the inside of her skull, and she couldn't force it to make sense. Bait for whom? Jeremy? No, that wasn't right. It's not like she had a family who would miss her. The friends she'd gathered at school and at work had been slowly drifting away from her as her relationship with Jeremy deepened. They were acquaintances at this point, if that.

"No one cares."

She'd meant it to come out as a question or a demand, not a whimper.

"I didn't think I would like you," Simon said.

She blinked as the sudden shift took her off guard. "And you think that bothers me?"

"You surprised me, though," he continued, unperturbed by her interruption. "Congratulations, that doesn't happen very often anymore."

"Oh, I feel so special."

He smiled at that. "You should. You are. Just"—he paused, twirling a long, slim finger in the air—"not quite special enough. I've been told that happens with sisters. One thinks she's never as good as the other."

"What did you say?"

"Sisters," he said, watching her with vicious expectation. "Sibling rivalry and all that."

"I wouldn't know." But her hand trembled where it was caught in rope.

"Oh, pet. Remember, I know you. I know you're not slow," Simon said.

"You don't know me," she screamed, but her tongue was lethargic. She knew what he was implying. "You don't know . . ." Her voice broke on a sob. Something heavy was pressing in on her chest. She wondered if it would crush her ribs, her heart, her spine.

He hummed again, unaffected. "I know that you never knew who your daddy was. Did you ever wonder, pet? Did you daydream that he'd ride in, a white knight to save the day?"

She dropped her head, the position bending her windpipe and taxing her already-struggling lungs, but she couldn't look at him. She couldn't give him that satisfaction.

But he took it anyway, tipping her chin up so that she had to meet his eyes.

She blinked up at him, the moisture making her lids heavy. "I didn't need to be saved."

He rubbed his thumb against her cheekbone. "I didn't expect to like you," he said again, then stepped away. "I'm going to tell you about him anyway."

It's not like he was waiting for her agreement, so she didn't offer it. She just waited.

"Your father met your mother while he was already married," he started, watching her. Like she was supposed to be surprised.

She lifted one shoulder and let it drop. She wasn't.

"You knew?"

For the first time since she'd woken up, she felt amusement tug at her lips. "I thought you knew everything about me."

He sniffed and touched a finger to his swollen nose. It hadn't been often that she could throw him. "He had another family."

While in her mind she'd known there was a possibility her biological father had been the married guy her mother always talked about after consuming too many glasses of wine, and that that meant there could be other children, it was another thing hearing it confirmed. She tried to keep her nonchalance wrapped around her like a blanket, a shield.

He saw through it anyway, his eyes lighting up at her confusion, her pain. "Your father was not a good man."

"Because you're the expert on good men?"

"So feisty." It seemed to please him. "No, I am not an expert on good men. The father figure in my life was a sadistic bastard."

"Am I supposed to feel bad for you?"

"No," he said. "I would never expect that from you."

"So what's the point of this little mindfuck?"

His eyes crinkled at the corners. "The point?"

"Or is it just that you get off on emotional torture?" she asked, knowing the answer. There was a sick excitement around him that he couldn't disguise despite his attempts at indifference. It made her want to push him, rattle him like he was doing to her. "Can't get it up any other way?"

That earned her a slap. "Ah, ah, ah. Don't push it."

She looked away, squeezing back the tears of pain that had sprung to her eyes. It had been worth it.

"Don't you want to know about that family your father had?" he asked. "The real one? The one he loved."

It was a taunt, like it was supposed to hurt. Maybe it would be better if he thought it did. She let two tears slip over onto her cheeks, looking away at the same time as if ashamed of her own emotions. He wasn't the only one who could play mind games.

"No," she whispered.

She heard the smile in his voice. “Mmm, I don’t actually care what you want. Funny that.”

There was a pause. Perhaps he was waiting for a reply, or perhaps he was settling in. She didn’t know and didn’t care to look up.

“Your father died in a car crash,” he finally said. “A tractor trailer slammed into his car. He was killed on impact, but his wife was alive until the paramedics got there. Their daughter watched them die.”

Their daughter. Their *daughter*.

“That’s who this is all about,” she said. Finally realizing.

His lips twitched up. “Yes.”

“Why?”

“Because we’re meant to be together,” Simon said, sending shivers along her raw nerves.

“So, what? What was Anna?”

Fury tightened his face into a stone mask. “Anna was a poor substitute.”

“And others? Have there been others?” She needed to know.

“It doesn’t matter. None of them have mattered.”

“Just her,” she said. That’s what this was all about. A sick obsession with some girl. *Jesus Christ.*

Before he could say anything more, though, she heard it. So did he. The sound of a boot on a squeaky floorboard.

The unwholesome anticipation that had been a low-level burn charging the air around them ramped up as he glanced toward the ceiling.

“Our visitor is here.” He glanced at the watch on his wrist. “A little early. That’s my girl.”

Bess couldn’t react. She was frozen. Absolutely paralyzed from her vocal cords to the balls of her feet. She wanted to shout out or throw herself toward the floor. Anything. Her body wasn’t listening to her, though. All it could feel was . . . *sister*. The word ran along her spine, snaked around her hip bones, and dug into the pit of her belly. Was this her sister? Was she drawing her sister to her death? Who was this woman who would come after a stranger? Blind terror warred with hope in a battle that left her helpless.

Simon wasn't wasting time, though. He held a finger to his lips and then faded back into the shadows of the room, where the weak light from the single bare bulb that hung from the ceiling didn't reach.

She'd lost track of the boots now, so Bess had no idea where the "visitor" was, or if she was coming down to the basement. If she did, would she be prepared to handle Simon? Was this person just walking blindly into a trap? God, Bess hoped she was smarter than that.

Bess tried to think, but her brain was foggy, and everything was a little bit sideways.

Focus.

Two against one could work in their favor, even if she was tied up. *Don't lose the will to fight. The will to survive.*

Before she could formulate any kind of plan, though, the door at the top of the short flight of stairs pushed open.

Bess couldn't make out anything but a shape, but then, gun first, the figure started making its way down, keeping sideways to create a smaller target. The weapon soothed Bess. Simon had at least a knife and one gun that she'd seen. But her potential savior hadn't rushed in empty-handed.

The woman finally stepped into the very edges of the light, and Bess realized she was holding her breath. She let it out as they locked eyes.

She didn't know what she'd been expecting. It wasn't this woman, though. She wasn't wildly beautiful, as Bess had been imagining. No Helen of Troy to inspire wars or psychotic serial killers, as it were. And she didn't look like Bess. At all. Maybe around the nose a little. But other than that, she didn't see a resemblance.

Her brown hair was pulled back into a ponytail. She was slim but toned, and several inches taller than Bess. She couldn't see her eyes.

But it was the general aura of confidence around her, the way she carried herself, that truly set her apart. Bess couldn't imagine the woman—her sister?—ever finding herself in the position Bess was in. So she just gaped at her. Unable to form coherent thoughts.

The woman's attention wasn't on her, though, even as she rushed over. Her eyes were searching the recesses of the room, where she couldn't see. Where danger was lurking. Bess wanted to tell her Simon was there. But the problem was that she couldn't get the words out.

"Hi," the woman whispered, kneeling by her chair. She slipped a little knife from the pocket of her coat. Only when she went to work on the rope around Bess's wrists did she meet her eyes. They were shocking and vibrant. And something in Bess slipped into place. *Sister.* The word thrummed around her racing heart, into the blood that was pulsing through every part of herself. "My name is Clarke Sinclair. I'm with the FBI. I'm going to get you out of here. Do you understand?"

The words were a rush against the pounding in her eardrums. Bess thought she understood them. FBI. She got that. Was her sister with the FBI? Or was this not the woman Simon was waiting for? Still, she wasn't able to say anything. Nothing was working. She screamed in her own head, feeling trapped and weak. Her mouth worked to form the words, but no sound came out.

"It's going to be all right. We'll get you out of here." Clarke Sinclair patted her arm with her free hand while she continued to slice through the thick bindings. She almost had one completely cut, even as her eyes were somewhere else, looking, searching.

Get it out. There was something important she had to tell Clarke Sinclair. *Say it. Do it, Bess. Don't fall apart now.*

She sucked in as much air as she could and let the rush of oxygen push through the confusion that had settled into her brain. Let it flow through all the crevices and folds.

"Simon," she finally gasped. Clarke Sinclair froze.

"What did you say, honey?"

Make her understand. Make her understand. Why was nothing working right? She'd just been talking. Swearing even. "He's here."

"Yes," Clarke Sinclair said, and that made Bess feel better. She knew. The knife sliced through the final strands, and her right hand was freed. "He's here?"

Bess nodded. It wasn't good enough. "He's down here."

Clarke Sinclair just nodded, her eyes tracking the dark corners of the room while she slipped the knife back in her pocket. She picked up the gun she'd laid on the floor.

"Come out, come out, wherever you are," she singsonged, moving to stand over Bess, her weapon tracking every movement in the shadows.

Simon's voice came from behind Bess. Smooth and cloying.

"Ah now, haven't we grown out of such games, Adelaide?"

CHAPTER TWENTY-SEVEN

Clarke

July 17, 2018

"You tell me, Simon. You're the one who likes to play games," Clarke answered, her gun trained on where she guessed he was. "And it's Clarke these days."

It was surreal to be this close to him again. For all that she'd talked to him, obsessed about him, hunted him over the years, she hadn't seen him since that night.

"Clarke," he said in that way of his, letting the *k* hit hard and sharp. Mocking. Derisive. "So ugly. Adelaide fits much better."

"Adelaide hasn't fit for a long time," she said, inching closer but staying in the light. Letting him pull her into the shadows would give him the advantage.

"And your hair." His voice broke as if it truly pained him. "Your poor, glorious hair. Brown is so boring."

"I was tired of being interesting," she murmured. A puzzle, he'd called her. Well, she'd never wanted to be one in the first place. Had never asked for that.

"We can fix it," he said, still lurking out of sight. She was caught between a desperation to finally see him again and the revulsion she knew it would bring.

At some point, she'd thought, she'd hoped, she'd prayed, for the memories of that night to fade, to become blurred images that shifted in her nightmares to something she couldn't really identify. That happened to people sometimes after traumatic events. They would forget. Black everything out. If only she had been so lucky.

For her, the images only became sharper so that she could never escape. She still knew the exact spot Mrs. Cross had scratched angry welts across his cheek with desperate fingernails, still saw the manic tinge in his eyes when she closed hers, still could picture the arc of steel the moment before it slipped into flesh.

Would seeing him now replace one nightmare with another? Would she slip back into the paralysis that had gripped her that night as he grinned at her across the room, his clothes saturated with blood?

Saliva gathered in the back of her throat, and the bile pressed up against her esophagus. She swallowed hard.

"Drop any weapons you have, Simon." The order, the reminder that she was here not as a terrified teenager but as a trained professional with a gun, helped quiet the wave of nausea. It was going to be different this time. "Come out with your hands up. Slowly."

"No, I don't think I'll do that, Adelaide," Simon said with a hint of laughter.

"You think that was a request?" The anger helped, too, to calm her and give her strength. She embraced it. She remembered endless nights she couldn't sleep because dreams were horrifying landscapes of knives and screams and pain; she remembered the blood that ran warm against her thighs with each slice of the razor blade; she remembered a life tainted by evil and never given a chance to become anything more than a twisted shell of a human just trying to survive.

He was going to pay for his sins. It would end now.

The beam of her flashlight still hadn't found him. She kept up the slow, torturous sweep of the darkness, but all she could see were walls and the dark shapes of long-neglected furniture.

"Where's your backup, Addie?" Simon asked instead of complying. "If you wanted to play the proper FBI agent with me now, I'm pretty sure you wouldn't be here alone."

She didn't answer. He had her on that one.

"That's right, pet. You don't want that. You never did. You want it to be just you and me in the end. That's why I could give you that final clue. I knew I could trust you."

Clarke bit hard on the inside of her cheek. *I could trust you.* What kind of ridiculous situation was this that a serial killer said that to the agent hunting him? What kind of ridiculous situation was this that she'd proved him right?

"I wanted it to be you and me at the end, Simon," she finally confirmed. There was no use denying it, anyway. "Because you don't deserve to go to jail. You deserve a bullet in the head. And that's what you're going to get."

"Tsk, tsk, pet," he said, finally stepping into the very edges of the light. She trained her weapon on him immediately, her eyes flashing down to his hands. He had both a knife and a gun held loosely in his long fingers.

Her gaze met his, and everything tilted for a moment. He was no longer as she remembered, but she recognized him in the way she knew she always would. He was older, of course, his hair now threaded with silver, the smoothness of his skin now creased with wrinkles. But his eyes were the same. The way he stood and the way his mouth ticked up at the corners in a smirk and the way he watched her were the same. It was Simon. He was the boy who loved her and the boy who broke her and the boy who haunted her. Now he was the man she would never let terrorize her again.

And just like that, the world righted itself once more.

"Drop your weapons, Simon," she said in a voice she didn't recognize. *Don't let him get in your head, kid.* It was almost like Sam was standing right next to her.

"But why would I do that when you just promised you're going to kill me anyway?" Simon asked. "So, no, I don't think I will. Self-defense and all that."

Her finger itched to pull the trigger. It would be over. So many years of pain, frustration, and torture could be ended in a single breath, a single press of flesh against metal. Why wasn't she taking the shot? Why had her body stopped responding to the voice that was screaming in her head to put a bullet between his eyes?

There was a witness, true. But it wasn't that. Clarke would gladly serve the sentence.

If it wasn't the witness, though, that meant she was actually hesitating. Something—something she didn't want to put a name to—was stilling her hand. Self-loathing coated the torn-open wounds of her past, and she saw it in his eyes. There was a victory there in the way he stood at the business end of her gun and didn't flinch. Because he knew her, like no one else knew her. That alone almost made her pull the trigger.

But still it wasn't enough.

Clarke spared a glance at the girl. Bess. Her sister. She was watching the exchange with wide eyes. Clarke shifted so that her body was between Simon and Bess.

Simon was amused at the gesture.

"Quite the little reunion, isn't it, Adelaide," he said, tipping his chin toward the girl. "Not only are we back together, but you also get to meet the sister you never knew. You can't imagine how happy I am to be able to facilitate this little arrangement."

"Why should I believe anything you say, Simon?" But she did. She believed him. Although he was a psychopath, he tended not to lie to her. There was no room for emotion right now. Later she would deal with it, the betrayal and the new responsibility and the tiny bit of hope that came with the idea of family. But in this moment, Simon had to take priority.

"You came, didn't you?"

"I would have come for anyone. It's my job."

"But you wouldn't have come alone for just anyone, pet," Simon said. "You would have brought your little friends. You would have planned and plotted, instead of reacting on that beautiful instinct you have. If that's the finale I wanted, I would have ended this long ago, Adelaide."

She wondered if that was true. Since she'd realized Bess was her sister, she had been raw and aching and unable to process much beyond a single-minded determination to find the girl. Would she have slipped away like she had if Bess were just the stranger she'd thought at the beginning of the chase?

At this point she wasn't even thinking straight, but she thought maybe she would have come alone anyway. There was nothing more important to her than ending Simon. She couldn't do that with Roger watching. He'd stop her before she could pull the trigger. No, this was never intended to involve anyone other than the two of them. Right back to where they'd started.

"So this was your endgame? To lure me here alone? This whole time you had me running around the country? Jumping through hoops."

He tilted his head. "Did you not have fun with our little games, Adelaide? I thought you would appreciate them. You always liked when I sent you pictures from my travels. You kept them."

"I kept them so when the police came, they would know what a sick psychopath you actually were," she spit back. The ghosts of the girls still whispered to her sometimes. How many of them had become his victims?

"Why are you lying, Addie? It's beneath you."

"Why are you? You didn't think I would enjoy it. You wanted to torture me," she said. "You're still punishing me."

He simply smiled.

"And taking Bess wasn't about getting me here alone," she said, some of the pieces clicking into place. "You knew I would come alone anyway. You know me well enough to know that."

The look he gave her was one of a patient teacher waiting for a slower student to catch on to the right answer. Her mind scrambled, chasing something she knew she should already understand. Something she should have known before stepping inside the house alone.

"It was the final punishment. Killing me isn't enough because I don't care about dying." And there it was. "This whole thing, it's always been about me. So of course the endgame is as well. I'd gotten numb enough to the other girls' deaths, so you had to up the ante."

"Lucky for me I had an ace up my sleeve the whole time," Simon said, smug. "You can thank your lovely cheating father for that one."

"How did you even find out about her?" She needed to know.

"Oh, he was so careless, pet," he said, with a dismissive flick of the wrist that made her tighten her grip on her own weapon. "Always follow the money."

"How long?"

"How long have I known about her? For years. If you haven't noticed, I'm a very patient man," Simon said. "Did you ever wonder what I was doing all that time? No need to answer that. I know you did. I know that I'm all you ever think about. Because you're all I ever think about. Don't you see how similar we are?"

She knew better than to lie. He was right, and it didn't matter. "I was hoping you were rotting in the desert as coyotes chewed slowly on your balls."

The taunt surprised a cackle out of Simon, and she grimaced at the sound. It was awkward and evil all at once.

"See, I told you. Feisty." But Simon wasn't looking at her. His gaze had flicked to Bess. Clarke moved so that he couldn't even see the girl. It forced his eyes back to her.

"Well, if you must know, I was actually hiding from those pesky FBI agents you sent after me," Simon said, refocusing his whole attention on her. "It wasn't easy. Matthew was dragging me down. We almost got caught in Albuquerque. He had to go."

Thank God for small favors. "And then what? You just stalked me?"

"I planned," Simon corrected. "Do you think this . . ." He waved his hands again. She'd seen this type of behavior before with criminals. Try to lull the agent into relaxing at small gestures. Shift slightly, frequently. Get the agent to drop her guard at the little movements. And then strike. "Just happened?"

"No," she said. "It was meticulously plotted out."

He grinned, pleased at that. "Of course it was, pet. It's my masterpiece. Everything in my life has been leading to this moment."

He looked around, savoring it. Her fingers itched, begging to slap the arrogance off his face. She gripped the gun tighter.

"All of it to torture me," she said. "Because, what? I left you after you raped me?"

His eyes tightened at the corners before he let his face relax again. "Because you left me, yes. After we made love. Because you were the only person I had ever loved, and you took my heart with open hands and then sliced it to bits."

It was odd to hear him talk about it. Like he had a heart that could be hurt. "You didn't love me, Simon. You were obsessed with the way I made you feel. That's not loving me. You don't do this to people you love. Even if they hurt you. You do this to people you hate."

"I did love you." The calm, measured facade he'd been wearing since she walked down the stairs cracked. Rage lashed at the air around her, and she nearly flinched away from it. "And you left me, you bitch."

This. This was easier to deal with than that broken boy who pretended to have a heart. This anger was something she could dismiss. It helped keep her balanced. "I escaped, Simon. You kidnapped me. You don't do that to someone you love."

"You wouldn't listen to reason. You wouldn't have believed me."

"We're having the same conversation sixteen years later, Simon. You threw a tantrum because you couldn't have what you wanted, like a two-year-old. It's led to the deaths of at least three women whose names you don't even care about. You just care that they looked like me, and when your fingers tightened around their necks, you could pretend it was me but still have me to look at. To manipulate. You had the best of both worlds. So you can drop this smooth mastermind act. You're nothing but a little boy who wants to break the toy because you don't get to play with it. You are a child."

The silence was taut. She didn't care if it was a mistake to taunt him. Her life, her entire life, had been shaped by the actions of a boy who couldn't take no for an answer. Every move, every breath, and every thought were shaped by her connection to him. And watching him pose and preen like he was playing some goddamn mind game with her was intolerable. This wasn't an elevated and elegant bout of chess. This was a particularly clever toddler in the midst of a hissy fit. And she was done indulging it.

"So, what now, Simon? If you kill Bess, that's it. You'll have broken the toy, and then what? Will it make you feel better?"

With that, the calm facade slipped back into place. He even smiled. "You know, you're right that killing you has never been my goal, Adelaide. Because you don't care. You only care that I am dead. That's your sole goal in life. But what would truly break you? That's what I had to think about. For years. What would truly break you?"

He doesn't have anything. He doesn't have anything.

"And then as I watched you find those girls, I knew. You were all torn up about them. But not really broken. Do you want to know why?"

She didn't answer.

"Of course you want to know why. It's because, though you were too late to save them, in your mind, you didn't cause their deaths. You, in the end, always blamed me for them. It's different, though, when your actions lead directly to someone's death, isn't it, Adelaide?"

"What do you mean?" But her mind raced. Trying to keep up, see the next step. That's never how it was, though. She never managed to get ahead of the bastard.

"That, my pet, would be a fate worse than death, wouldn't it? To live every day knowing, but not being able to end the torture because—well. That would be the ultimate punishment."

It was almost there. But the buzzing in her head started to drown out rational thinking. "What do you mean?" It was all she could manage.

"Oh, Addie. Do you really think the only person you have left to care about is Bess?"

Time slowed, and everything around her stilled as she met his eyes. "No," she whispered.

Bess hadn't been the target. She'd been the distraction.

Simon's eyes flickered to a spot over her shoulder. She blinked, slow and heavy, and behind her lids there were flashes of a life she always tried to forget. Summer nights and bike rides and giggles underneath a carpet of stars. She saw his face not as it was now, frozen in derision and lined with a rage that never seemed to fade, but as it was then. Sharp at the edges but sweet and kissed pink from the sun. She saw a mischievous smile and an outstretched hand begging her to come play.

She saw Simon.

It had been only a second, the hesitation. But when she opened her eyes, she knew she'd been too late. He was already moving, his hand gripping the hilt of the blade, to throw with his unerring accuracy.

She spared the extra second she didn't have to steady her hand and then she pulled the trigger. The bullet slammed into Simon's forehead, and he died instantly, with a smile on his face.

But she hadn't been quick enough. She knew it when she had felt the blade whisper past her cheek. She whirled when she heard the gasp of confirmation, the thud of a body hitting the floor.

No. No. No. No. It was a plea. A prayer. A mantra.

Her body reacted before she could force her mind to accept the reality before her, and she stumbled over to where Sam had fallen, the knife buried in his chest. Simon had always been handy with that throwing trick.

Clarke dropped to her knees, not even feeling the lightning bolts of pain that flashed through her as bone met concrete floor.

Sam was spread-eagled, his eyes at half mast. But he was breathing. That's what mattered. He was breathing.

She gathered the top half of his body into her lap as she dialed 9-1-1 on her phone and fished his out of his pocket so she could call Roger at the same time. She shouted off an address to the operator, but then Sam groaned and shifted beneath her.

"Hey, kid." It was so soft she almost didn't hear him over Roger's voice and the operators in each of her ears. She dropped the phones to the floor immediately.

"Sam." She leaned in closer. "Stay with me, stay with me."

Her eyes flicked down to the spreading stain on the front of his shirt. So much blood. But she heard the sirens. They were getting closer. "Hang in there. They're almost here."

"Kid," he said again. "This isn't your fault."

"No. Don't talk like that, Sam." She heard the panic in her own voice, but she couldn't quite tamp it down. "Yell at me. I was irresponsible. I'm a pain in the ass. You can't believe I left without you."

The corner of his mouth twitched, but her hands were covered now in red. "All that. Yes. But this is not your fault."

The tears started. Streaming down her cheeks, saturating the collar of her T-shirt.

"Sam, no. No."

"Kid. I need you to promise me." A racking cough cut his words off. She ran shaking fingers through his hair, soothing him as he grimaced against the pain it had caused. "Promise me, promise me you'll survive this."

Don't kill yourself. That's what Simon had meant when he said she wouldn't be able to end it. That she'd have to live with it the rest of her life. She could never deny Sam's request.

"I will, Sam. I will," she said, sealing her own fate.

"You've been worth it, kid," Sam said.

A sob caught in her throat, but she swallowed it. "You're not dying, Sam. You hear the sirens? They're almost here. Just hold on."

The lip twitch again, and his eyes slipped lower. "Did you get him?"

"Head shot," she confirmed. "It's over, Sam. We got him."

A tip of the chin. He'd heard her. He'd understood.

"Roger . . . ," he whispered, and then his eyes slipped closed completely.

The door slammed above their heads, but she didn't look up as feet pounded on wood. People were there. Surrounding her. Pulling at her hands. Tugging her away from Sam's body. She lashed out with boots and fists and screams. A few landed against soft flesh. But it wasn't good enough, because she was no longer holding Sam in her arms. There was a blanket thrown around her shoulders as if she were cold. That's not why she couldn't stop shivering, she wanted to tell them, but her lips weren't forming words, just sounds in between the sobs that racked her entire body.

Sam. Sam. Sam.

He wasn't there. Where'd they take him? She pushed at the hands that were holding her down in the chair. They didn't budge. Even as time passed, so much time, they refused to give. "Let me go," she managed. How long had they been holding her back? She had to get to Sam.

Then the person was in her view, kneeling in front of her. The hands came off her shoulders and cupped her chin, forcing her to meet his gaze.

Roger.

The name sank into the chaos that was whirling through her. *Roger.* He'd only be there, with her, if there was no hope left. If Sam didn't need him.

She fell into his arms, surprising them both. But he wrapped her tight, held her body to his as they knelt together on the floor two feet away from where the concrete was stained from Sam's blood. She buried her face in his neck and let his warmth seep into her bones, which had turned ice-cold.

His tears fell gently into her hair.

CHAPTER TWENTY-EIGHT

Adelaide

April 2002

The man slid a cup of coffee across the cheap plastic table to Adelaide while pulling out the chair across from her. And then just watched her.

She tried not to fidget, not wanting the coffee, but taking it so she'd have something to do with her hands. It had been twelve hours since they'd found her cuffed to the radiator right next to the bodies of the dead Mr. and Mrs. Cross.

Apart from managing to tell the first police officer on the scene who had done this to the couple, done this to her, she hadn't talked to anyone.

Her eyes flicked up to the man's when he didn't try to get any information out of her. Or buddy up to her. Wasn't that what they were supposed to do? Make her feel comfortable enough to give them what they wanted? *Good luck.* She wasn't even sure her vocal cords were actually working. That's what hours of screaming would do.

The silence filled the room, though, and he didn't seem to be inclined to fill it, like most people would. Maybe he was waiting for her to do that.

He glanced up as a second man entered. This one was tall and swarthy. Objectively handsome. He carried himself like he had some authority, and Adelaide immediately wished he would leave again. So that it would just be the stout teddy bear of a man. And his silence that was beginning to feel like a balm against the open wound of her emotions.

The second man didn't sit, just stood by the table, his hip brushing the first man's shoulder.

"Hi there," he said, and she glanced up to meet his eyes. "My name is Roger. This is my partner, Sam. We're with the FBI."

She didn't react. Was he waiting for acknowledgment? She knew they were FBI. The kind police officer had told her they were going to interview her next before he'd left her in the cramped, little interrogation room. She wasn't in trouble, the officer had informed her; they just wanted to have a private place for the interview.

"Right." The second man—Roger—cleared his throat. She made him uncomfortable, she realized. "How are you feeling? Can we get you anything else?"

He was annoying her with his voice and his questions, and she wanted him to go away. She let her gaze drop away from his and turned back to the teddy-bear man. "Sam," Roger had said. Kindness lurked in the little lines around his mouth and his eyes, ones that would be crevices in a few years. It meant that he smiled and laughed. Roger's skin was smooth.

Make him go away, she thought at Sam. He tilted his head as if he'd actually heard her. Then he leaned back, his shoulder sinking into the soft space next to Roger's hip. Roger looked down as Sam glanced up at him, and something passed between the two men. In a different situation she might have been surprised and intrigued, but it didn't make a dent in the numbness that had settled in around her.

And then, miracle of miracles, Roger left. Just turned and walked from the room. Sam turned back at her and quirked a brow.

"Thank you," she murmured, and realized she had indeed broken their little game of chicken.

"He's not so bad," he said with a grin, and she liked his voice. Rough and gravelly and tinged with a little bit of affection he didn't try to hide.

"He wants me to answer questions." Hers was raspy, but it wasn't completely gone, like she'd thought might be the case.

Sam nodded, his smile slipping. "Yeah."

"You want me to answer questions, too," she said.

"Well"—Sam considered—"I want to do what makes you comfortable. But I do want to catch whoever did this to you. And the only way we're going to do that is if we know what happened."

"You won't catch them," she said, weary, and for the first time since he'd come in the room, she saw the FBI agent in him. The way he tightened and sharpened, almost imperceptibly.

"We're actually pretty good at our jobs," he said, keeping his voice easy as if she wouldn't notice the way he'd snapped to attention. "Why do you think we won't catch . . . them?"

"Yes, there were two of them," she said, giving him that. "Simon Cross and Matthew . . . well, I don't know his last name anymore. Cross maybe. But maybe not."

His eyes flicked to the glass behind her. *Go agents, go. Scatter. Search out and eliminate the villains.*

"I told the EMT guy this already," she said.

Sam met her gaze once more. "You were a little under duress at the time, Adelaide."

She flinched at hearing her name. *I love you, Adelaide.* Those words tugged at her, wooing her back into a black place that held nothing but pain and death and blood.

Sam noticed. Of course he did. But he didn't comment on it, just let her regain the shaky control that was keeping her from breaking into a million pieces.

"So you knew these two men?"

"Just Simon. Matthew was before my time there," she said.

"With the Crosses?"

"Yeah. But I knew of Matthew. Simon left a few years back and met up with him. They've been hanging out since then, apparently." She didn't know if she was making sense. "It's all in a file somewhere, I'm sure."

Sam nodded. "Yes, we'll pull all the information."

They sat in silence again, and she sipped the coffee for lack of anything better to do. It was lukewarm and tasted like shit. Why were they giving a sixteen-year-old coffee anyway?

"Why don't you think we'll catch them?" he finally asked.

"He's wicked smart and a sociopath. Psychopath. I don't know the right term," she said. "Whatever. He'll crawl off to a hole somewhere. He talked about Colorado once. But he told me about it, so now he might not go there."

"Colorado. That helps. Thanks," he said, his eyes flicking back to the mirrored glass behind her.

She shrugged. "I have a lot of stuff that might help. Letters. Pictures. I'll give them to you."

"That's good, that's good," he said. But he didn't push. She was grateful for it. Now that she knew what Simon was truly capable of, the little box at the back of her closet was screaming at her. The voices clambering over each other to worm their way into the base of her neck and down her spine. She held them off, barely.

"So what's going to happen to me?" she finally asked.

He tipped his head at her. "What do you want to happen?"

It surprised her. She didn't think she'd have a choice. And she didn't have an answer ready. What did she want to happen? She wanted to be able to go to sleep without seeing the Crosses bleeding to death in front of her. She wanted to be able to hear her name without remembering Simon's sick voice saying it. She wanted to go back to last week when none of this was her reality. When she never would have believed it could be her reality. She wanted to go back to when she was seven and her caseworker was dropping her off with the Crosses. Instead of letting it happen, she wanted to turn around and march right back to the car. She wanted to go back to when she was six and Daddy told them they were going to the beach. She wanted herself to feign a sickness, throw a fit, anything to stop them from leaving the house.

But what did she want now? Was there really a future to be had in this new, altered reality? She didn't think so.

Instead of saying all that, though, she simply lifted a shoulder and let it drop in a half-hearted shrug.

"He'll just come after me again," she said. And she knew it was true in the very core of her being. They were fated to be, he'd told her, and it had been a promise.

"Hey, no. We won't let that happen." He leaned forward, elbows on the table, eyes fierce. "We'll make sure you're protected. We'll place you with a family that's prepared for this. Cut and dye your hair. Change your name. Hide you. Until we find him and bring him in. Because, believe me, we will."

It wouldn't matter. He read it there on her face. Saw the resignation.

"You don't believe me."

"No."

"What aren't you telling us?"

She laughed at that. “Where to start?”

“I find that starting at the beginning can usually be effective.”

“Do you?” she said, surprising him with her sarcasm. But pleasing him, too. She could see the humor and relief in his eyes. Maybe she seemed more catatonic than she’d realized.

“Actually, you know what? It’s your story to tell, kid. You can start anywhere you want. Just know in the end . . . in the end, I’ll be here. I’ll keep you safe. I promise you that.”

She had absolutely no reason to believe him. But she did anyway.

CHAPTER TWENTY-NINE

Clarke

October 2018

Clarke ran the tip of her finger along the edge of the chipped white coffee cup so that she didn't have to look at Bess. They met for lunch at least once a week in the shitty little diner around the corner from Bess's shitty little apartment on the outskirts of Silver Spring, Maryland.

It was awkward.

Clarke forced herself to come anyway. Made herself order a sandwich and eat most of it, because Bess would worry otherwise.

It was strange, that concern. Clarke wasn't used to someone caring about her well-being for the sole sake of caring for her well-being. It made her do things she didn't want to do, like order grilled cheeses and sit in tense silence every week.

When Clarke glanced up, the girl was watching her, eyes wide and mouth pursed. They weren't easy with each other. That was the problem. They tiptoed over eggshells and couched their words and spoke of Bess's job and the weather. Clarke asked about Anna every few weeks, as she knew the girls stayed in touch. Kept each other sane when the shadows got to be too much.

When those subjects ran dry, they simply sat and counted down the seconds until their self-imposed hour was up.

But still, they met.

Bess's eyes flicked to the big neon-rimmed clock on the wall behind Clarke's shoulder. The space between her eyebrows creased before smoothing out, and Clarke knew without looking that they weren't close to that moment where they could finally excuse themselves from each other's presence.

She liked the girl, she did. That alone had been a surprise in that dark time right after Sam's death. No one had talked much at all those days. They sat around in hospital rooms and pretended the bruises underneath their eyes were normal, and politely looked the other way when the crying became too messy.

Roger had put Clarke under careful watch, and she hadn't been able to explain why it wasn't necessary. All she'd demanded was to be able to see Bess.

"The nurse snuck me two cigarettes," Bess whispered one night. Clarke was curled in the chair beside the girl's hospital bed, in loose sweatpants underneath the flimsy gown they insisted she wear. There wasn't enough fight left in her to protest the indignity of it.

"I don't smoke," Clarke said, her voice rough from disuse.

Bess smiled back at her, a ghost of what it must have been at some point in her life. "Me neither."

For the first time since Sam had bled out beneath her hands, something other than guilt and hatred and overwhelming heartache pressed against Clarke's rib cage. It was soft and warm and felt almost like amusement.

She tilted her head toward the wide windowsill, and Bess scooted off the edge of the bed to follow her over. Clarke jimmied open the window the couple of inches it would allow, and they settled down with their backs pressed to the wall. Bess handed over one of the cigarettes, and neither of them mentioned the fact that they didn't have a lighter.

Clarke touched the seam of the paper and then dug her fingernail under it, wanting to rip it apart, deconstruct it until it was no longer the sum of all its parts, until all that was left was a collection of random pieces that once used to actually be something.

"I'm sorry about your friend," Bess finally said, her voice low and hesitant, like she knew she was wandering into dangerous territory but decided to do it anyway. There was something about intense situations that bred a closeness that wasn't supported by years of building up trust.

Clarke pressed her lips together so the sharp words that sat on her tongue wouldn't spill out into the fragile space between them. She wasn't angry at Bess. But whenever she so much as peeked into the dark emotions that roiled within her over Sam's death, the void yawned out in front of her and threatened to woo her into its soothing numbness. And she refused to break her promise to Sam to survive.

"I'm sorry we couldn't get to you earlier," Clarke said, instead of any of those thoughts. She wondered what she would have said if Sam were here instead of this stranger, who was really her sister.

"No. Please." Bess cut herself off, swallowed hard. "Don't start with that, please."

Clarke turned the cigarette over between her fingers. "Why?"

Bess was quiet for a moment. Then there was a hitch in her breathing, as if she'd made some decision. "Abusers do that, you know? Manipulate fear and sadness into self-hatred. Soon you're blaming yourself for things you had no control over. Soon you're believing you're responsible for something you could never have stopped in the first place."

Clarke wanted to protest. Of course it was her fault. The self-loathing was justified. But Bess shifted so that her shoulder pressed against Clarke's, stopping the thoughts before they could form into coherent words.

"Everything, all of this, was Simon's doing," Bess said. "Don't let him win, Clarke, by blaming yourself for it instead. He wanted to destroy you, and he never could. Don't finish the job for him."

Clarke didn't say anything. But she didn't move away, either.

She looked at Bess now. She liked the girl, she did. But there had been something in that moment they hadn't been able to replicate since. Understanding.

"Do you have plans?" Clarke asked.

The girl blinked at her, slow and confused. "After this? No."

Clarke nodded once and then dropped a twenty on the table before standing up. "Come on."

She didn't check if Bess was following her as she pushed through the door of the diner. They climbed into Clarke's car, and Bess didn't ask where they were going. For the first time in months, it was comfortable, easy.

It wasn't long before she was taking the familiar turn onto the long, bumpy path. The slim trees rose up around them, blocking the farmhouse until almost the last moment. Clarke parked beside the sleek black BMW and tried to ignore what its presence meant.

Bess trailed after Clarke as she got out of the car. The girl faltered slightly when Clarke headed toward the woods instead of the farmhouse, but then she jogged lightly to catch up. Any questions Bess may have had remained unasked. They just walked until the wind changed and the trees thinned out and the gentle gurgle of a nearby stream replaced the quietness of the woods.

Clarke stopped when the pond came into view, and then found the large, flat stone at the edge of the water so she could sit. Bess followed suit, leaving some space in between them.

"He didn't want to be buried," Clarke said, her voice too loud after so much silence. "Sam. He grew up here. We scattered his ashes here."

Bess made a little startled sound in her throat but didn't push further.

"It's funny how we don't think of our parents as real people," Clarke continued. "That's what he was to me, you know. A father. More than anyone else could claim."

It was a challenge, but Clarke didn't regret it. They had yet to talk about their biological father, and a part of her wondered if they ever would. But Bess wasn't defensive about this man neither of them had known. Instead, her eyes were eager and bright, hungry for personal information after months of stilted conversations and empty words.

"When I met Sam, I was so damaged and young—God, so young," Clarke said. "And everything became about me. I didn't realize it at the time, of course, and even when he tried to tell me that later, I still didn't get it. Everything was through my lens, and I never saw him as a real person with flaws and a history and a life of his own."

She smiled without any real humor. "I didn't even know he had the farmhouse. He inherited it after his parents died, and came out here on weekends sometimes. It was his favorite place. This. This was his favorite place."

"It's beautiful," Bess whispered.

"It's a strange sensation learning about someone you thought you knew everything about," Clarke said. "I could tell you his Chinese-takeout order, but I couldn't tell you he used to play guitar in a cover band in college. I could explain his theories on childhood abuse and how it's tied to the compulsion to commit serial murder, but I couldn't tell you that his sister died when he was eleven."

"Oh," Bess breathed out, and shifted closer. Her shoulder pressed against Clarke's, a warm reassurance that she was listening.

"He was in the house. With her. When she died," Clarke said. Savior complex, she'd accused all those years ago. The memory of it was a hot slash of fire against tender skin. "A simple break-in gone wrong. She was older, and she shoved him in a closet to hide. He heard her die."

"Shit."

"Yeah." Clarke rested her cheek on her upturned knees and watched Bess for a minute. She breathed in deep and let the heavy smell of damp earth ground her. "He's my family."

"I know."

Clarke met her eyes. "You can't replace him."

Bess flinched, but didn't look away. "I know."

Clarke's lips tipped up in a ghost of a smile. The girl was stronger than she probably realized. "Okay."

"I won't push, Clarke," Bess said, her voice wavering only slightly. "But you should know you're *my* family now. And I'm not going to give up on that."

Clarke looked back toward the lake. "Good."

They were quiet for a bit, but it didn't take long before the itch on the back of her neck became unbearable. "How much did you hear, you nosy bastard?"

Bess jolted slightly. She must not have known Roger had been standing there, in the shadows of the trees.

"All of it," Roger said, without any shame. Clarke rolled her eyes, and Bess looked back and forth between them.

"I'm going to . . ." Bess waved a vague hand and pushed to her feet.

"I left the back door open," Roger told her. "Just follow this path and you'll see the farmhouse."

It took a minute for Roger to take Bess's place. Despite being out in the country, he was still dressed in nice slacks and slick shoes, so he was more careful about sitting down.

"I didn't mean to interrupt," Roger half apologized. "I saw you pull in."

Clarke shrugged. "We said what needed to be said."

"I'm glad."

And she knew he was. Despite everything, despite their history, and Sam's death and the mess following it, he held no ill will toward her. They'd settled into something that wasn't quite friendship but was more than two guilty survivors clinging to each other. He told her about Sam, the one he knew. The one who played guitar and owned a farmhouse and swam in the pond in the mornings, even in the middle of February. She told him about her Sam. The one who laughed at her wiseass comments and insisted Katharine Hepburn was really the best and most underrated Hepburn.

Roger cooked her dinner, and sometimes a haunted look would come into his eyes when he turned to include Sam in the conversation before remembering he was no longer there. They would be quiet for the rest of the evening after that happened.

But they tried to be kind to each other in those wounded moments. Because that's what Sam would have wanted, and while Clarke had never succeeded in becoming a better person for herself, she thought maybe she could do it for him.

"Why don't you hate me?" She couldn't look at Roger when she asked it, because for all that they were gentle with each other these days, there was a part of her that was terrified he would say, *I do.*

"I know you're never going to believe it, because you're incredibly stubborn, but it wasn't your fault," Roger said instead.

Clarke started to protest, and he held his hand up. "No. I can't believe you haven't figured it out yet. Use that big brain of yours, Clarke. What do you think happened that night? You think Sam didn't know what you were doing?"

That threw her. "But he didn't stop me."

Roger smirked, but it was sad at the edges. "Neither did I."

The simplicity of the answer punched the air out of her lungs. "What?"

"When I was younger, I did something stupid that you never forgave me for," Roger said, and Clarke scrambled to keep up with the topic shift. It was hard, though; she was off balance and confused. "I picked my career over him. It was more complicated than that, of course. But you never really were one for nuance when it came to him. To us."

Clarke shook her head. Not agreeing. Not disagreeing.

"Sam wanted him dead, Clarke," Roger said. "More than anything in the world. He dragged you back into the case against everyone's better judgment—that's how much he wanted it. Last time I picked my career. This time I picked him."

And it clicked. "You two let me go."

"Self-defense is a little less believable when you have the entire cavalry there," Roger murmured.

"But . . ."

"We couldn't let the chief and the rest of the local cops suspect," Roger continued, as she just stared at him at a loss for anything coherent to say. "An agent gone rogue is something you can explain away. Three agents becomes a conspiracy to murder."

"He wouldn't have let me go into danger alone like that." But it made a sick kind of sense.

Roger tilted his head as he studied her face. "'We don't see our parents as real people.' Isn't that what you just said? I loved him, Clarke. But he was far from perfect. You're a damn good agent. He made sure of it because I think he always knew it was going to come down to you against Simon."

The vise that had been tightening, slow and sure around her chest, released, and oxygen flooded her bloodstream. The rush of it made her light-headed.

"He thought he'd be able to get to you in time, of course," Roger continued. "We split up, and I took the locals off to some other location.

He wanted to give you backup in case you weren't able to take down Simon on your own."

"I don't—" Clarke stopped, swallowed, and tried to get air in at the same time. Three months of shame and guilt and darkness were difficult to shrug off. "Why are you telling me this?"

"You asked why I don't hate you," Roger said, simple and easy, as if he hadn't just completely upended her entire world.

"Do you hate him?" The question hurt. But everything hurt right now. "Do you hate yourself?"

He huffed out a breath. "Him? No. Never. He was an arrogant ass who had a blind spot as big as yours when it came to Simon Cross. The only thing he cared about more than you was killing him."

"Yourself, then?" she pushed, ignoring that last bit. Maybe this was the more important question anyway.

"Do any of us not?" Roger dodged, and she let him. It was true anyway.

They fell silent once more, and she thought of Sam. Of his insistence she join the case, of nights at the practice range, of that cagey look in his eyes when he'd first suggested she might want to think about becoming an agent all those years ago.

But layered over those memories were the ones of him talking her off a ledge in the early hours before dawn, of him threatening his way into her hospital room so he could be there when she woke up, of him promising to always be there. Of him always being there.

"I don't want you to think less of him," Roger said, reading her easily. "That's not my intention."

"I don't." She was only slightly surprised when she realized it was the truth. Everything between them had always been complicated. There had been deep gratitude and resentment and friendship and disappointment. She was used to dealing with complexities when it came to Sam.

"So. What are you going to do now?" Roger nudged her shoulder with his own, his tone light despite the undercurrents. He'd put her on six-month leave after the Simon case, but neither of them expected her to come back when it was done.

Before, the resentment would have gnawed a vicious hole in her belly. But now . . . now it tasted like something unfamiliar and sweet and heady. It tasted like freedom.

For the first time since she could remember, her life wasn't being dictated by anyone else. It was hers alone. The idea was simultaneously terrifying and glorious.

She looked over at him and found him watching her back. She smiled, a rare thing these days.

"I don't know."

ACKNOWLEDGMENTS

Thank you to Abby Saul, my fantastic agent, cheerleader, editor extraordinaire, advocate, answerer of questions, the calm voice at the other end of the phone, and all-around amazing person. Thank you for everything, but most of all for seeing potential and fighting to bring it to life.

To Megha Parekh, who not only helped make *It Ends With Her* a reality but made that reality stronger, sharper, and better. Your skilled eye, killer instincts, and boundless energy were appreciated every step of the way. Thank you for believing that we could make this shine.

A huge debt of gratitude goes to Charlotte Herscher, my wonderfully talented editor. I am so grateful for your keen insight, thoughtful feedback, and deep understanding of exactly what this book was and could be.

And thank you to the entire team at Thomas & Mercer; this could not have happened without each person who helped on the project.

Last but not least, thank you to all my family and friends, but especially Dana Underwood, for being the best first reader I could ever ask for; and Deb and Bernie Labuskes, for always supporting me unconditionally.

ABOUT THE AUTHOR

Born in Harrisburg, Pennsylvania, Brianna Labuskes graduated from Penn State University with a degree in journalism. For the past eight years, she has worked as an editor at both small-town papers and national media organizations such as *Politico* and *Kaiser Health News*, covering politics and policy. Her historical romance novel, *One Step Behind*, was released by Entangled Publishing. She lives in Washington, DC, and enjoys traveling, hiking, kayaking, and exploring the city's best brunch options. Visit her at www.briannalabuskes.com.